MAHU VICE

A HAWAI'IAN MYSTERY

MAHU VICE

A HAWAI'IAN MYSTERY

NEIL S. PLAKCY

ALYSON books

Mahu Vice

Published by Alyson Books
245 West 17th Street, Suite 1200 New York, NY 10011
www.alyson.com

First Alyson edition: August 2009

Library of Congress Cataloging-in-Publication data is on file.

ISBN-10: 1-59350-111-0
ISBN-13: 978-1-59350-111-2

10 9 8 7 6 5 4 3 2 1

Cover design by Victor Mingovits
Book interior by Jane Raese

Printed in the United States of America
Distributed by Consortium Book Sales and Distribution
Distribution in the United Kingdom by Turnaround Publisher Services Ltd

DEDICATION

To Marc, once again. If you were a castle, I'd be your moat, and if you were an ocean, I'd learn to float.

ACKNOWLEDGMENTS

My agent, Richard Curtis; Don Weise and Paul Florez at Alyson Books; and PJ Nunn of Breakthrough Promotions have all done terrific work on my behalf, and I appreciate it.

Thanks to the usual suspects as well: my mother, Shirley Globus Plakcy, and friends Andrew Schulz, Anthony Bidulka, Christine Kling, Eileen Matluck, Jim Born, Joe Pittman, Lois Whitman and Eliot Hess, Mike Jastrzebski, Pam Reinhardt, Pat Brown, Steve Greenberg, and Vicki Hendricks.

The members of the Stonewall Library GLBT book group and many online friends have provided support and encouragement. Once again, Cindy Chow helped me make sure Kimo's world was authentically Hawai'ian. And the baristas at many different Starbucks kept me caffeine fueled to get this book finished.

Richard Parker's donation to Equality Maryland provided for his friend Sean Hackbarth to become a character in this book—congratulations to both of them! And it was great to get back in touch with high school friends Karen Gold, Ed Millner, and Stephen Viens, who as requested can be found in these pages. Thanks also to Cara Black for the chapter title "Nobody Dies in Chinatown."

Thanks again to my colleagues in the English department at Broward College, to my Florida International University classmates and friends, my fellow members of the Florida chapter of Mystery Writers of America, and everyone who's e-mailed me or stopped me at a conference to say they've enjoyed meeting Kimo and learning about his life.

MAHU VICE

A HAWAI'IAN MYSTERY

Chapter 1

A RETURN TO SURFING

"YOU'VE GOT A problem, Kimo," my brother Lui said.

Lui is ten years older than I am and an inch shorter. Our Japanese grandfather's genes seem to predominate in him, while I look more *haole,* or white, thanks to our father's mother, a blue-eyed blonde from Montana.

My other brother, Haoa, eight years older, sat next to him, nodding in agreement. He's the most Hawai'ian of the three of us, beefy and round faced. Though we look like we've taken a different dip in the gene pool, you can still see the resemblance between us. At thirty-four, I have a slim physique, though I put on some weight when I stop exercising. Black hair, brown eyes with flecks of green, and dimples that come out when I smile give me a package that the guys seem to like.

"Ever since you dumped that fireman, you've been going downhill," Haoa said. We were sitting outside under the palm trees decorated with fairy lights at the Rod and Reel Club, a gay bar in Waikīkī. The fact that my brothers had tracked me down there at six o'clock on a Friday evening, instead of being at home having dinner with their families, meant that they were serious.

"Mom and Dad say you never come over to see them," Lui said. "And you don't go surf, either."

Haoa drained the beer in his bottle. "And your buddy Gunter said he took you to the emergency room."

I looked at him in surprise. Gunter was my best gay friend, the guy who'd helped me navigate the shoals and reefs of queer culture. A few weeks before, when a sexual adventure had gone wrong for me and I couldn't stop bleeding, I'd called Gunter for help. I hadn't known that he'd rat me out to my brothers.

"You getting cozy with Gunter now, Haoa?" I asked. "Thinking of coming over to play for our team?"

"Don't talk stink," Haoa said. "This is serious, brah. You're screwed up."

I took a long pull on my beer, the second I'd had since I'd left police headquarters in downtown Honolulu, where I was a homicide detective. Haoa was right, of course; I was screwed up, and I could trace it all back to my breakup with Mike Riccardi, the handsome, sexy fire inspector I'd met on a case.

I'd fallen hard for him; he had a sense of humor, he was smart and kind, and fun to be around. We had a connection that began with hot, smoldering sex, but quickly deepened in a way I'd never experienced before. Mike is half Italian and half Korean, and we both knew what it was like to be a part of many different worlds and yet not feel like you fit in to any of them. We both worked in jobs that required us to be strong and masculine and joke around with other guys—and it was a joy to be able to express doubt, feel emotion, and point out sexy, half-naked men to each other.

He was my first real boyfriend, and I was so thrilled to be in love that I didn't pay attention to the warning signs that things might not work out. He was very closeted, and I was very out—with my friends, my family, my coworkers, and the general public. It wasn't always my choice, and indeed when I'd been outed I had freaked out, hidden with my parents for a while, and agonized over something I should have accepted years before. And even though it was still hard, two years after coming out, I felt I had a responsibility to be honest in my personal life, to be a good role model.

Mike tried; I know he did. But guys started talking stink about him at the firehouse, kidding him about his friendship with me, and that made him back off. We stopped going out to dinner together, getting takeout instead. We didn't go to the movies, or shopping, or any place we might be seen together.

When he went to an arson investigation conference in Santa Cruz, where I'd gone to college, I wanted to go along. "Nobody has to know we're together," I'd said. We were sitting in the living area of my studio apartment in Waikīkī. "I won't go to any of your events with you. We'll just share a room, and while you're in your meetings, I'll surf."

Mike shook his head. "I can't do that. These are guys I've known for years. Nobody's bringing a wife or a girlfriend. We're just going to hang out in the bar after the conference and talk about fires."

I believed him. Maybe that was my problem. Or maybe it was the gonorrhea he brought back with him, after a careless night on the town in San Francisco. Either way, when I discovered that he'd lied to me—the other guys all brought spouses—and cheated on me with a skanky guy he picked up at a bar on Castro Street—I dumped his ass.

I felt lousy about doing it, and about myself. I went into a spiral of bad behavior. I screwed around, and then avoided my parents, my brothers, and my old friends, because I was ashamed of myself. Sitting there with my brothers I knew it was time for a change. I sighed deeply. "I know I've got a problem. But I don't know what to do about it."

"Come surf with us tomorrow," Haoa said. "North Shore waves building."

It was late October, and Haoa was right, the North Shore swells were growing. I hadn't been up to Haleiwa in two years, since I'd gone undercover up there after I was outed.

"Don't you guys have stuff to do?" I asked. Lui was the general manager of KVOL, "Erupting News All the Time," Honolulu's most tabloidlike TV station, riding every celebrity scandal. He had a wife and three kids. Haoa ran a successful landscaping business; he was married, too, with four kids of his own.

"It's time we looked after you, little brother," Lui said.

Lui invited my friend Harry Ho, too, and Harry picked me up early on Saturday morning. Skinny and Chinese, with bowl-cut hair and a couple of PhDs from MIT, Harry had been my best friend since high school, and like my family, he'd stood by me when I was dragged out of the closet, taking me surfing then, too. He had been so calm and matter-of-fact, giving me a handhold when inside I felt like I was being churned in the roughest waves I'd ever experienced.

We strapped my board on the roof next to his, then stopped in St. Louis Heights to pick up my brothers. The roomy SUV accommodated all of us, though I had to yield the front seat to Haoa, whose six-foot-four bulk couldn't squeeze into the back. Harry had Israel Kamakawiwo'ole's last real CD in the deck, and we blasted "In Dis Life," as we cruised up the H2 toward the North Shore.

We were surrounded by newly harvested fields, and the decimation around us mirrored the way I felt inside. But when we crested the last mountain and began to descend toward the shore, it was as if all that stuff was wiped away. Ahead of us we could see bits of bright, blue-green ocean, interrupted by white swells, the sun shimmering on the water as if it were a bed of diamonds. When we turned off the highway into old town Haleiwa, I felt that familiar sense of anticipation.

The streets were crowded with weekend surfers, shirtless guys in patterned shorts toting boards longer than they were tall, little kids eager to play in the surf, women in one-piece bathing suits that showed off tattoos up and down their arms. Like all of Hawai'i, the people were a mix of Asian, Hawai'ian, and *haole*. You could tell the locals by their even tans, the tourists by their sunburns.

It was an eye candy feast, all those muscular men, shorts hanging off hips and showing a hint of butt crack, tribal tattoos around biceps and ankles. I felt like a dog who'd been out in the sun too long, my tongue hanging out. I wanted to surf, and I wanted to get laid, and I was so happy to be spending the day with my brothers and my best friend.

For the three of them, it was a day away from responsibility, from kids and errands and household chores. For me, it was a chance to reconnect with guys who had always known me and still loved me, no matter what. I'd forgotten how much I enjoyed getting out on the water, challenging my body and satisfying my soul.

None of us was that agile anymore, so we headed for a good break that wouldn't kill us, creeping along in traffic and then snagging a lucky parking spot on the Kam Highway. The beach stretched out in both directions, miles of sand and surf, and the sun blasted us as soon as we left the cool comfort of the SUV.

The waves crashed against the shore, big and small, delivering some surfers upright, while others churned around in white foam as if they were inside a washing machine. The best surfers were out the farthest, tiny toy figures suddenly popping up and riding the top of an incoming wave. There were bodysurfers close to shore and little *keikis* frolicking at the water's edge.

We raced for the water and launched ourselves in, hopping onto our boards and paddling past the breakers, duck diving under the incoming waves, until the four of us were sitting on our boards waiting for the right waves to break and take us in.

It was a magical moment—until Lui claimed rights as oldest boy and took the first wave, and then we each followed him, repeating the in-and-out process until the sun was high in the sky and it felt good to collapse on the sand and have it warm our tired muscles.

"You want to talk about what's going on?" Harry asked, lying next to me on the sand while my brothers walked up to the road to get us all something to eat from one of the lunch trucks.

"Nothing much to say."

"Yeah, there is," Harry said. "You've turned down every invitation to come to dinner with Arleen and me, to hang out, to surf. Gunter called me after he took you to the ER, you know."

"Asshole," I mumbled.

"Nope. He was scared. I get the feeling that he's into some kinky stuff, but whatever it is you're up to freaked him out."

"I'm not up to anything."

Harry sat up, shaking the sand off, and I realized how much he'd been working his upper arms. He'd always been a skinny kid, and when he'd gone away to the mainland for school he'd spent all his time in labs and classrooms instead of out on the water. Now that he was back in Hawai'i, he'd joined a gym to get back in prime surfing shape.

"You know what?" he said. "Fuck you. You don't trust me enough to talk to me? What, you think I'm going to judge you? Shit, Kimo. If I'm going to judge you for anything, it's for not being able to keep your balance on a board. Not for who you like to fuck, or how you like to get fucked."

He stood up, ready to follow my brothers up the beach.

"Harry," I said. "Wait."

He looked down at me. "You going to talk?"

I sat up, and he sat down, so we were on the same level again. He looked at me expectantly, but I didn't know what to say, how to start. I realized that I was crying.

"Shit, Kimo, I'm sorry," he said. He reached around awkwardly and hugged me. "You are messed up, aren't you?"

I nodded.

"This is about Mike?"

I rubbed my hand across my nose and sniffled. "How'd you know?"

"I know how I feel about Arleen," he said. "If we broke up, I'd go nuts, too." He looked at me. "Come on, Kimo, why are you punishing yourself?"

"I thought Terri was the one who had all the emotional insights," I said. She was my other high school best friend, a cop's widow with a young son. She had always been the one we turned to for advice on feelings, as we looked to Harry for logic. Me, I was the one who just pushed through and got things done. "You're supposed to be the computer geek."

He wouldn't meet my eyes. "Come on, Harry. You talked to Terri about me?"

"I didn't tell her the specifics," Harry protested. "Just that it sounded like you were getting into some very dark stuff, and I was worried about you. Your brothers were worried, too. Hell, even Gunter was worried."

I pulled my knees up to my chest and hugged them. I'd become so accustomed to keeping secrets, never telling my family or friends I was gay until I was publicly dragged out of the closet. When those secrets were torn away from me, I felt lost and vulnerable. As I got more comfortable with myself, I swore I wasn't going to hide anymore. But I'd gone back to my old habits, and that failure to share the load was hurting Harry as much as it was me.

"I never told you what Mike did." I explained to Harry about the conference in Santa Cruz, the sleazebag he slept with in San Francisco, the gonorrhea he brought back to me as a souvenir.

"What a dick," Harry said. "You're better off without him."

"I should have gone easier on him," I said, suddenly feeling defensive of Mike. "Hell, I know what it's like to be stuck in the closet, the kinds of things you do without thinking because you're screwed up. I should have given him another chance."

"Why? So the next time he could give you HIV?" Harry looked at me. "That's not it, is it? You're not positive, are you?"

I shook my head. "Nope. I've been careful. And I get tested all the time. I may want to get roughed up a little now and then, but I don't want to die."

"You ever talk to Mike again?"

"Nope."

"Then how do you know he's not happy? He's found some other guy stuck in the closet, and they're both having a gay old time screwing in the dark, while you're beating yourself up."

"You're right. I don't know that." I smiled. "Did Terri tell you that, too?"

He shook his head. "Nope. Came up with that one all by myself."

My brothers came back then with bottles of water, plates of grilled shrimp, piles of sticky rice, and slices of fresh, sweet pineapple sprinkled with *li hing* powder, and we ate, and drank, and then dozed for a while. Then we surfed again, until, in succession, all three of their cell phones went off. Harry's first; then Haoa's. Lui's cell phone rang next, and we were sure it was his wife—but it was the station, notifying him that there was a big fire at a warehouse in Salt Lake, and that the evening news was going to lead with the story.

I thought of Mike, but for the first time in nearly a year, I didn't feel anything more than mild curiosity about whether he'd be investigating.

Or at least that's what I told myself.

Chapter 2

FEEL THE HEAT

A COUPLE OF weeks later, I took a shooting victim in to the emergency room at The Queen's Medical Center to get a bullet pulled out of his butt, and I pegged the handsome, *haole* ER doc as gay as soon as he introduced himself, when he made lingering eye contact. One thing led to another, and once the victim was wheeled off for surgery, the doc asked me to dinner.

Since the surfing expedition with Harry and my brothers, I'd been celibate, resisting any temptation to get in trouble, trying to get back to the things that mattered to me—seeing my family and friends, reading, surfing, beating my body back into shape.

Intellectually, I knew I ought to say yes to the doctor's invitation. His name was Phil, and he was in his mid-forties, trim and well groomed, though his face was a bit too angular to be considered handsome. Emotionally, I was worried that I wasn't ready for a normal relationship yet.

Then I looked at him and he smiled, and my dick stiffened. I said, "Sure. That'd be nice," and we made plans to meet on Saturday night.

To celebrate my return to dating, I treated myself to a cleanup at my friend Tico's hair salon. Saturday morning, I pulled up in the parking lot of the strip mall on Waialae Avenue where Puerto Peinado claimed an end location. Until recently, my father had owned the center, one of a few he'd built around O'ahu. He'd sold them all off in the last couple of years, investing the money in T-bills and CDs.

For an older shopping center, it was meticulously maintained, with rich green grass between the parking lanes, expertly trimmed hedges, and kukui trees surrounded by perfect rings of mulch. The center had been Haoa's first client when he began his landscaping business, and he still treated it as a jewel. Fearing my father's disapproval might have had something to do with it, too.

Tico, who is also my sister-in-law Tatiana's best friend, embraced me like a long-lost relative. "Kimo, it's been so long!" He looked at me front and back. I knew I'd let my hair get shaggy, and my normal tan was just starting to come back. "You are here just in time. I think if I work my magic I just might save your looks."

He leaned close. "Though you know, the closer you get to forty, the more you have to work to keep them."

"Forty!" I squawked. Tico was at least ten years older than I was, if not fifteen. "I'm not even thirty-five yet."

"And you want the boys to know that," he said. "So you have to take care of your hair and your skin."

"I leave myself in your capable hands."

He led me past a row of old-fashioned hair dryers he loved because they reminded him of an *I Love Lucy* episode. The salon was filled with stuff like that—lavish murals, painted by a former lover; postcards of Puerto Rico, Tico's home island; and a collection of Barbie dolls with extravagant hairdos, bought for him by clients every Christmas. When I walked in, Bruddah Norm was singing on the CD player about his Hawai'ian-Samoan heritage, and I couldn't help swaying to the beat.

Tico sat me down in a chair and motioned a boy over to me. "Jingtao will wash your hair," he said. He made some hand signals to the boy, which led me to believe he didn't speak much English, and then the boy turned me around in the chair and gently pressed down on my shoulders, lowering my head to the sink.

I rested my neck on the porcelain indent, closed my eyes, and tried to relax. I'd been working like a madman since the surfing expedition, trying to make up for my slacker attitude.

My boss, Lieutenant Sampson, hadn't said anything to me in my low period, but now he'd begun lavishing praise on me, as if recognizing that I needed some extra pushing to make it back up from my depths. I'd closed out three homicides that week, all as the result of dogged police work, and I was feeling good.

Jingtao's long, slender fingers massaged my scalp, first with shampoo, then conditioner, and I wondered how a boy—and he couldn't be more than sixteen—who couldn't speak English ended up shampooing at a hair salon. When I moved to Tico's chair for my cut, I asked.

"I found him in the back alley," Tico said, leaning close to my ear. The back of the center faced a narrow alley. "He was scared of his own shadow. I coaxed him inside, cleaned him up, and let him sleep in the back room."

"Doesn't he have family?"

"Not that I know of. There's a Chinese girl at the travel agency next door, and all he'd tell her was that he'd run away from somewhere."

"You should call social services. They can find out what's going on."

"In a few days," Tico said. "I gave him a safe place to sleep, I feed him every day, and he collects a few bucks in tips. He's safe enough, for now."

He began to snip at my head, and black hair began to fall around me. "Now let me work my magic, young man. You need some help here."

I relaxed to Bruddah Norm's island beat as Tico cut, and when I left the salon I felt handsome. I've been lucky enough to get the best genes from my Hawai'ian, Japanese, and *haole* grandparents: a light olive skin, a slight epicanthic fold over my eyes, and thick dark hair. I have toned my body for years through surfing, rollerblading, bicycling, and other sports. I'd put on a few extra pounds in the past year, maybe the beginning of a potbelly, but I'd been working it off with a fresh round of exercise.

Gunter came over that night to help me pick out the right clothes to wear. I'm no fashion bug; if it was up to me, I'd wear aloha shirts, board shorts, and rubber slippers every day of the year. I sprawled on my bed, playing the air ukulele with Jake Shimabukuro on the sound system, while Gunter picked through my closet, most of which did not meet with his approval. "You need new clothes," he said. "Actually, you need new taste first."

"Just pick something," I said, strumming along with one of Jake's killer riffs. "It's a date, not a job interview."

"Honey, every date is a job interview," he said, striking a pose. He's an inch or two taller than I am, skinny as a coconut palm, with close-cropped blond hair. He's a muscle queen, with bulging biceps and abs as taut as guitar strings. He likes to pretend to be some kind of Teutonic god, but I know he's just a suburban boy from New Jersey. "You're interviewing for a position. Husband, boyfriend, or just flat on your back with your legs up in the air." He flipped through my shirts, pulling out a black T-shirt with a designer label, something Tatiana had given me for my birthday. "I may be looking for a new job myself," he said.

"Really? What's up?" Gunter was a security guard at a fancy condo in Waikīkī, a job that suited him because he got to wear a uniform and boss people around. He was good at that.

"This new company took over the contract for services at the Kuhio Regent," he said. "They're subcontracting valet, security, and maintenance. We've all been hired by the new company—but who knows how long that will last. They may want to bring in all their own people."

The music gave us a nice vibe, and a couple of beers added to the mellowness of the evening. Gunter moved on to pants. "Have you ever heard of this thing called dry cleaners?" he asked, pulling one rumpled pair of khakis after another out of the closet and throwing them into a pile on the floor. "You take these dirty, smelly, wrinkled pants like these and they return them to you a few days later, all nice and clean and pressed."

"Who has time for that?"

"You have time for surfing," Gunter said. "And what did you do this morning? Rollerblade? Bike ride? Jogging?"

"I ran through the park," I said. "After surfing."

"See? You could have dropped these pants off on your way, and picked them up the next time you go for a run."

"Save me the lectures," I said. "Just find a pair of pants I can wear."

"My new boss is hot, though," Gunter said, inspecting a pair of black pants for stains. "He's over fifty, but built like a brick shithouse. And he's hung like a horse."

"Gunter. You haven't seen his dick in person, have you?"

"The man's a wannabe cop," Gunter said. "He wears these tight uniform pants stretched across his crotch, white shirts with epaulets. His nipples are pierced, too."

"Too much information," I said. "Those pants going to be OK?"

He tossed the slacks to me. "They'll do. But I am taking you shopping," he said. "The outlets in Waikele. As soon as I get my next paycheck."

I met Dr. Phil a little later outside Raimundo's, an Italian restaurant on Kuhio Avenue. "You look handsome," he said, scanning me up and down. "The night we met you were kind of ragged, but you clean up very nicely."

I wasn't sure that was a compliment. "My friend Gunter picked out my outfit," I said. "He's always telling me I don't sell myself enough."

"That's a good friend to have."

It wasn't until we were seated that I remembered Raimundo's was a place where Mike and I had eaten when we'd dated. I wondered if I'd picked the place as a way of reclaiming it, banishing his memory.

To a soundtrack of Frank Sinatra and Don Ho, Dr. Phil and I traded basic information, shared some sushi, and started on that long process of getting to know each other. "When did you know you were gay?" he asked, over the salad.

"I knew there was something strange when I hit puberty," I said. "I'd always liked girls, been friends with girls, but the feelings I had for guys were . . . different."

"The locker room," Phil said.

I nodded. "I'd see other guys naked and I'd start to think about touching them, doing things with them. I knew it wasn't what I was supposed to feel, though, so I compensated by dating girls." I shrugged. "I was lucky, because the girls liked me, and I never . . . you know . . . had trouble."

I sipped some wine, and he waited. "And then there was this case, a couple of years ago. A bust that went bad, and my adrenaline was running like crazy, and I suddenly thought, 'Is this the way I want to live? If I died today, would I feel like I'd lived the life I was supposed to?'"

He smiled. "We all have to come to that decision," he said. "For me, I was in medical school." He told me a long story about a homophobic professor, and how that experience had spurred him to come out. He poured the last of the wine, and we finished it up over dessert. He said, "I'd like to see you again, Kimo, but my schedule gets crazy starting Monday. I'm going to nights, and I'm supervising a new crop of residents, so I won't be able to get away for dinner."

"That's a bummer," I said. "Tomorrow's my last night shift, and then I have two days off before I switch to days."

I licked my lips, and looked at him with raised eyebrows. In my past experience, this was the point when we figured out whose place to head to. But I hadn't gotten much of a sex vibe from him and so I wasn't sure what would happen next. I stuck my leg out and made contact with his.

"I don't have sex on the first date," Phil said, answering my unasked question. "I've found in the past that it doesn't lead to second dates. And I'd like a second date with you."

"I'd like one with you, too," I said, smiling, and meant it.

"I've got your number," he said, standing up. "I'll call when I have a day off."

"That would be great," I said. We walked out to the parking lot together. In the distance, a street performer was imitating Keali'i Reichel in a reedy tenor. Maybe I wasn't going to sleep with Dr. Phil, but I certainly was going to kiss him; if he couldn't kiss, then there wasn't much point in a second date. In the shadow of my truck, I leaned down a bit and kissed his lips lightly.

He kissed back, and it was pretty good. Fireworks didn't go off and my heart didn't race, but it felt nice to chase a little romance. Then he backed off and said, "See you soon—hopefully not in a professional capacity."

I slept in on Sunday morning, then spent a couple of hours in the surf off Diamond Head. I started my shift at eleven that night, and almost immediately my cell phone rang. When I saw it was Lui's number I got scared.

My father had been in declining health, getting a new heart valve and taking a host of pills, and I was always worried that the next news about him would be bad.

"What's up, brah?" I asked. "Mom and Dad OK?"

"They're OK, but shook up. You know Dad's favorite center, the one on Waialae Avenue? It's on fire. He and Mom are freaking out."

I knew my dad had a sentimental attachment to that center, even though he didn't own it anymore. "I was just there yesterday," I said.

"Mom and Dad are heading over, and so am I. Can you get up there, too?"

"See you there." I told my partner, Ray Donne, where I was going, and drove my truck up to St. Louis Heights.

By the time I arrived, the flames had been doused everywhere except the acupuncture clinic at the far end from Tico's salon. A single fire engine remained on Waialae Avenue, and bright arc lights illuminated the scene. The long, one-story building was now just a skeleton, and the air was filled with the acrid smell of burnt lightbulbs, drywall, electrical wiring, and plastic.

My parents stood at one side, supported by Lui's wife Liliha. All of them looked like they'd dressed hurriedly, my father in sweatpants and a UH T-shirt, my mother in a housecoat. Even Liliha, who never appears in public without perfect makeup and elegant clothing, looked rumpled and tired. I went over and hugged them all. Since my teen years, I've always been a little taller than my father, though he's shrinking as he gets older, and his normally sturdy body felt frailer in my arms.

"Terrible thing," he said, shaking his head. My mother grasped his hand and squeezed. Though he has a blustery temper, she's always been the strong one in their relationship. She's only about five seven, but she has a take charge attitude. Perhaps it comes from her childhood as a daughter of a Japanese father and a Hawai'ian mother, living in near poverty on the windward coast. Or maybe they just feed off each other, the big, strong builder and the petite housewife, who made an exceptional team raising three sons.

Lui came over and said, "We heard that there's a victim inside. Ralph wants a sound bite from someone in Homicide. Come talk to him, OK?"

"It's not my case. There's probably somebody coming up from downtown right now."

Lui looked at his watch. "If I can get this wrapped up in the next few minutes, we get something at the end of the eleven o'clock news. There's a chance somebody who's watching will have some information. Don't you want to make sure they know where to call?"

My oldest brother is a master manipulator. I couldn't argue with that, so I followed him to where Ralph Kim was setting up a live shot. He was a trim, dark-haired Korean guy in his early forties, and we had a history; he was one of the newsmen who'd dogged my coming out, and I didn't trust him, but as the ranking police representative on the scene I'd have to talk to him.

The lights went on and we were rolling, the shot framed by a couple of restless palm trees behind us. Ralph spoke first to an assistant fire chief, and then turned to me. "Also on the scene is Honolulu Homicide Detective Kimo Kanapa'aka," he said. "We understand that there was a fatality here. One of the tenants?"

"The victim has not been identified yet," I said. "But anyone with information about this fire, or about the victim, should call CrimeStoppers, 955-8300, or dial star-C-R-I-M-E on your cell phone."

When we were finished, I walked over to the far corner of the site, where Lui and Haoa were standing in front of what had been Puerto Peinado. The air was filled with acrid smoke, the arc lights from the fire engines casting eerie shadows. They were talking to someone, and it wasn't until I was there that I realized it was Mike Riccardi. I caught a mouthful of smoke and started to choke.

As I fought for breath, my heart raced, and I felt an emptiness at the pit of my stomach. I'd always known I could run into Mike somewhere; it's a small island, after all. But seeing my parents so upset, and then having to be on TV with Ralph Kim, had raised my stress levels, and Mike made them go off the charts.

The first time we met, after another fire, I'd been floored by his looks. He was handsome, with thick, dark hair, and a black mustache over full, sensual lips. He looked like the same guy I'd fallen in love with and spent six months dating and sleeping with, except around the eyes. His eyes had always been dancing and full of fun, with a bit of an epicanthic fold over them, courtesy of his Korean mother, but in the glare of the arc lights, they looked tired and somber.

"Kimo," he said, sticking out his hand. "You look good."

I shook his. "You too, Mike." The electricity of his touch raced through my body, and I wondered if he felt it, too. I struggled to stay professional when all I wanted to do was touch him, hold him— and maybe beat the crap out of him for betraying me. I cleared my throat. "My brother said there's a body inside?"

He nodded. "In the back of the salon."

I looked over at Tico, in sweatpants and an oversized T-shirt. He was hugging Tatiana and crying, resting his head on her thick, blonde hair. I was about to go over to them when my cell phone rang, and I saw from the display that it was Ray. "Hey, we caught a case," he said.

I listened to the details and said, "Already on the scene, partner. You want to come up here?"

Ray shared a car with his wife, a graduate student in East Asian studies at UH, and I drove us wherever we had to go. But on nights, he was able to get around on his own, so I gave him directions, then slapped the phone shut. I told Mike that my partner and I had caught the case.

In the low light I couldn't tell if he was smiling or not. "Looks like we'll be working together," I said.

"Just like old times." There was a flatness to his voice I couldn't interpret.

We walked over to his truck, and just as we'd done the night we first began working together, we stepped behind it and pulled off our shirts, pants, and shoes, getting ready to don a pair of yellow fire suits. That first night, the air had nearly crackled with sexual tension, as I kept stealing glances at Mike's body, and my dick rose up in appreciation of his finely chiseled abs, his biceps, and strong calves.

This time, though, the sexual tension that had been between us that first night was gone. There was a sadness in Mike that hadn't been there before, and as I stepped into the pants, pulled them up by the waist, and then shrugged into the upper part of the suit, I kept remembering how we had broken up. I knew that I couldn't trust my body's reactions, because the last time I'd done so I'd gotten my heart broken.

The hood of my suit got tangled, and Mike had to help me fix it. I felt his hot breath on the back of my neck, the closeness of his body to mine. My traitorous dick jumped to attention and I had to force myself to ignore the way his hand passed over my back as he popped the hood into place.

Once dressed, we walked to the back of the salon, where we saw the charred remains of a body. Logic indicated it was the Chinese boy Tico had been sheltering in his back room, Jingtao, but it was going to be a pain to identify him, since there would be nothing to connect him to—no dental records, no fingerprints. We'd be lucky if his body type conformed to that of a pubescent boy of Asian origin.

Had the fire been set to kill him? Tico knew nothing about him, just a guess that he was on the run, that he had been abused. I regretted not forcing the issue the day before, when I had been in the salon. Perhaps if I'd called social services myself, had the boy taken away to a group home somewhere, the fire might not have happened.

But that was getting ahead of myself. I looked at the burned-out ruin, finding it hard to believe that it had been a beautiful, lively hair salon just the day before. I could still make out the walls, the wash station, and a crumpled shelf that had once held Tico's Barbie dolls, which were now a pile of melted rubber and charred fabric.

Looking down the center, through what had been the demising walls between premises, I could see the travel agency, karate studio, acupuncture clinic, cell phone store, and pharmacy were all gone, too. "Any idea where the fire started?" I asked.

"Behind the acupuncture clinic," Mike said. "But the place went up fast. The wind carried the flames down the block—when the first engine got here the beauty parlor was already engulfed. The guy in the back didn't have a chance, especially if he was asleep. Doesn't look like there were fire alarms or sprinklers."

"And now it's up to us," I said. "To figure out what happened."

"Yup," Mike said. "You and me."

Chapter 3

GHOST MARKS

RAY SHOWED UP a little later. He's about five ten, wiry and tough, with sandy brown hair. He'd just made detective in Philadelphia when his wife announced she wanted to pursue a master's degree in Asian studies at the University of Hawai'i. He'd joined HPD a little over a year before and become my partner.

He was Italian, very laid back, with an ironic sense of humor. He was also a savvy investigator, and though he was a newcomer to the islands, or *malihini*, he had a keen understanding of human behavior.

Two crime scene investigators were behind him, and I briefed them all on what we knew. We blocked off the site with tape, and Ray and I walked out to the edge of the parking lot. The night was dark away from the arc lights; there was only a single street lamp half a block away. I could see the pattern of streetlights that rose into the mountains around us, broken in places where the ridges were too steep for housing.

With all but one of the fire engines gone, traffic had resumed on Waialae Avenue: trucks and motorcycles and low-riding sedans. "We know who made the 911 call?" I asked.

"Nope."

I looked across the street. Most of the block was taken up with a two-story office building—insurance agents, doctors, and so on. Next door to that was a used car lot, dark behind a high fence. "No neighbors to see anything," I said.

"Nope."

"Got any ideas?"

"Nope."

"Know any words other than nope?"

"Yup."

The perils of having a partner who thinks he's a comedian. There wasn't anyone to canvass, though perhaps the next morning our 911 caller might resurface, or a passing driver might call in a clue. Mike came over and said, "They're working on the overhaul now."

"What's that?" I asked.

"Once we think the fire's been extinguished, we send some guys in to search for any bit of fire we might have missed. They pull out the furniture, open the walls and ceilings. We want to prevent any possibility of rekindle—when the fire starts up again, after it's been extinguished."

In the glow of the arc lights next to the remaining fire truck, I followed Mike's gaze back to the smoldering ruin. "I've got to stick around for the overhaul," he said. "If they don't do it right, they could remove evidence I need to determine the cause and origin of the fire." He stretched his shoulders back and flexed his arms. "Going to be a long night. After that, I'm going down to company 22 to talk to the guys there. How about we meet back here at six? Should be first light then, not too hot."

"Ray and I are just finishing a night shift," I said. "We're supposed to have two days off, then go back to days, but I'll talk to my lieutenant and see if I can go straight to days tomorrow morning," I said. "How about you, Ray?"

"Julie's in school," he said. "Won't matter to her if I'm off or at work." He smiled. "Will get me out of a bunch of chores, though."

The crime scene techs went off to look for anything related to cause of death—spent cartridges, rope that might indicate the victim was bound. Then the medical examiner's office took away the body, and Ray and I waited around until they had cleared the site. Then we went back to the District 1 station, inside the police headquarters downtown, and spent the next few hours clearing our desks so that we could focus on the dead body at the back of Tico's salon. I believed it was Jingtao, who had so carefully touched my hair on Saturday, and felt that I owed it to him, to Tico, and to my family to figure out what had happened to him and bring his killer to justice.

Sampson came in at seven, and I explained the circumstances to him. He told us both to go home, get a couple of hours' sleep, then clock back in. Ray left for home, but I drove directly up to Waialae Avenue. I was tired, but at the same time my adrenaline was high, and I was determined to work through my fatigue.

I wasn't sure I could work with Mike again without all the baggage of our personal relationship. On the way up to the center, I wondered if I could shift coordination with Mike to Ray. That would be the coward's way out, though. I would have to suck it up and work with him, and avoid being distracted by memory or sexual attraction.

By the time I got to the burned center, Mike had set up a temporary command post in an Army tent in the parking lot and it was already hot and humid. The night's strong winds were gone; no breeze came down from the Ko'olau Mountains, and not a single cloud blocked the sun's rays. I parked on a side street, out of the way, and walked across to the center, waving at an officer I knew named Lidia Portuondo, who was keeping foot and vehicle traffic out of the center while consoling the pharmacist and his wife, who had seen the morning news in disbelief.

The trees my brother Haoa had carefully planted and tended over the years had burned, leaving no shade anywhere except under the tent, and when I met Mike there it was swelteringly hot.

Mike had two firefighters delegated to him, who were already out in the ruins looking for clues. "The ME hasn't given us a cause of death for the body we found," he said. "And it was burned so much that he might not be able to tell. Looks like the work of a pro. I want to isolate the ignition point and see if I can identify any accelerants. Every pro has his own signature; if we find the clues we find the guy."

Mike had a pint bottle of water in his hand, and he unscrewed it, then took a deep gulp. His radio buzzed and he stepped away to take the call, leaving his water bottle on the table. I used the sleeve of my aloha shirt to wipe my sweaty forehead, and grabbed the bottle for a drink.

As soon as the liquid hit my tongue, though, I knew it wasn't water. Way too much kick for that. I jerked the bottle back, spilling a few drops on the counter, and then sniffed. The liquid was odorless and colorless, but I thought it was vodka.

I capped the bottle, wiped the spilled drops with a tissue, then put the bottle back on the table and went out to the ruins of the shopping center my father had built, in part with his own hands.

As I walked, I yawned, and wondered if I'd have passed the call to another detective if I'd known Mike would be involved. Maybe. But how could I have justified that to my family? They had met Mike a few times before we broke up, and liked him. No one had ever questioned why we'd stopped seeing each other, and until I told Harry when we were surfing, I'd never volunteered an explanation.

And what was up with the vodka bottle, at eight in the morning? When we'd dated, Mike had been a wine drinker, preferably red and Italian. He'd gotten a little loopy sometimes, but I had too. I'd never considered that he had a drinking problem.

In the daylight, the center looked worse than it had at night. Traffic slowed on Waialae Avenue as onlookers gaped, but Lidia kept the cars moving, and prevented foot traffic from getting in our way. The devastation the fire had caused was clear, and the acrid smell of burnt wood and plastic was still everywhere. I stifled another yawn as Mike and I started at the far end of the center, by the acupuncture clinic, looking for anything we could find.

"A fire needs three things," he said, as we began investigating. "Oxygen, heat, and a fuel source. Last night, I talked to a bunch of the guys about what they found when they started fighting the fire. The flames were light yellow, almost white, and the smoke was black. That means gasoline was part of the fuel source."

He pointed at a charred piece of wood framing. "This building had a lot of wood. If the wood was the only material burning, the flames would have been more red, and the smoke brown."

I nodded, writing notes for myself.

"You can see various points throughout the center where the fire seems to have burned hotter and stronger. Those were the places where the gasoline was spread. The rapid progress of the fire indicated that those places were linked with some kind of accelerant."

He pointed to the ground behind the clinic. "The fire was started on the exterior of the building. So our arsonist either didn't have access to the clinic, or didn't want to waste time breaking in. There was an alarm system, yeah?"

"An old one—just a keypad outside each back door, and sensors on the front and rear exits. If you broke down the door, you'd trip the sensor, but that's about it."

It was weird working with Mike again. I couldn't help looking at him when his attention was elsewhere, remembering the wiry feel of his hair against my chest, noticing the curve of his ass in his dark jeans. The ghost of our failed relationship hung between everything we said to each other. He felt the tension, too; I could see it in the set of his shoulders, the awkward way he tried to avoid touching me.

"You said the third thing the fire needs is oxygen," I said, pushing my attention back to the case. "But isn't there oxygen everywhere?"

"There is. A fire needs oxygen to keep burning. If the arsonist had set a fire in one store that was airtight, it would have burned itself out. But by setting the fires outside the building, he guaranteed a supply of oxygen. And the narrow alley is perfect; the wind channeled the flames down alongside the building."

I saw something on the ground behind the hair salon and leaned over to look closely. "Think our arsonist was a potato chip fan?" I said to Mike, pointing at a scrap of a chip bag.

"Not necessarily." He leaned over next to me, and his head was so close to mine that I could have turned just a bit and kissed him. I could tell he felt something, too, from the quick way he pulled back.

"Potato chips are greasy, yeah?" he said, standing up and stepping a little away from me. "So they're a good accelerant. You lay a trail of chips away from the ignition, and the fire runs down the trail. Soon you've got a wall of flames going up."

He pulled out an evidence bag, and scooped the fragment of chip bag into it. "Good eye," he said.

He looked at me, and for a moment I saw a flicker of the old Mike in his eyes, as if he wanted to make a joke but then thought better of it. That connection between us was like an electrical spark in the air, only there wasn't anything to fuel the combustion.

We walked all the way down the alley to the beauty salon at the far end. "We're not only looking for things that shouldn't be here," Mike said, "but things that should be, too."

"What do you mean?"

"Well, there isn't much reason for a gasoline can to be in a travel agency, for example," he said. "But people decorate their workplaces with personal items." He motioned through the damaged wall to the travel agent's desk, where we could see the remains of photographs in twisted metal frames. "If she'd cleared her desk, that might mean she knew the fire was going to happen."

"So I guess we can wipe her out as a suspect."

"We can't eliminate anyone as a suspect yet," he said. "We're just looking for clues, remember?"

"Yes, boss."

"Gee, I remember when you used to say that and mean it."

My eyebrows shot up and I was about to say something when I saw Ray pull in the parking lot. "There's my partner," I said. "Let me go fill him in."

"I'm not going anywhere," Mike said.

"I've got to pick Julie up at two," Ray said, when I got over to his car. "If we're still working, can you follow me down to UH and bring me back up here?"

"Sure. Listen, I need to talk to you before we get started in there."

There was a hole-in-the-wall *malasada* shop across the street, and I steered Ray over there. A *malasada* is a kind of Portuguese donut popular in Hawai'i, and I figured I would tell Ray about my background with Mike over a big dose of sugar. We'd started working together just as I was breaking up with Mike, and I hadn't felt comfortable enough with Ray then to say anything.

Since then, we'd gotten closer. I remembered one of the first conversations we'd had together on personal subjects. We were in my truck on our way back from a case—an old man whose pills had been tampered with by his son. The daughter was a lesbian, and she'd been our primary suspect until her brother had done something dumb that gave him away.

I said I worried that I'd bent over backward to think of the sister as innocent, because I empathized with her. I took a deep breath. "Because I'm gay, too."

"No shit?" he asked. "That's cool. My cousin Joey was my best friend growing up—we used to have a hell of a time together. He turned out to be gay."

"You still in touch with him?"

Ray shrugged, and turned to look out the window. "Joey got it into his head when we were about twenty that he wanted to own an X-rated porno store. He used to say he wanted to sit behind the counter with his pants open, jerking himself off while the customers shopped."

"Not a pretty picture." I realized I had been gripping the steering wheel tight, and relaxed a little.

"He did some stupid stuff to raise the money. Started selling drugs, got killed. That was that for Joey."

"Wow. Must have been tough for you."

"That's when I decided to be a cop," he said, turning back to me. "I mean, I always knew cops growing up, had a few in the family, but I hadn't been thinking about it for myself till then."

I still didn't talk much about my personal life to Ray, but he'd known I'd been burned by a guy in the past, and when I told him about my date with Dr. Phil he'd cheered me on.

We sat down at a rickety table in the *malasada* shop with a plate of hot, puffy donuts dusted with grainy white sugar and a pair of coffees, some funky Japanese pop music playing in the background. "So you remember I told you a little about that fire investigator I broke up with a couple of months after you started working at HPD?" I asked.

Ray had a mouthful of *malasada,* so he just nodded.

"And I never would tell you much about him, because he was so closeted? Well, that's the guy. Mike."

"You OK to work with him?" Ray asked.

I shrugged. I wasn't really OK to work with Mike; just the short time we'd spent together had already shown me that there was still a lot of unfinished business between us—half machismo and half sexual tension. But I was going to have to get over it. "Don't have much choice," I said. "He's the fire department side of this, and I want to figure out who torched the center. My dad built a lot of that place with his own hands. That makes this personal. Plus there's the boy."

I told him about getting my hair cut on Saturday, and Jingtao. "You think that's our victim?" Ray asked.

"Most likely. Hard to ID him, though."

We finished the *malasadas* and coffee and walked back across the street, where Mike was making notes on a yellow legal pad, sitting on a folding chair under the tent. Though the wind had picked up, it was still brutally hot, the sunlight glaring off the windshield of a Menehune Water delivery truck parked across the street.

"I've still got to walk through the last two businesses," Mike said, putting down his pad and capping his pen. "Want to walk it with me?"

"Sure." I noticed that the vodka bottle was gone and wondered if that meant Mike had finished it. But as we walked toward the acupuncture clinic, I couldn't see any evidence of intoxication. I'd been on road patrol early in my career, and seen a number of roadside sobriety tests given, and I'd seen guys I knew were completely drunk pass with flying colors. So just because Mike didn't stumble or slur his words didn't mean he wasn't plastered.

As we walked, we went over the report from the crime scene techs, who hadn't been able to find much. There was no evidence that Jingtao had been restrained in any way, no bullet holes in the remaining walls, no spent cartridges. The fire had done a very efficient job of burning what was flammable; what was left held few clues, if any.

We walked through the cell phone store, a scrap heap of mangled metal and plastic. The acupuncture clinic was the last step before we went back to the station, and I was eager to get it over with.

When I walked into the front room where there was a reception desk and a couple of chairs, I felt something was wrong. The place was too empty. Though the fire had begun behind the clinic, the wind had whipped it down the center before it could cause much damage. There had been no decoration on the walls beyond a couple of cheap posters of Chinese sights, and no personal items at all.

"See the stains on the floor tiles?" Mike asked, pointing to the strange outlines on the floor. "We call them ghost marks. They're produced by dissolution and combustion of tile adhesive."

While Mike and Ray surveyed the back of the building, analyzing the point of origin, I nosed around the reception area, looking for the stuff I expected to find—insurance forms, appointment books, and so on. Nothing. I found only couple of ballpoint pens, a deck of worn playing cards, and a box of rubber gloves in one of the drawers. Each of the three small treatment rooms was similarly barren—the remains of some built-in cabinetry, a tiny restroom with a single toilet.

"Looks like they pulled out," Ray said, coming inside to join me. "You said your dad used to own the center, didn't you? He know the current owners?"

"I'll ask him. See what he can give us on all the tenants."

Mike was behind him. "You know whether the center was profitable?"

"Last year, when my dad was sick, we all sat down and talked about money. Back then, the center was owned by a trust—with my parents as the trustees. No mortgage. My dad called it a cash cow, mostly income and little expense. But he's getting older, and he wanted to sell off the real estate to make things easier for my mom in case anything happened."

I took a deep breath. I didn't like thinking about the possibility that my dad would pass away. I relied on his quiet strength too much.

"He went to a shopping center convention in Arizona and hooked up with some big mainland company that was looking to expand here in the islands. I think he sold them seven properties in all. He walked away with cash, though I'm not sure what kind of financing they have."

Ray was snooping around the inside of the acupuncture clinic while Mike was taking notes. "My sense is that the new owners are landlords rather than builders," I continued, "so the place was worth more to them intact, even after the insurance."

"Good information. Let me know if your dad knows anything else." He hesitated for a moment. It felt like there was something charged in the air, and it wasn't just the smoke. "Tell your folks I said hello."

There it was. That sense that he had once been part of my life. "I will."

"I'm going to stick around here for a while," Mike said. "I've got a couple of the guys from the fire last night coming over to walk around some more with me, see what they remember. I need to do some calculations, figure out the fire load."

"What's that?" Ray asked, coming back to join us.

"The total amount of fuel that might be involved in a fire. I count up what was here in the building that might have been fuel. I figure out the origin of the fire, then I examine that spot for sources of ignition. Then I evaluate those ignition scenarios to see if they're capable of creating sufficient heat energy to cause the fuel that was present here to burn."

"We'll leave all that stuff to you," I said. "Science was never my strong point. You'll call us with whatever you find?"

"You show me yours, I'll show you mine," Mike said.

"We've already done that," I said. "And see where it got us."

Chapter 4

BETRAYAL

ONCE I DROPPED Ray at UH to meet Julie, I couldn't stop yawning. But since my father had sold the center only a few months
before, I knew his records would be relevant and I wanted to pick
up whatever he had. Since his heart surgery, he had closed the office he'd kept in Salt Lake, moving all his paperwork into Haoa's
old bedroom.

"Are you sleeping enough?" my mother asked, as soon as she
opened the door. "You look very tired."

"Just temporary," I said, leaning down to kiss her cheek. "Shift
change."

"You should go to your room and take a nap. I'll make up the
bed for you."

"Thanks, but I want to get back home." I sniffed the air. "What's
cooking?"

"Chicken long rice. I'll make you a plate."

My father was sitting at the kitchen table, a pile of papers around
him, half-glasses perched on his nose. An old Alfred Apaka CD
was playing softly in the background, and he wore a T-shirt pro-
claiming him the world's best grandfather. "Aloha, Tūtū Al," I
said, kissing the top of his head and calling him by the nickname
his grandchildren had given him.

I sat across from him and he started handing me papers. "Lease
agreements for the center," he said. "Liliha kept the records for
me, on computer. She's going to e-mail you the spreadsheet up to
the time the center was sold."

I hadn't known that Liliha was involved in my dad's business, but it made sense. She had been a secretary and bookkeeper at KVOL when Lui met her, quitting her job when their first child was born.

My father shook his head. "When this center first opened, I knew every tenant personally. They gave me the rent, in cash, and I gave them a paper receipt. Now, everything is on computer. Some tenants were on automatic pay—the bank sucked the money out of their account, dropped it into mine the first of the month."

"Made it easier for you," I said.

He shook his head. "Nothing easy about business these days. That's why I wanted to sell everything. I won't be around forever, you know. I want things to be easy for your mother."

"Enough, old man," my mother said. "You know the saying, only the good die young. You will live forever."

I laughed. My parents had bickered like that for as long as I remembered. Mike and I had done the same thing, a combination of our family legacies and all that free-floating testosterone between us.

We talked for a while, and I kept yawning, even as I devoured the shredded chicken and the short, gooey noodles. Finally I couldn't stay any longer, and I gathered the papers up, kissed my parents, and got into my truck.

Only by blasting a CD could I stay awake enough to keep my truck on the road down to Waikīkī, and as soon as I pulled into my parking space I had to lean my head against the steering wheel and rest for a minute before I went inside.

I fell asleep almost as soon as I crawled into bed, though it was only six o'clock outside. I slept till midnight, when I awoke with a full bladder and an empty stomach. After I took care of the bladder, I pulled on shorts, a T-shirt, and rubber slippahs and headed out to Kuhio Avenue to handle the stomach.

Sitting at a table by the window at Denny's, listening to an instrumental number by Hapa coming out of the speakers, I stared out at a couple of drunken twentysomething guys laughing and mock brawling on the street. The way they were having so much fun reminded me of the good times Mike and I had had—and then of the vodka in Mike's water bottle.

There was something seriously wrong with that. But what could I do about it? I could say something to Mike, but I doubted it would do any good. If anything, it would make the relationship between us that much more strained.

I could go to his boss—but that would mean a suspension, maybe losing his job. I could never do that to him, even after what he'd done to me.

I didn't know any of his friends; he'd always been careful about keeping our relationship a secret, though he'd met my family and Harry, Terri, and Gunter. He'd never introduced me to his parents, either. But I had met them once.

A week after Mike returned from his conference, I woke up with a yellowish discharge and pain when I tried to urinate. I did a little online research before I had to leave for work, and that's when I figured it out.

Mike had given me an STD.

Which meant he'd been with somebody else, when we'd agreed to be faithful to each other. We'd used condoms for any penetration, but because the chance of transmitting something was so slim with activities like blow jobs and rimming, we'd been less careful with those.

I'd had this romantic ideal when Mike and I were dating, but now I saw that I'd been foolish. It was the first real relationship for both of us, and we were both feeling our way along. How much time did we want to spend together? How much did we have to share about our past, and about who we saw and what we did?

Mike was stingy with details. I told him about every guy I'd slept with, each bad date and embarrassing rendezvous. But all he said was that he'd gotten his first blow job from another guy in college and that he'd fooled around with a couple of men he'd met online—nothing serious.

I see now that he just wasn't ready to commit to a serious relationship. He still had wild oats to sow; he had to date a bunch of jerks in order to recognize a keeper. He was still figuring out what he liked in bed, too, as I was, and we both needed more experience before we settled down to monogamy.

Sitting at my computer that morning, with the evidence on my screen in front of me, I was so angry with Mike I was tempted to drive over to Fire Department Headquarters and out him. But hell, I didn't even know what I had. And then, fear jolted through my body. If Mike had passed me an STD, was there a chance he'd passed me HIV as well? Had I ruined my life by trusting a guy who couldn't be trusted?

All I wanted was to curl back up in bed and cry—out of fear for my life, out of sadness that Mike had cheated on me. Out of general despair that a world that had seemed so happy and full of possibility the night before had suddenly turned dark and deadly. My limbs felt heavy, as if I could barely stand up, and I kept imagining tiny viruses circulating from my dick throughout my body.

But I had to go to work, and I wasn't going to create an audit trail on my office computer that showed me visiting gay Web sites or googling STDs. All day long, it felt like the bottom had dropped out of my stomach, and I couldn't concentrate on anything. Ray made a couple of cracks about my grouchiness and distraction, and I wanted to confide in him, but something held me back.

We were working the homicide of a teenaged girl who had also been raped, and the sense of violation I felt pushed me over the edge as Ray and I interrogated the suspect, a lowlife friend of the girl's mother who already had two convictions for sexual assault under his belt. When he refused to answer and I raised my hand to smack him, Ray grabbed my arm.

I turned on him, vicious as a caged animal. "Don't touch me!" I snarled.

Ray dropped my arm and held up his hands. "Cool down, Kimo," he said. "Don't do anything you'll regret later."

"It's too late for that," I said, but I recognized I was out of control. "Can you finish this up? I need to get out of here."

Ray agreed and I signed out a couple of hours before the end of the shift, telling Lieutenant Sampson I needed personal time. He was busy with a funding request so he just nodded his head and I hurried to my truck.

By the time I got there, my hands were shaking, my throat was parched, and I felt like I could burst into tears at any moment. All the way home, I gripped the steering wheel and repeated "maintain" to myself as a mantra. I nearly knocked the computer off the table trying to get it turned on, and kept fumbling the keys as I tried to type.

I remembered Mike had told me his parents volunteered at an STD clinic out near Tripler, the Army medical center where they both worked. His father was a doctor, his mother a nurse, and I thought it was poetic justice that I go out to their clinic to get tested.

It was like the planets were lining up. I checked the clinic's Web site, which listed the doctors and their schedules, and found his dad was scheduled that day. I drove out there, my stomach in knots the whole time. I just missed hitting an SUV that darted in front of me on the Moanalua Freeway, and yelled my fool head off at the driver, even though he was cocooned behind tinted glass.

I pulled up in the parking lot of the clinic and sat there for a couple of minutes, scared to start the whole thing in motion. What if I was HIV positive? How would my life change? I'd come out of the closet two years before, and every part of my world had shifted, from my relationship to my family and friends to how I acted on the job. What would another shift do to me?

Ever since I told people I was a *māhū*, the Hawai'ian word for a gay man, I've faced the things that scared me—whether it was chasing down an armed suspect or telling Mike that I loved him when I didn't know how he'd respond. So I knew I had to get out of my truck and find out what was wrong with me.

Inside, I filled out a sheet of paper that I was assured was confidential, and I was assigned a number—1423. There were three other people in the room, and I took a seat next to a middle-aged Hawai'ian woman in a blue Wal-Mart smock. Across from us were two men: a long-haired young guy, and an obvious military type, from his brush-cut hair to his erect posture.

The woman was called in first, then the military guy. I figured the longhair was next, but the receptionist called "1423," and I went up to the door, where a middle-aged nurse who looked Korean led me back to an examining room. As I followed her, I realized that she had to be Mike's mother, and my decision to come to the clinic where she and Mike's dad worked started to look really stupid.

When I was sitting on the white paper sheet, she took my medical history. "Have you experienced any anal discharge?" she asked me, and I thought, not for the first time, how glad I was not to work in the medical field. I'll take dead bodies any day over anal discharge.

"No," I said.

"How about pain or swelling in the throat?"

"No."

"How many partners have you had in the last six months?"

"Just one." I took a deep breath. I could out Mike to his mother. But that would be childish and hurtful, and I just couldn't do that to him, even after what he'd done to me. "I did see some discharge around the head of his penis once, a few days ago. I didn't think anything of it until I had the same problem."

She smiled. "It sounds like gonorrhea," she said. "But I'm going to need throat and rectal cultures, and a urine sample, too." She must have seen my evident discomfort. "Don't worry, I'll be gentle," she said.

She stuck a swab down my throat and gave me a kit for a rectal swab and a urine sample. "I have a son about your age," she said. "I can just imagine how he'd feel in your circumstances."

Back in the waiting room, the housewife and the longhair were gone, but the brush cut was waiting for his results, and we were joined by a teenaged Japanese girl. It was getting late, and the clinic was closing soon. I hoped I'd get my results before then; I didn't want to wait days to find out my fate.

I had enough time to read two different *People* magazines, both a couple of months old, and learn more than I needed to know about the drug and alcohol habits of the rich and famous, before the receptionist called "1423" again.

The nurse I thought was Mike's mom led me back to the examining room, and said, "The doctor will be with you soon."

A few minutes later, a tall, handsome man in a white lab coat came in. I knew immediately that he was Mike's dad, even before he introduced himself.

I thought Mike's parents didn't know he was gay—but what if they did? What if he'd mentioned my name, or described me? How stupid was I to have put myself in this soap opera situation?

But Dr. Riccardi didn't appear to make the connection. "There are a number of different tests we can do," he said. "Here in the clinic, we're only equipped to do the gram stain test, which showed that you have garden variety gonorrhea. That's good news. The infection is localized in your penis, but you should refrain from any kind of sexual activity until the medicine has had a chance to work its magic."

He smiled, and I could see Mike in his eyes and the turn of his mouth. He was clean shaven, where Mike had a mustache, but his lips were just as full as his son's.

"We'll give you penicillin to kill the gonorrhea bacteria in your body," he said. "One oral dose of Ofloxacin." He smiled again. "That is, unless you'd prefer Ceftriaxone. We administer that as an injection in the buttocks."

"The oral dose will be fine," I said, my voice rough and a little squeaky. I still couldn't get over the fact that he was Mike's dad, that I could see Mike's face in his.

"I thought so." He scribbled something on my chart. "Cheer up. I hope you've learned a mildly painful lesson about safe sex. If your symptoms persist you should see your regular physician, or go to a hospital facility that is equipped to perform advanced tests."

He put the clipboard down. "Now, let's talk about your partner. You told the nurse that you've been monogamous with him?"

I nodded. Damn. Was he going to ask me for names? I couldn't tell him his son was the one who had infected me. "The most important thing is honesty. You'll have to tell this partner about your infection, and you'll have to refrain from any activity with him, or anyone else, until you're cleared up."

"That won't be a problem. I have no intention of any intimacy with this partner. Ever again. But I will tell him to get treated."

The doctor nodded. "I'll send the nurse in with your penicillin."

As I finished the last of my meal at Denny's and asked for the check, I thought that Dr. Riccardi would be proud of me. I'd stayed healthy despite the rough sex I'd put my body through.

My heart, though, was another story. It wasn't until that surfing trip with my brothers and Harry that I had realized how much Mike's violation of trust had hurt me, and despite the sparks between us, I wasn't sure I could stand to go through that kind of pain again. That, I saw now, was why I had quelled my sexual desire with a series of one-night stands that I knew could never lead to anything romantic.

But no matter how things had ended between Mike and me, I still cared about him, and I couldn't stand by and let him ruin his life. It was time for another visit to the clinic near Tripler. I hadn't, and I wouldn't, out Mike to his father as a homosexual. But if I didn't out him as a drunk, who knew what misery he would bring on himself. His father was the only person I could think of who could help him.

Chapter 5

WE ALL HAVE OUR CLOSETS

I HAD TROUBLE getting back to sleep after my big meal at Denny's, and around five I gave up and went out to Kuhio Beach Park to surf at first light.

When I was a teenager, I lived to surf. I majored in English at UC Santa Cruz because most classes met later in the day, and I could surf every morning and read books on the beach between sets. After college, I spent a year on the North Shore, figuring out that despite all those years, I wasn't good enough to make a living as a professional surfer. When I gave that up, due at least in part to a sexual assault by a guy I'd considered my friend, I went to the police academy—the most macho thing I could think to do.

As a patrolman, and then a detective, I kept on surfing. I'd see a dead body, and then having to focus on the way the wind blew would clear that vision away. I'd comfort a victim of a mugging or rape, and the waves would wash away some of the pain I picked up from them. An investigation would help me understand the reasons why a criminal acted the way he did, and the relentless action of the surf showed me the potential for renewal. The faces of the dead stayed with me, but at least I was able to refresh myself for another day.

It was just before six, and the sun was about to rise over the Ko'olau Mountains, illuminating all of Waikīkī in a watery, golden light. Next to me, I saw a dark-haired guy a few years younger than me, burly and tattooed, with a kid who couldn't have been more than five or six. He was teaching the boy to surf in the gentle waves, holding him up on the board at first, then letting him go, cheering him on when he made it safely to shore.

I paddled out beyond the breakers and lay there on my board for a while, remembering the times my father had brought me down to this very beach to teach me how to ride the waves. I was the same age as that boy, my brothers in their early teens. I wanted to be like them, to be accepted by them, and so I worked my little butt off to be a good surfer. I pestered my dad to drive me down to Waikīkī every weekend, and somehow he made the time, between all the hours he spent starting his business, doing the work of every trade he couldn't afford to hire. My brothers worked with him, then, and they were my allies when I wanted him to skip work and go to the beach.

I rode a couple of waves, the white foam rushing toward shore and then the undertow receding. Fingers of sunlight peeked out over the Ko'olau Mountains, and Kalākaua Boulevard buzzed with early deliveries, joggers, and tourists who hadn't adjusted their body clocks yet.

I couldn't stop worrying about Mike and thinking about the dead boy, about the teenagers I used to mentor at the Gay Teen Center on Waikīkī, who I'd forgotten about once I got so caught up in my own problems, about all the people I'd let down. So I quit and went back to the station. Maybe there I could do some good.

When Ray showed up, I gave him the list of tenants and he started setting up appointments with them. The only number we had for the acupuncture clinic was disconnected, though, and the lease had been signed on behalf of a corporation, Golden Needles, Inc. The signature was illegible, and the rent payments had been transferred directly from the corporation's bank account.

I called Imperial Bank, a small, Chinese-owned bank where the clinic had an account, and discovered that the account had been closed two days before the fire. The branch manager couldn't give me any information without a warrant, but I got him to confirm that the only address and phone number he had were for the clinic's location at the center.

While Ray was busy on the phone, I went down to Honolulu Hale, our city hall, to check corporate records on Golden Needles, Inc. Nothing new, there, though; the same address and phone. The owner of Golden Needles was another corporation, Wah Shing Ltd., based in Hong Kong.

On my way back to the station, I called the STD clinic and found out that I could catch Dr. Riccardi there Thursday night to tell him his son was a drunk. Great. Add that to my datebook. Then I called my sister-in-law Tatiana. She was at Hawai'ian Graphics, an art supply store downtown, and when I got there she was browsing through paint brushes. Who knew there were so many different options? I'd done some house painting for my dad as a teenager, and I'd played around with watercolors in elementary school. You had a big flat brush for one, and a skinny little one for the other.

She wore a puffy hot pink blouse, jeans, and jeweled sandals. Her blonde hair was piled loosely on her head, wisps escaping all over the place. She was big boned and almost as tall as I was. After some small talk about Haoa and her kids, I asked, "Did you ever see the Chinese boy Tico had staying in the back room of the salon?"

She nodded, then leaned down to pick up a black-handled brush from the bottom shelf. "Beautiful boy," she said. "Cheekbones to die for."

I hadn't noticed. "You think you could do a sketch of him?" Tatiana was a talented artist, and I'd been amazed in the past at how she could capture the essence of family members in just a few lines.

"Sure. You trying to find someone who knew him?"

I nodded. "It'd be a lot easier if I had a picture of him."

"You buy me a coffee, I'll draw," she said. "Let me pay up here."

We went to a Starbucks down the street, and she brought in a sketch pad and a bunch of pencils from her car. While I ordered her a tall soy, no foam cappuccino and a raspberry mocha for myself, she started sketching.

By the time I picked up the coffees and joined her at a round table in the window, she'd almost finished the rough drawing.

There in front of me was the boy I'd seen on Saturday. I sipped my coffee and watched Tatiana sketch, her fingers almost dancing over the pad, shading here and there, erasing and redrawing a line.

She sipped her coffee and considered. She erased his hairline and moved it back, shaded a little behind his ear, and then handed the pad to me. "Look like him?"

"You're amazing. How can you do that so quickly?"

"Years of observation and practice," she said. "Sort of like being a detective."

"Sort of."

She leaned back against the padded chair and drank some coffee. "So, I saw Mike there on Sunday night," she said.

"You did."

"Don't get cagey with me, Kimo," she said, nudging my leg with her sandal. "What did you think when you saw him?"

"He looked hot," I said. "But maybe that was just the shopping center burning."

"You've got to get back in the dating pool," she said. I'd kept my sexual activities my own business, and Tatiana had the idea that I'd been celibate since Mike, too emotionally overwrought to consider dating again. A few months before, her gay brother, Sergei, had come to Hawai'i from Alaska, where they grew up. He'd been working for Haoa, and she had been trying to fix us up since he arrived.

"Playing matchmaker?" I asked.

"My brother is adorable," she said. "You two would make a cute couple. Why don't you want to go out with him?"

"I don't need complications."

"It would be great if you two got together. I admit, Sergei's had some trouble in the past, but he's cleaning up his act." She nudged me with her foot. "He's coming to dinner on Friday. Why don't you come, too?"

My sisters-in-law are even more determined than my brothers when it comes to getting things done. Both of my brothers married women with personalities similar to our mother—the iron fist in a velvet glove deal. I figured resistance was futile. "What time?"

"Seven. The monsters are eating early, and I'm paying Ashley to keep the younger ones entertained and out of our hair."

"Seven it is." By the time I got back to the station, Ray had set up appointments with all the tenants. Our first was with the clerk at the cell phone store, who was picking up a shift at the downtown location, in the other direction from the café where I'd just hung out with Tatiana.

The downtown streets were crowded with tourists in convertibles, delivery trucks, and a wedding couple in a white horse-drawn carriage. Both bride and groom were decked out in colorful leis and plumeria headbands. The newlyweds reminded me of my romantic fantasies when Mike and I were dating. I asked Ray what he thought about Mike.

"Seems like a good guy," he said. "He knows his shit. You think you're going to be able to work with him?"

He'd gotten into the island way big time, wearing aloha shirts and mirrored sunglasses. The Philly was still there inside, just covered with a layer of Honolulu.

"Going to have to."

"You still have a thing for him?"

"Nah, I'm over him," I said, though I knew it was a lie. I had Dr. Phil in the background, but that wasn't going anywhere fast. Maybe Tatiana's brother would be just the distraction I needed to keep my mind off Mike Riccardi.

"Didn't look that way to me," Ray said. "The way you were looking at him."

"Excuse me?"

"I'm a detective, hotshot. I notice things about people. And I noticed there was enough heat rising off the two of you to start another fire."

I wasn't sure which attitude made me more uncomfortable. A guy like Akoni, my former partner in Waikīkī, who avoided the topic of my sexuality whenever possible, as if it was something smelly on the bottom of his shoe. Or Ray, who was so comfortable with it that he wanted details. He treated me like any other guy, telling stories of his own and expecting me to reciprocate.

I wasn't that comfortable with myself yet. I'd only been out of the closet for two years, and I was still shy about sharing. Further discussion was forestalled because we reached the cell phone store. Ginny Tanaka was a chunky girl with a pretty face and long dark hair that hung straight over her left eye. As soon as she was finished setting up a calling plan for a young guy with a Mohawk and multiple tattoos, she came over to talk to us.

"You see anyone suspicious hanging around the center?" I asked.

"The only suspicious thing was that acupuncture clinic," she said. "Men coming and going all the time. Some businessmen, some skanky. Lots of old Chinese men. And the place was busy all the time—even late at night. I mean, who goes to get acupuncture at eleven o'clock?"

"You open that late?" Ray asked.

Ginny shook her head. "I go to HCC, and I live with my parents and three brothers. There's never a quiet time in that house. So I stay at work late and do my homework. Use the computer and stuff."

"You think you could identify any of these men you saw?"

"Nah. Never looked at them that carefully. I mean, it wasn't like any of them were young and cute." From the way her eyes darted over to the Mohawk guy, who was browsing for accessories, I got an idea of her taste in men. "Plus, they kind of gave me the creeps. I didn't want any of them to think I was spying on them."

Ray had already spoken by phone with the day clerk, who hadn't had anything to contribute, so we thanked Ginny Tanaka and drove back to the station, stopping to pick up lunch on the way. Ray had developed a taste for *saimin,* a Japanese lunch, and I teased him that he'd never get that back in Philly.

"Who says we're going back?" he asked.

"I figured once Julie's done with her degree, you guys would go home."

He slurped up some noodle soup and then said, "She's got three, maybe four years left on her PhD. By then, who knows where we'll go? We might stay here."

I nodded. When I transferred downtown from Waikīkī I had spent six months working on my own. I figured it was because nobody wanted to work with the gay guy. Then Ray had walked in, refreshingly without prejudice, and once again I had a partner. We worked together well, and I was glad he was planning to stick around.

After lunch, we drove out to Kahala, where the pharmacist had been transferred, along with his assistant, who was also his wife. The pharmacy was a small chain, and he told us they were lucky that the owners were willing to accommodate them, transferring another clerk so he and his wife could continue to work together.

He was a skinny Filipino named Louis Cruz; his wife Lorna looked enough like him to be his sister. "I tried to get the old woman in charge to buy from us," Lorna said. Louis stood behind the counter, Lorna in front. "But she said everything had to come from the owners."

I could tell from the face Lorna made that she didn't trust that at all. "I used to work near a clinic like that," she said. "They were always running out of stuff—rubber gloves, ballpoint pens. They were good customers."

"Can you describe this woman?" I asked.

"Old Chinese lady. I think her name was Norma. Looked about a hundred. Shorter than me." Since Lorna herself was barely five feet tall, that made the old lady pretty small.

"There was another lady who worked there," Louis said.

"Her," Lorna snorted.

"A very attractive young woman. Chinese, too." I could see he was hesitating, as if knowing too much about the attractive young woman would make his wife jealous. "I only spoke to her once or twice," Louis continued. "In the parking lot."

Lorna was glaring at Louis and I caught Ray's eye. He nodded, and said, "Mrs. Cruz, could I talk to you for a minute? I'd like to see if you remember anything else about the elderly woman."

They walked toward the front of the store, and Louis lowered his voice. "I think the woman's name was Jewel, or Treasure, something like that," he said. "I only spoke to her once or twice, but she was very friendly. Friendly enough that my wife was upset."

"Can you describe this Jewel?"

"Tall. A little taller than me, in high heels. Black hair, always in one of those French braids. She wore those Chinese dresses, very tight. Silk, in bright colors."

"Cheongsams?"

"That's it. I'm sorry I can't tell you anything more. That was a very busy location, and I never had time to talk to her."

Louis Cruz was hiding something. If it turned out to be relevant to the case, we'd have to come back to him. If not, I would let him slide. We all have our closets, after all.

Chapter 6

A DEADLY CLAUSE

ON OUR WAY back to the station, I told Ray what Louis had told me, and he said, "Wife confirms what the cell phone girl said. Lots of customers, all men. Some of them came into the pharmacy afterward, and as she said, 'They didn't look like somebody had been sticking needles in them.'"

We both laughed. "What do you think was going on in that acupuncture clinic?" I asked. "My guess is not acupuncture."

"Back in Philly, we had a case like this," he said. "In Chinatown. They were using a clinic as a cover for a gambling operation." He pressed one knee up against the dashboard of my truck. "I got called there for a multiple homicide. I walked in, there was this big round table, six guys sitting around it. Every one of them shot. Blood and guts and brains everywhere."

"That's grim." I'd seen a couple of those cases myself, the ones that were so gruesome you kept seeing them in your mind for months or years after. I took a breath and tried to focus back on our case. "You get a lot of men coming and going from a place like that. Like the cell phone girl and the pharmacist's wife said."

"Skanky guys, too," Ray said.

"And the beautiful girl could be some kind of waitress. Like in Vegas."

"You know anybody in Vice?" Ray asked. "Maybe they heard about this place."

"I can ask," I said. "But we can make a little detour to China-town ourselves."

I continued *ewa* toward Chinatown. In Honolulu, we don't use directions like north, south, east, or west. *Mauka* means toward the mountains, *makai* toward the sea, and Diamond Head is in the direction of that extinct volcano. *Ewa,* which is in the other direction, is toward the city of the same name.

"Remember that bookie, Hang Sung?" I asked as we drove.

"Guy looked like a weasel?" Ray asked.

"That's the one. If anybody knows about gambling in Chinatown, he does."

I pulled up at a seedy building on River Street, next to Nu'uanu Stream. "Last I heard, Hang was hanging out here. Up on the second floor."

Hang was on a cell phone when we pushed past his secretary into a small office that overlooked the street. "Gotta go," he said into the phone, hanging it up quickly and slipping it into his pocket. "Detectives. What a nice surprise."

"Talk to me about acupuncture, Hang," I said, sitting down in a hard wooden chair across from his desk. Ray sat next to me.

"Acupuncture? Helped me quit smoking."

"You ever hear of somebody using an acupuncture clinic as a cover for a card game?" I asked. "Dice, betting, that kind of thing?"

Hang gave me a half smile. "Why would I know of such a thing?"

I leaned back in my chair and put my feet up against Hang's wooden desk. I had known Hang since I was a kid; he was a business acquaintance of my Uncle Chin, my father's best friend. In his day, Uncle Chin had been a major figure in one of the Honolulu tongs, the Chinese gang operations. Growing up around his house, I'd met a whole lot of guys like Hang, never realizing their criminal connections until I'd joined the police force.

Of course, Hang knew that I knew who he was and what he did, but we went through this little dance every time we met. "You're a wise man, Hang," I said. "You know a lot of things, I'm sure. And if you knew anything about a gambling ring operating out of an acupuncture clinic in a shopping center on Waialae Avenue, you'd tell me, wouldn't you?"

"The shopping center your father owns?"

"Owned. He sold it last year."

Hang nodded. "I know the center. I know a little about the clinic. But there's nothing I can tell you about gambling there."

"Nothing you can tell us, or nothing you will tell us?" Ray asked.

"Your partner is a man of great discernment," Hang said to me, smiling. "Let me rephrase myself. I do not know anything about gambling at that facility."

I wasn't satisfied, but it was clear we weren't going to get anything more out of Hang Sung until we had something to bargain with. I figured a trip to Vice was still in order. I put my feet down on the ground, dusted off the place on Hang's desk where they had rested, then stood up, Ray following me.

"See you around, Hang," I said.

Our next appointment, the head of the karate studio, a short, wiry Japanese guy in his early thirties, was waiting to see us by the time we got back to the station. His name was Yuko Mori, and he wore sweatpants and a sweatshirt with the arms ripped off—the better to show off his muscles, I guessed.

It wasn't hard to get him to talk about the acupuncture clinic. "I tried to make an appointment," he said. "The dragon lady kept putting me off. No appointments, very busy. Every time I tried to talk to Treasure, the old grandma pushed me away."

"Treasure?" I asked.

"Beautiful," he said, making motions with his hands to indicate the girl's measurements. "I like a tall girl. You know where she is now?"

I shook my head. "We're trying to get in touch with all the tenants, see if anyone saw anything suspicious."

"Only suspicious thing I ever saw was how nice the gardener keep the grass," he said. "Like somebody pay him extra. All the time guys working out there, trimming hedges, cutting grass. Waste of time."

We thanked him, and he grumbled about having to find a new location for his *dojo*, which had just started to become profitable. He'd only had liability insurance because of the expense, so he was worried he'd have to take a job somewhere else in order to build up his savings.

So far, none of the tenants had shown a motive for arson. The cell phone store and the pharmacy were both chains; the fire was an interruption in business. Yuko Mori would suffer financially, so he had no motive either. Ray had talked to a guy from the mainland company that owned the center. They were in the process of hiring a new manager for their island properties, and he knew little about it more than its numbers. He confirmed it had been profitable and said the company had no idea what it was going to do with the burnt-out buildings and the land.

The acupuncture clinic was looking more and more suspicious. Could it be a front for a gambling operation? I went over to see Ricky Koele, a guy I knew who worked at the Business Registration Division, a state agency that's a division of the Department of Commerce and Consumer Affairs. They maintain the business registry for all corporations and other businesses in the state.

Ricky had been two years behind me at Punahou, the private school Harry, Terri, and I had attended, though we'd known each other through a couple of extracurricular activities. He had come to me a year before when his drug-dealing brother had been killed in a drive-by shooting in Wahiawa, one of the more dangerous parts of the island. Ricky was concerned because he'd overheard one of the investigating officers refer to the crime as NHI—no human involved.

Though Wahiawa was outside of my district, I'd reached out to a detective I knew there, Al Kawamoto, and he'd made sure that Ricky's brother's killer was brought in.

"That's the Professional and Vocational Licensing Division," Ricky said, when I met him at his desk and asked him about acupuncture. "There are twenty-five professional boards and commissions and twenty licensing programs. You're looking for the Board of Acupuncture."

"Can you tell me whose license is behind the Golden Needles Clinic?" I gave him the address on Waialae Avenue and he turned to his computer. It took him a couple of minutes, hitting keys and browsing screens. I listened to Lite 94.7 playing anonymous slack key guitar music over the office sound system while I waited.

"The clinic is run under the license of Dr. Hsing-Wah Hsiao," Ricky said eventually. "Reason why it took so long, I looked up Dr. Hsiao. Turns out he licensed three other clinics as well—all of them since shut down. I'm printing you a list of all the clinics under his license. Looks like he's a signologist."

"What's that? Some kind of specialist?"

Across from his desk I saw a printer kick into action. Ricky walked over to it and pulled the pages off. "Not really," he said. "When a doctor signs off on a lot of different licenses, we get the idea maybe he's nothing more than a guy who likes to sign stuff for money. A signologist."

He handed the pages to me. "Thanks," I said. "I appreciate your help."

"I owe you, Kimo," he said. "Come to me anytime."

I stuck my hand out to shake his, but he pulled me into a hug.

On my way back to the station, I thought about why someone would burn the center. To cover up a gambling operation? But they'd already shut down. Could the boy have worked for them, perhaps as a runner? Hang Sung had been hiding something, but I didn't know what.

Could the fire have been a ploy to break a lease? The clinic's two-year lease still had six months to run, and the penalty for breaking it was stiff—the clinic had to cover the rent until the landlord could find another tenant at comparable rent, or until the end of the term. Was that a good clause for that mainland company—or a deadly one for the rest of the tenants, and the boy Jingtao?

Chapter 7

ARSON PAYS WELL

BACK AT MY desk, I faxed Ricky's list to Mike, to see if any of the other clinics licensed by Dr. Hsiao had been burned. Ray said, "I nosed around while you were out. Organized Crime has a task force investigating gambling in Chinatown." He handed me a list of the guys on the task force. "You want to call Akoni?"

Akoni Hapa'ele had been my old partner in Waikīkī. I didn't see him much anymore, though we were both working out of downtown; he had been moving around from operation to operation. As soon as I left Akoni a voice mail, our next interviewee arrived: Robertico Robles, or Uncle Tico, as my nieces and nephews called him. He managed to fit us in between scouting spots for his new salon, which he announced was going to be bigger and better than Puerto Peinado—which as far as I could tell meant "hair port" in Spanish, a sly pun that he and Tatiana loved.

We went into a small conference room decorated with artwork prepared by our Police Explorer troop—pictures of cops and palm trees and one of a hula dancer on the hood of a blue-and-white. Tico accepted a Styrofoam cup of coffee. "Thanks, I need the caffeine," he said. Despite his natural ebullience, I could tell he was troubled. "I feel so terrible for that boy. I shouldn't have let him stay in the back room. I should have done what you told me, Kimo, and called social services. Either that, or taken him home with me."

Since I knew Tico so well, we'd decided Ray would take the lead on questions. "You see anyone suspicious hanging around the shopping center?" he asked.

"Suspicious how? A guy with a gasoline can? Honey, I cut hair. All day long. I flirt with the ladies, I listen to them complain about their husbands, I try to steer them away from bad hair choices. I don't get to lounge around outside looking for suspicious characters."

"Tell me about the center. The new owners keep it up well? You ever get a sense that they're letting it run down?"

"They used to have a local manager, but he quit and they haven't replaced him yet." Tico took another sip of the bad coffee. "As soon as a store closes, another is ready to take its place."

"Anyone have a gripe against you, or any of the other businesses?"

He shook his head. "Not that I know. Most of our clientele is local, little old ladies and businesswomen from St. Louis Heights. I try to make them all happy."

"What about the boy. You told my partner that you thought he was scared of something. You get any idea what that was?"

"Not a thing. I didn't want to push him."

"He ever tell you where he came from?"

"Just China. That's all. I asked Li Po, the girl from the travel agency, to talk to him, but he wouldn't tell her much either."

Tico didn't know anything about the acupuncture clinic, since his salon was at the opposite end of the center. "Better tenants than the last ones," he said, referring to the Church of Adam and Eve, an anti-gay group that had been closed down a year and a half before.

When we left the conference room, Li Po was waiting at my desk. She and Tico embraced, both of them crying a little. She was a Chinese woman in her mid-fifties, a little too plump for the bright blue silk dress she wore. Her black hair was piled up on her head, kept in place with a pair of chopsticks.

She and Tico chattered for a few minutes, and then he left. We led her back to the conference room, where she sat with a big sigh. She said that she was swamped with trying to retrace all her client activity, since her computer had been destroyed in the fire, and with it all her records.

"We'll try not to keep you too long," I said. "Can you tell us anything about the Chinese boy who was sleeping in Tico's back room?"

"His name Jingtao," she said. She had a strong Mandarin accent, and I could see Ray straining to understand her. "Only sixteen, seventeen. No more. He come from Gansu, very poor part of China."

"Do you know how he got here?" I asked.

"He never say. I think someone bring him here to work illegal."

"At the center?" I knew there were sweatshops on the island, places where illegal immigrants worked long hours sewing and working assembly lines.

She shrugged. "He no say much. He very afraid."

From the way that Li Po fiddled with her hands, and avoided looking Ray or me in the eyes, I could tell she, too, was afraid. But of what? Had the boy told her something—did she know about the gambling at the acupuncture clinic? A travel agent has a lot of different clients. It made sense that one or more of them might have said something about placing a bet. Or did she know something else about the arson that she didn't want to say?

I tried to get her to open up, with no success. She didn't know anything about acupuncture, or gambling, or how Jingtao might have ended up in Honolulu. Shifting gears, I asked, "Did you ever talk to any of the other tenants?"

She shrugged. "Little bit, now and then. Nice lady in pharmacy. Sneaky husband. I feel bad for her."

"How about the two women in charge of the clinic—you ever talk to them?"

She shrugged. "Once or twice, in parking lot. I think maybe they need help with travel some time, they come to me. But no."

Between the language gaps, and Li Po's fear, it was clear we weren't going to get anything more out of her. After she left, Ray and I went over what we had. None of the tenants we spoke with had any motive for arson. The acupuncture clinic had closed their bank account and cleared out of the clinic before the fire, which was suspicious, but until we could get a lead on one of the employees, either the elderly dragon woman or the beautiful Treasure, we didn't have anything to go on.

I called Akoni again, and he picked up the phone. "Eh, brah," I said. "Howzit?"

"Not bad, not bad. Keeping busy." I heard his fingers clicking on his computer keyboard in the background.

"You guys know anything about gambling out of an acupuncture clinic up in St. Louis Heights?" I asked, moving some papers around on my desk. "Place that burned the other night."

"Don't think so. Hold on." He put the phone down while he called out to another guy in his unit. "Nope. Tony doesn't know the place, either," he said, when he picked the phone up again. "But that doesn't mean it was clean. What you got?"

"Just suspicions."

"You get anything else, you let me know?" I heard Tony Lee say something in the background, and then Akoni said, "Gotta go, brah. Take care."

Another lead down the drain. I was fiddling around on the computer, checking my personal e-mail while Ray and I both let our brains roam over what we'd learned, when I saw a message with the subject line CONTACT ME ABOUT FIRE.

I didn't recognize the sender's address, except that it came from a student at UH. I clicked it open.

KIMO: SAW U ON TV. I CALLED 911. CAN U MEET ME 2 TALK? There was a cell phone number below. I called Ray over and showed him.

"You know this guy?"

"Don't know yet. Don't recognize the e-mail or the number."

Since I came out of the closet, I've occasionally been contacted by gay people in trouble. I've worked both sides of the street whenever I could. I help the person, if I can, and at the same time I try to provide a compassionate voice inside the station. Was this e-mailer someone I already knew—or just someone who recognized my name? But how could he have gotten my personal e-mail address? I was careful about giving that out.

Or at least I'd tried to be. During my dark time, after breaking up with Mike, I'd hung out online a lot, and every now and then I'd given out my e-mail address for some hot cybersex, or as a way to hook up with some guy I met online. The more I thought about it, the more I figured this guy was someone I'd known—perhaps, I thought wryly, in the biblical sense.

I used my cell phone to call the number from the e-mail. "This is Kimo," I said. Fortunately, Kimo's about as common a name as you can get in the islands. Since I didn't know who I was calling I was reluctant to start out with name and rank.

"Thank God," the man said. "I have been very upset about what to do."

He had a South Asian accent. "Well, let me see if I can help. You know something about the fire Sunday night?"

"I do not wish to talk about it on the phone," he said. "Can you meet me?"

I looked over at Ray, who was listening to the conversation from across the desk. "You at UH?"

"Meet me in front of the law school library. Half hour?"

"I'm downtown. I'll get there as soon as I can. Will I recognize you?"

"I know you," he said. "And when you see me, you'll recognize me, too."

He hung up. "You want to take a ride up to UH?" I asked Ray.

"Sure. Let me call Julie and tell her I'll meet her up there."

Clouds had swept in off the ocean, wrapping Diamond Head in ribbons of white, and a stiff breeze shook the palm trees on South Beretania Street as we left the parking garage. In the half hour that it took us to climb the hilly roads to Mānoa, though, the trade winds had swept the clouds away and a brutal sunshine glared off every reflective surface. I parked at a meter near the law school. "You want to go over there alone?" Ray asked.

"Why don't you hang back, but keep me in visual."

He nodded, and I strolled up to the law school library, where students were congregating on the concrete steps and under the giant kukui trees, and walking on the paths. Somebody was playing Keola Beamer's *Wooden Boat,* and the gentle rhythm of the slack key guitar made me smile.

I was looking at a notice board covered with decades of staples and the remnants of hundreds of flyers when a guy appeared next to me.

I did recognize him, though I'd never known his name. As I thought, he was one of my hookups from MenSayHi.com, an island dating site for gay men. He was about five ten, very handsome, with short, dark hair and skin the color of a coffee bean.

I knew the first time I signed on to MenSayHi.com that it was a mistake. All it would take is one disgruntled trick to report me to the department, or start spreading vicious rumors about me being a sloppy bottom who loved to get plowed, and my career could go up in flames. I already had guys teasing me about working for the Department of Homo-land Security, or snickering behind my back. Cops are among the most homophobic guys I've ever met, pouncing on the straightest guy who mentioned seeing a chick flick, asking if he'd started pissing sitting down—anything to get a rise out of you.

But when it came to getting laid, I was willing to take a few risks.

I'd tried meeting guys in ordinary ways. I'd met my first boyfriend on the beach, and I'd met Mike on the job. I'd picked up, and been picked up by, guys at bars and clubs. But after I broke up with Mike, I didn't want to go out. I just wanted to get laid, frequently, and in ways that reminded me what a lousy human being I was for the way I'd dumped Mike without giving him a chance to explain.

So I logged into MenSayHi.com and answered a couple of ads, and had some sexual encounters that went from bland to disturbing. The things I got off on scared me a little—mostly men treating me badly, physically, tweaking and slapping and pounding various body parts. Somehow I got punishment confused with sex; I thought because I'd been a jerk when I broke up with Mike, I should be treated that way by every guy I met. I'd always been a little intrigued by S&M, and I indulged myself and my throbbing dick.

A few of the guys had simply been closeted, though, and if I recalled correctly, this was one of them. "I'd rather not give you my name, if you don't mind," he said. I couldn't place the accent, though it was South Asian.

We walked off to a bench in the shade of a big kukui tree. I saw Ray leaning up against a palm across from us, watching, and I said, "I remember you. You didn't give me your name then, either."

"My situation is difficult," he said. "My wife doesn't know what I do. Her father is paying my law school tuition, and he will cut me off and force my wife to divorce me if he ever finds out."

"Wait a second," I said. "I thought this was about the fire?"

He frowned. "I was here at the library Sunday night. Studying. I got a text from a man I had met on MenSayHi. He was working late, had the whole office to himself. Wanted me to come over."

"Office on Waialae Avenue?" I asked.

"Across from that shopping center that burned. We finished, like maybe ten o'clock, and I walked out to my car."

"Where was your car parked? In the lot in front of the office building?"

The guy shook his head. "I was afraid someone might see my car. So I parked around the corner, on that side street that dead-ends into Waialae Avenue."

I pictured it in my head. "Facing toward the street, and the shopping center?"

He nodded. "I sat in the car for a while, thinking. I knew that what I had been doing was wrong, and that I needed to stop." His mouth set into a frown and his brows came together. His palms were sweating and he wiped them on his pants.

I knew the feeling. I'd had it myself, more than a few times. It wasn't until I'd come out of the closet that those feelings of shame began to fade away.

"After a while I knew I couldn't just sit there forever, and I was about to leave. I saw this guy, like a ninja or something, all dressed in black, come running out from behind the shopping center. From where I was parked, I couldn't see where he went, but about a minute later, a dark sedan came zooming across the parking lot, turned onto Waialae Avenue, and drove off."

A group of students passed us, laughing and fooling around. One of the guys was shirtless and buff, and I watched my caller's eyes track him as he passed. I could see beads of sweat pooling on his forehead. "Just then my cell phone rang, and I saw that it was my wife. She wanted to know when I was coming home."

He wiped his forehead. "I told her that I was just leaving the campus. She wanted me to stop at the ABC Store near our apartment and get some milk for the morning. We talked for a couple of minutes, and I was so scared that she knew I wasn't at the library at all."

A gray cloud passed overhead, heavy with rain, throwing us into shadow. "When I hung up the phone, I turned the car on and rolled down the windows. As I drove away, I smelled smoke and realized it was coming up from behind the center, and I called 911."

"That was pretty good of you," I said. "Considering the circumstances."

"I'm not a bad person," he said. "I believe in the law." He paused. "I saw you on TV, and I thought I could trust you. That you'd understand."

A cool breeze swept past us, rustling the dead leaves under the kukui tree. "I do. I understand. Tell me about this ninja. Man or woman?"

"Definitely a man. I saw the way he ran."

"Height? Weight?"

He shrugged. "Too far away to see much. Maybe a little on the chunky side, average height, but I didn't pay a lot of attention."

"How about the car. Did you notice anything about the car as it drove away?"

"Fancy sedan," he said. "BMW or Mercedes. I have to drive a piece of crap Toyota. I tell you, as soon as I pass the bar I'm leasing one of those nice cars."

"Color?"

"Dark blue," he said. "With a white interior."

"You saw that in the dark?"

"Oh, the ninja's car. I thought you were asking about the car I want."

I wanted to bop the guy on the head. He was cheating on his wife, and maybe he'd married her just so that her father would put him through law school. But he thought he was honest and righteous because he'd called me. I did understand the pressure he was under, though, so I cut him a little slack.

"The ninja's car," I said patiently. "Notice anything about it? The color?"

He shook his head. "Dark color, that's all I saw."

I pulled out a business card and scrawled my personal cell on the back. "If you think of anything more, please call me," I said.

"You don't need to know my name?" The relief was evident on his face.

"I appreciate your call, and the information you've given me," I said. "But I have your e-mail address if I need to get in touch with you. I don't want to know your name because I don't want it to get into any paperwork."

"Thank you." It felt as though he wanted to hug me, but it was a public place—and after all, we'd done a lot more than hug the one time we'd hooked up. He settled for shaking my hand once again.

I watched him leave, and Ray came over to me. I told him what I'd learned. "Ninja, huh?" he said.

"Yeah. A ninja in a fancy sedan."

"Arson pays well," Ray said.

"Better than police work," I said.

Chapter 8

FINALISTS FOR MISS CHINATOWN

RAY HUNG AROUND UH to wait for Julie, and I walked to my truck. On my way, Mike called my cell. "I've got a lead," he said. "You going to be home tonight?"

"I'm on my way there now," I said, then regretted it. I was having enough trouble dealing with Mike on neutral ground, with others present. What was I doing inviting him over? And what was he doing asking?

It was just after five, the height of rush hour, and the sun was setting. The streets were alive with neon and with car stereos blasting hip-hop as the tropical night descended rapidly. The air was hot and humid, without a hint of a trade wind. The slow traffic and intermittent showers made me edgy, combined with the sense that our case wasn't moving forward either. Or maybe it was just knowing that I was going to see Mike.

When I pulled into my parking space, he was sitting in his truck on the street, the same one with the flames painted on the side that he'd been driving when we dated. "I had an idea," he said, getting out of the truck and walking toward me. "I cross-referenced a bunch of unsolved arsons, and I think I found a pattern."

He showed me a list of ten arsons over the past two years, but the sun was setting and it was too dark to see clearly, so I led him upstairs to my apartment. Fortunately, I'd cleaned up on Sunday so most of the clothes and sports equipment were put away, and there were no crusty dishes in the sink or dirty underwear on the floor to embarrass me.

He sat down at my kitchen table, and I got us a pair of Long-board Lagers from the fridge—only realizing as I popped the caps that if Mike was an alcoholic, based on that vodka in his water bottle, it was a bad idea to give him a beer.

He accepted the bottle gratefully and took a deep swig. "Long day," he said.

I sat across from him and looked at the list. The other fires had been at a massage parlor in Waikele, a quick mart in Kaneohe, a coffee shop near the airport, a Christian religious shop downtown, and a lingerie shop in Chinatown. "They were all places where the business closed down before the fire," Mike said. "I want to see if there's anything else that connects them. Business licenses, phone numbers, that kind of thing. You have any ideas?"

There was something familiar about that lingerie shop, and I struggled to make the connection. Then it hit me. "I know this shop."

Mike looked at me, his eyebrows raised. "My old partner from Waikīkī, Akoni, and I went there when we were investigating Tommy Pang's murder. Tommy owned the place. I wonder if any of these others were owned by tong guys."

"Can you run them by your Organized Crime unit tomorrow?"

"I will." Something was tickling around the edge of my brain. "The pharmacist's wife told me that she thought the old Chinese woman at the clinic was named Norma. And at this lingerie shop, there was another old Chinese woman named Norma." I reached over to the sofa, picked up my laptop, and brought it to the table, where I turned it on. "If I can pull up the report online, maybe I can find her last name, and we'll see if we can connect her to both places."

Mike scooted his chair around next to me and looked on as I logged on to the department's intranet and searched for the right files. Being so close to Mike unleashed a wave of pure longing, followed by sadness. I had loved him, and I'd been devastated to find out that he'd cheated on me, thinking at the time that it meant he hadn't loved me the way I'd loved him. I'd overreacted—but if we hadn't broken up over that incident, something else would have happened to tear us apart.

Mike still wore the same lemon-scented cologne, and I wondered if he'd reapplied it in his truck while waiting for me to pull up. What did he want from me? Why couldn't this meeting have waited until the next morning, and included Ray?

I multitasked—talking to Mike, searching the files, and at the same time considering Mike's motives. I'm no computer geek; I leave that to Harry Ho. It took me a lot of searching, because I wasn't giving it my full attention, to pull up the reports from Tommy Pang's murder.

It wasn't an investigation I was happy to recall, since it was the one that had dragged me out of the closet two years before. But I found Norma Ching's name in one of our reports. "You think this might be the same old woman?" Mike asked.

"Worth checking," I said. A few minutes later, I'd run out of options. There was no listing for Norma in the phone book, or in Yahoo's people search, and she had no criminal record.

Tommy Pang, who had owned the lingerie shop, was my Uncle Chin's illegitimate son. Would his widow, my Aunt Mei-Mei, have known Norma? I looked at my watch. It was dinnertime, and I knew if I showed up at her house she'd ply me with delicious food. Mike, too, if he was along for the ride.

"Want to take a trip up to St. Louis Heights with me?" I asked.

On the way to Aunt Mei-Mei's house, I reminded Mike of my relationship with her and Uncle Chin. "This is the guy whose wake was going on when we were fighting that fire in Wa'ahila State Park?" he asked.

"Yup. You met her there, or maybe at my parents' house."

Mike had come over for dinner a couple of times, and was being gradually absorbed into the Kanapa'aka clan when we'd broken up. Both of us were quiet, probably thinking the same things, when I pulled into Aunt Mei-Mei's driveway.

She came to the door in a flowered dress, with a white apron over it. From inside, I could smell something delicious cooking. "Kimo! You just in time for dinner," she said. "Jimmy on his way from college with bunch of friends."

A year and a half before, just before Uncle Chin's death, they had taken in Jimmy Ah Wong, a gay teenager whose father had kicked him out. Since then, he had completed his GED and been admitted to the University of Hawai'i, where he'd started as a freshman a few months before.

"Do you remember Mike?" I asked Aunt Mei-Mei. "He's a fire inspector, and we're working on a case together—the fire at the center my dad used to own. We wanted to ask you a question."

It was strange to introduce Mike that way, without mentioning all that had gone between us. But if Aunt Mei-Mei was surprised to see Mike, she didn't mention it. "You ask while you eat." She hugged us both, then led us into the dining room, which had been set for a crowd. "Always room for more," she said. "Sit."

She brought out a platter of tiny dumplings, delicately fried, and sat with us as we ate. "What you want to ask?"

"You know a woman named Norma Ching?" I asked, and Aunt Mei-Mei's face darkened.

"What you want with Norma?"

"I think she might have been working at an acupuncture clinic in the center."

Aunt Mei-Mei laughed, exposing a row of tiny white teeth. "Acupuncture," she said, and it was good to see her smile. She hadn't done enough of that since Uncle Chin's death. "No acupuncture if Norma there."

"That's what we were thinking," I said.

"Do you know how to get in touch with her?" Mike asked. "These dumplings are amazing, by the way."

I'd been so busy eating I hadn't stopped to tell Aunt Mei-Mei how good they were, but I did.

She waved her hand. "Just dumplings," she said. "Lots more food in kitchen. Jimmy's friends, they always hungry."

"Norma Ching," I said.

"I no want to talk about Norma," Aunt Mei-Mei said. "You eat."

I was about to protest, but a car pulled up in the driveway, with the sound of loud music and laughter. Aunt Mei-Mei's face broke into a smile again, and she hurried to the door. "You OK to stay?" I asked Mike.

"If the rest of the food's as good as this, I'll move in," he said.

Jimmy's friends were all guys from his dorm, mostly straight, as far as I could tell, and as Aunt Mei-Mei had said, they were all hungry. We ate honey chicken, white rice, wonton soup, more dumplings, spare ribs—the woman must have been cooking all day to generate so much food.

The guys were all curious about being a cop, and a fireman, and we carried on rapid-fire discussions, even as Norma Ching kept percolating in the back of my mind. One of the guys said, "Man, you guys must get a lot of babes in your jobs."

I looked at Mike, and he looked at me, and we both burst out laughing. Jimmy laughed, too, then looked at his friend and said, "Dude, can't you tell? They're both gay. They used to be boyfriends."

The guys didn't seem to care, just kept peppering us with questions. It was almost nine before we finished.

The boys left first, after lots of compliments to Aunt Mei-Mei, and kisses and hugs from her. "The poor woman's going to spend the next two days cleaning up," Mike whispered to me as we watched them pile into somebody's old Chrysler LeBaron convertible, a rental car reject from the 1980s.

They turned up the car's meager stereo and backed away, heading downhill to the tune of some Jawaiian reggae. "The future of America," Mike said, as we walked back to the kitchen, where Aunt Mei-Mei had begun loading the dishwasher.

"Let us help you," I said.

"No, no, you go," Aunt Mei-Mei said.

"About Norma Ching," I began, but Aunt Mei-Mei held up a tiny hand with pink lacquered fingernails.

"I have to ask for address for you," Aunt Mei-Mei said. "Someone tell me."

We had to be content with that. But there was something else there, and I knew I couldn't let it loose. When we were back in my truck, I picked up my cell phone and dialed my parents' number.

My dad answered. "Hey, Tūtū Al," I said. "Howzit?"

"I'm not your tūtū, boy," he said. He was grumpy, which probably meant my mom was watching his diet. "You can call me Dad."

I laughed and said, "I'm driving, Dad, so I'm putting you on speaker. You ever hear of a woman named Norma Ching?"

There was silence on the other end of the phone, and for a minute I worried he really was angry that I'd called him grandpa. "What do you want with Norma?"

"Why does everybody ask me that? Aunt Mei-Mei said the same thing."

"You asked Mei-Mei about Norma? Are you stupid?"

"Hold on, Dad. I'm missing something here."

He sighed. "Your Uncle Chin was a good man, but he had many weaknesses. Pretty women were one of them."

I remembered meeting Norma. "Dad, she's an old woman."

Mike poked me in the side and I looked across at him.

"She used to be one of the most beautiful women in Honolulu." There was a wistfulness in my father's voice that made me wonder a little. "She had Chin at the tips of her fingers. He bought her the apartment in Chinatown where she lives."

I'd always heard rumors that Uncle Chin was a womanizer, but in the past my father had been cagey when I asked him. I knew that Tommy Pang had been Chin's *manuahi,* or illegitimate son, from a woman in Hong Kong, but I'd never paid much attention to any women he might have had after that.

"You know where that apartment is? Aunt Mei-Mei said she didn't know the address, though she was going to try to find it for me."

"Best to let Mei-Mei," my father said. "She and Norma, they go back a long way. They were both finalists for Miss Chinatown, you know, way back when Chin and I were in college."

"Aunt Mei-Mei?"

The disbelief must have crackled in my voice, because my father laughed. "We were all young once," he said.

I thanked him and hung up. "I can see that, you know," Mike said. "I'll bet Aunt Mei-Mei was quite the looker when she was young."

"What do you think she meant when she said that if Norma was around there wasn't any acupuncture going on?" I asked.

He shrugged. "Could be she knows about the gambling. You said her husband was a crook, yeah? You think she knew about his business?"

I shook my head. "She was always just a housewife," I said. "Uncle Chin never let her know anything that could have hurt her." I paused. "I'll tell Ray about your list tomorrow. I can take it down to Honolulu Hale, and run it by Akoni, too, in case Organized Crime knows anything. You got any other ideas?"

I realized I wanted to know if Mike had any ideas about the two of us—but I didn't say that. Mike shook his head. "Making the connection to those other fires was my big leap. I'll start going over the case files tomorrow. Maybe there's a lead."

I pulled into my parking space, wondering how the night was going to end. Mike yawned theatrically. "Got to get my beauty sleep," he said. We stood next to each other beside my truck, both of us unsure how to part. Should I hug him? Shake his hand? Or just walk away?

We both made little movements toward each other, and I gave up and hugged him. It felt good to be close to him again. "It's been good seeing you again, Kimo," he said, as we pulled apart.

"Me too. See you around." There was a warmth in his voice that thrilled me a little, and as he walked away I tried to make myself stop thinking about him, about the way his body had felt against mine. I watched him get into his truck, then wave as he drove past. I waved back, unable to shake the feeling that the evening had felt almost like a date.

I was too antsy after that encounter with Mike to go upstairs and go to sleep, so instead I walked through the evening tourist crowds to the Rod and Reel Club. A tall Chinese transvestite and a *haole* surfer dude were laughing and talking in front of an ABC Store, and tiny orange-billed mynah birds pecked at crumbs on the sidewalk. Slack key guitar music spilled out of every other shop. I put my hands in the pockets of my board shorts and felt like whistling.

My neighborhood gay bar, the Rod and Reel Club, was like a second home, and as I hoped, Gunter was there, having just come in from his shift at the Grand Kuhio. There was another guy with him, a *haole* in his fifties wearing what looked at first glance like a police uniform—but wasn't.

"Hey, Kimo, I want you to meet my new boss," Gunter said, waving me over. "Stan LoCicero, Kimo Kanapa'aka."

"The homicide detective," Stan said, reaching out to shake my hand. "Nice to meet you. I admire everything you've done."

He had an unlit cigar in the corner of his mouth, a ruddy complexion, and the lines and wrinkles that come with a life well lived. But I could see he'd been quite handsome when he was younger. "You don't know everything I've done," I said, and we all laughed.

I ordered a beer and we talked for a while. I couldn't help checking Stan out; as Gunter had said, he was hot. His body was in good shape for a guy his age—but it was something about his attitude that made him attractive. He looked like the kind of guy who'd learned a few tricks, and who'd be happy to show them off.

"You know, you're not the only gay cop in Honolulu," Stan said to me. "I could tell you stories about a captain in the traffic division, for example."

"Really?" I didn't know every cop in Honolulu, but I had a feeling that if there was a gay captain somewhere I might have met him.

"No names, of course," Stan said. "A fella has to be discreet. But if this guy ever pulls you over, it won't be for speeding. And once you start blowing him, he never says stop."

We all laughed. "He's in traffic?" I asked. "*Haole,* Hawai'ian . . . what?"

Stan pretended to run a zipper over his lips. "My lips are sealed," he said. "That is, unless there's a dick in the vicinity."

He looked at his watch. "Speaking of which," he said. "I've got a date with a hot little piece of Japanese ass. Much though I'd like to hang out with you gentlemen, Big Stan needs to have his fun."

He stood up, shook our hands, and said it had been nice to meet me. "I'll see you Friday, Gunter," he said. He laid a bill on the counter. "You guys have a round on me, all right?"

"Thanks, Stan," Gunter said.

When he'd left, I said, "Big Stan?"

"I told you, he's hung like a horse."

"But come on. Do you have a name for your dick?"

"Dick?"

"More like Little Richard," I said.

"You didn't say that the last time I plowed your ass," Gunter said.

"Speaking of assholes," I said, "I saw Mike Riccardi tonight." I told him about seeing Mike at the fire on Sunday night, about working with him, and then about our dinner at Aunt Mei-Mei's.

Gunter had never liked Mike much, because Mike was so closeted, and Mike disapproved of Gunter's flamboyance and sexual adventuring. "You're not getting back together with him, are you?" Gunter asked. "Because if you say you are, I'm going to tie you to your bed until you come to your senses."

"You mean tie me to my bed and fuck me till I'm senseless?" I asked.

"You are the best-looking guy in the bar at the moment," he said. "Well, second best, after me."

I could go home by myself, I thought. Be good, be celibate. But I was damned horny, after the date with Dr. Phil, seeing Mike, then flirting with Stan LoCicero. Chances were, if I went home by myself, I'd end up online, looking for sex at MenSayHi, and I knew that was a bad idea.

Sex with Gunter wasn't the smartest idea in the world either. But at the time, it seemed like the safest path to take. I drained the last of my beer and said, "Well, you're not Big Stan, but you'll do."

Chapter 9

BEAUTY AND HIDDEN DANGER

I SURFED IN the early morning, trying to avoid thinking about Mike, Gunter, or the fact that the arson investigation had stalled. We'd interviewed all the tenants except the owner of the acupuncture clinic, whose ties back to China we could not trace. Everyone we spoke to represented a successful, thriving business without a motive for arson. Even the corporation that had bought the center from my father checked out.

We knew nothing about the victim, other than that his body type matched that of Jingtao, the boy Tico had picked up in the alley. Jingtao may not even have been his name. We passed Tatiana's sketch out to the cops in the area, and Ray and I canvassed the stores and offices to see if anyone recognized him. No one did.

Ray and I got roped into a stakeout for another case, and we spent most of the day sitting in my truck, hoping that a teenaged gangbanger would show up at his mother's house in Wahiawa. The gangbanger was a suspect in the murder of two drug dealers in Waikīkī, one of whom was his girlfriend's brother. "Want to get this case resolved before Thanksgiving," Ray said. "Be awkward having that big family dinner when you're worried your boyfriend might have killed your brother."

"Think about bringing him home to meet Mama," I said. "Nice to meet you. Did you kill my son?"

We sat like that most of the day, just shooting the shit, and I felt damn lucky that Ray was the guy who'd stumbled into the department when I needed a partner. He was smart, in brains and street knowledge, he was patient, and he had a good heart. Plus he liked Hawai'ian music, so we went through CD after CD of Sam Alama and his Islanders, Pua Almeida and his Club Pago Pago Orchestra, and the Brothers Cazimero.

Most days, you spend more time with your partner than you do with your significant other. You've got to find a guy who's on the same wavelength you are, or else you butt heads all day long. Ray and I argued sometimes, but neither of us held a grudge for long.

"Any more ideas on tracking the dead kid?" he asked late in the day. "I was thinking maybe homeless shelters. This might not be the first time he ran away."

"Good idea. There's a gay teen center on Waikīkī, too. A lot of those kids live on the street. Maybe one of them has seen him."

I'd volunteered at the center myself, leading a group of kids once a week through workouts and some self-empowerment stuff. I stopped going after I broke up with Mike, when I started thinking that I didn't have anything good I could say. But maybe it was time to go back.

Just before the end of our shift, the radio crackled with the news that the gangbanger had been nabbed in Waikīkī, and I dropped Ray off on my way home. I was feeling at loose ends, so I walked through the humid evening, tiki torches being lit on the street around me, to the Gay Teen Center.

Cathy Selkirk, the tiny, half-Japanese lesbian who ran the center, was in her office, and I settled into the big comfy chair across from her desk to pour out some of my troubles. But first I had to apologize.

"I'm sorry I blew off the group," I said. "I was going through some stuff and I didn't feel much like a role model."

"Anytime you want to come back, the door's open."

"I was thinking about it."

"How about a week from tonight?" Cathy asked. "That'll give us time to get some posters up, see if we can draw a crowd."

I agreed, and then I showed her Jingtao's picture. She didn't recognize him, but she promised to get it passed around among the kids.

I kissed Cathy good-bye, sent my regards to her partner Sandra, and walked down Kalākaua Boulevard for a while, showing the hookers and the street vendors Jingtao's picture and not getting any response.

There was a steady stream of traffic down Kalākaua—buses and rental cars and delivery trucks, the occasional horn or screeching brakes blending in with the hawkers selling heritage jewelry and the sound of slack key guitar music coming out of a T-shirt shop. It was just after six, and the sun was setting over the ocean. Tiny white lights wrapped around the trunks of the palm trees, and car headlights bounced off the elegant storefronts and the homeless oddballs equally.

It's a strange thing, living in a tourist paradise. Every day, you go to work, live your life, and all around you are people who've saved all year to spend just a few days in this beautiful place you sometimes take for granted. Every now and then I like to see it through their eyes, and I always end up surprising myself with its beauty and hidden danger.

Thursday morning, Ray and I caught another case, a vehicular homicide near the Aloha Tower. We spent most of the day interviewing witnesses and tracking the suspect car. Just before the end of our shift, the driver turned himself in, accompanied by his attorney. Since I had to go out to the STD clinic that evening, Ray agreed to stick around and walk the guy through the system. "Hell, I can use the overtime," he said. "Maybe someday Julie and I can afford a second car."

I felt sorry for him. He was already pulling temporary duty whenever he could: security gigs at the Aloha Bowl flea market, Hawai'ian nationalism rallies, special events at the Blaisdell Center. I was lucky that my living needs were simple, and my parents had announced a week before that they were going to start giving each of us an advance on our inheritance, so if I needed anything I'd have that money to fall back on.

On the other hand, I knew I'd rather be sitting around a court-room waiting for our errant driver to be arraigned than going out to the STD clinic near Tripler to tell Mike's parents that their son was a drunk. But if I stalled, I'd have to wait another few weeks for them to be on duty, or attempt to corral them somewhere else.

At the clinic, I showed my badge to the receptionist and asked to speak with Dr. Riccardi. "He's with a patient now," she said.

"I'll wait."

Once again, the reception area was filled with an interesting cross-section of locals who wanted discretion. I avoided eye contact with anyone, and sat in a corner—the location expressing something about how I felt being there. The *People* magazines I'd read the last time I was there were gone, replaced with newer yet still out-of-date editions. I was skimming one when the receptionist called.

I was struck again by how much Mike resembled his father. Mike had a slight epicanthic fold to his eyes, and a mustache, but the shape of the face, the cheekbones, the curve of his lips—they were all the same.

"What can I do for you?" Dr. Riccardi asked, escorting me to a run-down office that was clearly shared by a bunch of different doctors, since there was nothing personal there—just a collection of posters and pamphlets about STDs. "I hope you know I can't reveal any information about patients without a warrant."

"I'm not here on an official basis," I said. "My name is Kimo Kanapa'aka, and I'm a detective with the Honolulu Police Department."

"I know who you are, detective," Dr. Riccardi said, turning to face me. "You're the man who broke my son's heart."

Every now and then, in the homicide business, you run across someone who says something so totally unexpected that you don't know how to respond. Sometimes it's a confession, from someone who wasn't even a suspect. Sometimes it's the revelation of a life behind the façade we all present to the world.

Dr. Riccardi's statement was one of those. I'd been so concerned about not outing Mike to his father that I'd never considered his father might already know.

"I may not have been the greatest father, detective, but I know my son. I'm sure Michael has had a few choice words to say about me, and my expectations of him, but I love him, no matter what." He motioned me to a hard chair across from the desk, and he sat down behind it in a worn armchair.

"Michael's mother and I always wondered why he never brought any young women home to meet us," he said. "Was he embarrassed of us? Living in New York, we knew he was uncomfortable that his mother was Korean, and maybe that was why he didn't bring friends home, but we thought that moving to Hawai'i had helped him get over that."

He steepled his fingers and stared at me. It wasn't a comfortable stare at all. I'm accustomed to being the interrogator and I didn't like the role reversal. From the glare in Dr. Riccardi's eyes it was clear he didn't like me, and I didn't know how I was going to tell him about the vodka in the water bottle without seeming like a tattletale as well as a heartbreaker.

"About a year ago, Mike stopped joining us for dinner, and he didn't do anything except go to work and then lock himself up in his side of the house. One day, I got fed up."

I could see from Dr. Riccardi's eyes that it wasn't a happy memory. But he worked in an STD clinic; he was accustomed to tough conversations.

"I found him passed out on the sofa, an empty six-pack of beer next to him. I woke him, and had some harsh words for him." He sighed. "Not one of my finest moments as a father, I know. I demanded to know what was wrong with him. I said that I'd put up with a lot—his poor academic performance, which was far below what I knew he was capable of. His choice of a dangerous career. His Peter Pan complex—trying to remain a boy forever."

"That must have been difficult for both of you," I said.

"I suppose I should thank you for prompting the conversation, but I'm afraid I can't." Man, if looks could have killed, I'd have been dead in my chair. "He told me about you then." A hint of a smile crossed his lips. "I still think of him as my little boy, you know. I want to fight his battles for him, though I know I can't. When he told me how much you had hurt him, I wanted to hurt you in return."

"Mike hurt me plenty on his own," I said.

"But you were the one who broke up with him," Riccardi said. "Because he wouldn't become the kind of poster child you've made yourself for gay rights."

"I haven't made myself a poster child," I said. "I accepted the responsibility that comes with who I am and what I do. But that isn't why Mike and I broke up."

He waved his hand. "This is all old news, isn't it, detective? Is that why you came here today? To 'out' my son to me?"

"Not at all." I took a deep breath. "Mike and I are working together on a case again, and Monday morning I picked up a water bottle he'd been drinking from—just to take a sip myself. It wasn't water."

Dr. Riccardi's brows closed together and he sighed again. "I was afraid something like this would happen. Seeing you has driven him to drink again. Why can't you just leave my son alone?"

At that point I'd had enough of Dr. Riccardi's attitude, and I stood up to leave. "I guarantee you, Dr. Riccardi, I didn't want to come down here and speak to you. But I didn't know who else to tell, and I do care about Mike and want to make sure he gets some help." I took a deep breath. "But if you want to know the truth about why we broke up, it's in your records here. Patient number 1423."

I shouldn't have said anything, and as I drove back to Waikīkī I felt lousy. Not only had I told Mike's dad that Mike was a drunk—I'd branded him as a careless slut as well. From the little I knew of Mike's relationship with his parents, I could imagine his father's icy stare, the disappointment radiating from him. I remembered

Mike telling me that every time he got sick as a kid, his father took it as a personal affront. "How does it look when a doctor's son is so careless about the flu," I remembered Mike repeating to me.

How much worse would it be when it wasn't the flu Dr. Riccardi was complaining about, but gonorrhea. Especially when he and Mike's mom volunteered at the safe sex clinic.

It was after eight by the time I got home. I picked up a mystery novel I'd been reading, one of Charles Knief's Honolulu private-eye books, but I couldn't concentrate. I got online and started making lists of homeless shelters and places that helped teenagers that Ray and I could check out the next day.

Around eleven I looked at the clock, yawned, and stripped down for bed. I'd just turned out the lights when somebody started pounding on my front door. "Jesus, hold on," I said, jumping up and fumbling around in the dark for a pair of shorts. I looked through the peephole and saw Mike Riccardi there.

"You know what time it is?" I said, when I opened the door. "You're gonna wake up the whole neighborhood."

"You had to go and do it," he said, slurring his words and pushing past me. I closed the door and turned around to look at him. "You had to tell my parents."

"I was worried about you."

"Fuck you, Kimo. You were pissed." A wave of alcohol fumes washed over me. Mike was pissed, too—in more than one sense of the word. He was angry, and he was drunk. "Jesus, Mike, take a look at yourself," I said. "You're drinking vodka out of a water bottle at eight o'clock in the morning. You don't think that's a problem?"

"What I do is my business. I'm maintaining." He wavered a little on his feet, and I was worried he'd fall over on me.

"Yeah, and the first time somebody from the fire department catches you, you're out on your ass," I said. I poked him in the chest and pushed him back. "Take a look at yourself, pal. How much have you had to drink?"

"None of your fucking business," he said, and he burped.

I shook my head. "I couldn't just walk away and pretend I didn't see what I saw. I had to tell somebody, and the only person I could trust was your dad."

Mike's eyes glazed over, and suddenly he threw up—all over himself and the tile floor in front of my refrigerator. He looked at me and then he just collapsed. I caught him, getting his vomit all over me and my shorts, and he passed out.

I figured it was my penance. I stripped him, sponged him off, and laid him down on my bed. It was a level of intimacy we'd never shared when we were dating; we'd both been pretty self-sufficient, and the only times we'd undressed each other had been as a prelude to sex. But there was something sweet about the intimacy, despite the stink of vomit.

He started snoring as soon as his head hit the pillow. I cleaned myself up, scrubbed the tile floor, then took his dirty clothes and my shorts downstairs to the washing machine on the first floor of the building. There was a comfy chair there, and I sat there and read my book and dozed while the clothes washed and then dried.

It was almost two o'clock when I went back upstairs. Mike was still asleep, still snoring, spread-eagled on my bed. I grabbed an extra pillow and lay down on the sofa. I was asleep myself within a few minutes, despite the noise emanating from the other side of the Japanese screen.

It was just after daylight when I woke up to see Mike, naked, standing at the foot of the sofa. "What happened to my clothes?" he demanded.

"Good morning to you, too," I said, yawning.

His body looked good—better than good, actually. Muscular forearms dusted with black hair. A broad chest that narrowed to his waist, meaty calves, and a half-hard dick that I remembered was more than big enough to fill me up completely, front or back. "What happened last night?"

"You showed up at my door drunk off your ass," I said, sitting up. I pulled the comforter over my crotch so he wouldn't see that I was hard just from looking at him. "You threw up all over yourself, me, and my floor. Then you passed out. I washed your clothes for you—they're over there."

I pointed toward the front door.

"For real?" he asked.

"For real. You don't remember?"

He shook his head. "I guess I am fucked up."

"Guess so."

I watched as he pulled on his clothes. "I'm sorry," he said, as he was getting ready to leave.

"Me, too," I said. "For everything."

Chapter 10

THE FIREMAN OR THE TIGER

ON FRIDAY, RAY and I went around to homeless shelters and showed pictures of Jingtao, without making any connections. I was glad we had Saturday and Sunday off; maybe something would break over the weekend.

Ray was doing special duty both days—security for a gun show at the Blaisdell Center—so he was fine with an easy Friday. Me, I was bored and antsy, trying not to think about Mike, or about my dinner that night with Haoa, Tatiana, and Sergei.

Sergei, like his sister, was tall, sturdy, and blond. He'd bummed around a bunch of jobs in Alaska—working the pipeline, cooking at a diner, helping train dogs for the Iditarod. It didn't sound like we had anything in common except being gay. Not the kind of fix up I was looking forward to.

I arrived at my brother's house just before seven. My truck was making some unhappy noises on the steep, twisting climb up into St. Louis Heights, and I thought that I'd have to make an appointment to take it in for what would turn out to be some very expensive repair.

Most of the houses in the neighborhood had no yards to speak of, front or back, but Haoa's was on a wedge-shaped corner lot. Walking into his backyard is like entering a tropical exhibit at a botanical garden. Combine my brother's intuitive feel for plants and flowers with Tatiana's artistic sensibility, and you get a lush landscape full of short and tall palms; spiky red and orange heliconia; the five-petaled plumeria with orange centers and a frosting of white at the edge; dark red anthurium; and single, double, and triple hibiscus in red, pink, purple, and white. The sensory overload is amazing—from the bright colors of the flowers, to the glossy green leaves, to the scent of the tuberose. It's like being draped in a full-body lei.

I'd met Sergei before and liked him. Maybe it was a physical thing; I prefer my men big and beefy, and he had that in spades—six-two, broad shouldered, with thighs like tree trunks. He had tribal tattoos around both biceps, which bulged out of his short-sleeved aloha shirt. He wore long board shorts and rubber slippers, and his hair was the same honey blond as Tatiana's and nearly as long.

My brother was grilling steaks, and Tatiana went inside to get the salad. I asked Sergei, "What brings you to Hawai'i?"

He laughed. "It's Tatiana's turn to watch me. Everybody else in the family has given up." He downed his wine in one big gulp. "I was staying in our sister Natasha's guesthouse until her husband caught me screwing the neighbor's teenaged son in the sauna."

I raised my eyebrows. "Hey, he was eighteen, and horny. Nothing illegal about it. Of course, Arnie had the whole sauna ripped out and rebuilt afterward. Tasha was pissed about that."

Tatiana returned and the meal passed quickly. I laughed and joked with my brother, my sister-in-law, and Sergei. At some point his bare toes were tickling the inside of my leg, and at another point he reached over to touch my hand and an electric current shot through my body.

I helped Haoa clean up the grill after dinner. "You ever go over to the center on Waialae Avenue?" I asked, scrubbing a grate with a bristled brush.

"The one that burned? Sometimes."

I knew Haoa placed the occasional bet on ball games, and that he and his college buddies played poker together. And once he'd narrowly escaped a raid on a *pai gow* game in Chinatown. "You know anything about gambling over there?"

He looked up from tying up a bag of trash. "You still investigating that fire?"

"Yeah. We think there might have been gambling going on out of the acupuncture clinic."

He shrugged. "Not that I knew of."

Sergei was house-sitting for Haoa and Tatiana's neighbors who were on a round-the-world cruise, and after dinner I walked down the hill with him so he could show me his digs. I was pretty sure he'd be showing me something else, too, and I was fine with that.

The living room, dining room, and kitchen were all fine; what I wanted to see was the master bedroom suite. Sergei flipped on the overhead lights as we walked in, and I flipped them off.

He turned to me, and I wrapped my arms around his broad back and pulled him in for a kiss. "Hey, there, sexy," he said, when we parted.

Sergei unbuttoned my aloha shirt and dropped it to the floor, then attacked my nipples with his mouth. First one, then the next; starting with a gentle licking and sucking, then just the hint of teeth, then it felt like he'd grabbed them in his jaws and started twisting.

All I had to do was whimper and moan and rub his head and shoulders. Every now and then he'd pull off for a deep kiss, and by the time my nipples were tender and achy the rest of me was hungering for his touch. We stripped in the moonlight and tumbled into bed, talking in low voices as we touched and stroked each other.

Sex with Sergei was like a return to a more innocent past, before all the kinky stuff I'd gotten involved in. I was relieved that I could enjoy sex that was romantic and gentle once again. Though he was wild, everything he did was approached in the spirit of fun. "You like that, Kimo?" he asked, as he tickled my butt hole with his tongue. "That turns you on?" he whispered, as he stroked my sensitive inner thigh and I squirmed under his touch.

His body was like a candy shop I hadn't visited in a long time. I remembered how much I enjoyed sucking cock, kissing a guy, feeling the weight of a big man sprawled on top of me. We had sex in a couple of different positions, him in me, me in him, until we both were so wiped out all we could do was lie there and breathe.

As Sergei was drifting off to sleep I remembered the sound of Mike in my bed, me on the other side of the Japanese screen, and despite the thorough fucking I'd just gotten from the sexy Sergei, I missed the touch of my hunky fireman.

As I drove down to Waikīkī the next morning, after a little more romping with Sergei, I was feeling cheerful. I'd had some great sex with a guy who knew how to enjoy another man's body, and I had two days off to relax and forget about the arson and murder at the shopping center. I was just trying to decide what to do with my free time when my cell phone rang.

Harry wanted to know if I'd join him and Arleen for lunch. One of her many cousins had opened a little café in Aiea and they wanted to give him some business. I arranged to meet them at noon, and spent the morning Rollerblading, reading, and puttering around the apartment.

My truck groaned again as I climbed up Aiea Heights Drive, and I reminded myself to make an appointment at the garage. "We've got some news," Harry said, after we'd been seated at a café table. "Arleen and I are getting married."

"About time," I said.

"We wanted to make sure Brandon was OK with it," Harry said. Brandon was Arleen's eight-year-old, from a guy she'd forgotten before the boy was born.

"What's not to be OK?" I asked.

"Harry loves Brandon, and Brandon loves Harry," Arleen said. "I think it was just your friend here taking his sweet time."

"So when's the wedding? And am I going to be the best man?"

"April," Harry said. "And yes, you're the best man."

"There's more," Arleen said. "We're buying a house. Just up the street from here. We wanted to show it to you."

The rest of the lunch was taken up with details—buying the

house, fixing it up, selling Harry's condo on Waikīkī, where Brandon would go to school, and so on. I think I zoned out for a bit, thinking about the case, wondering if my brother had known more than he let on. Was he gambling at the clinic?

When we finished eating, I followed Harry's SUV up a couple of winding streets to the new house. They hadn't closed the sale yet, so they didn't have a key, but we walked around outside, peering in the windows. "Looks great, brah," I said, as we came back to the street. "I'm sure you'll be very happy here."

We hugged, and then he and Arleen piled into the SUV and drove off, and I got into my truck.

It wouldn't start.

I cursed a couple of times, then reached for my cell phone to call for a tow.

The phone battery was dead. I was sure it had been charged when I used it earlier in the day, but it must have been low then, and run down while I was at lunch.

I cursed again. I was stuck in a residential neighborhood, no pay phone in sight. I could always walk up to a random house, but it was the middle of a Saturday afternoon and most of the driveways around me were empty.

I could walk downhill to Aiea Field, where I could find a business, maybe hail a patrol car, if one passed me. I was staring out over the steering wheel at the street ahead of me when I saw the sign at the intersection, and realized it marked the street where Mike Riccardi lived.

He'd driven me past the house once, pointing it out, but I'd never been inside. I have a pretty good visual memory, so I thought I could recognize it again. But did I want to?

Hell, he owed me a favor, after that drunken visit Thursday night. And all I needed was to use the phone and call a tow truck. If Mike was around, and feeling generous, he could drive me home. But that was it.

Before I could change my mind, I got out of the truck and

started walking to the corner. I turned onto his street and began climbing. After a couple of twists and turns, I saw his truck ahead of me, parked on the street, the yellow and red flames streaking the side.

There was just one problem: I couldn't tell which half of the duplex belonged to him, and which half to his parents. It was that "the lady or the tiger" dilemma—from the short story we'd read in high school English class. Behind one door lurked a tiger; pick that door and get ripped to shreds. Behind the other door was a beautiful lady—or in my case, a handsome guy. Pick the right door and live happily ever after; pick the wrong door and confront the doctor who'd diagnosed my gonorrhea, and who blamed me for breaking his son's heart.

I stood on the street, rethinking my plans. Suddenly, the idea of walking down to Aiea Field seemed a lot better. But anytime I think about running away from something that scares me I know I have to man up and face things.

I took a guess that Mike's half was the right-hand side, because there were a couple of weeds under one window. I didn't think his father would tolerate any unwanted foliage. I walked up the path and knocked on the door.

The man who answered didn't look happy to see me. "What are you doing here?" he asked.

Chapter 11

TRUE CONFESSIONS

MIKE STOOD BEFORE me in a pair of ragged athletic shorts and nothing else. "You stalking me now?" he asked.

"In your dreams."

He looked behind me. "Where's your truck?"

"Invite me in, and I'll explain."

Mike's house was nothing like I'd imagined it. First of all, it was a mess, and I'd always had the idea he was a neat freak. Second, it was nondescript, and I'd thought he'd have beautiful, simple things.

Maybe he wasn't as gay as I thought.

"Want a beer?" he asked, leading me into the living room. Newspapers were scattered everywhere, along with dirty clothes. The place had an unpleasant smell, too—sweat overlaid with dirty dishes and garbage that hadn't been taken out.

"How many have you had today?" I asked.

He turned around to face me. "Fuck you," he said. "You come up here just to harass me? Gonna tattle on me to my folks again?"

"Somebody had to," I said. "Jesus, Mike, you can't bring a bottle of vodka with you to work at eight o'clock in the morning."

"I needed a little pick-me-up," he said. "What's it to you?"

What was it to me? Before I could think, the words spilled out of my mouth. "Because I still fucking love you," I said. "I don't want to see you kill yourself."

Mike grabbed me and kissed me hard on the lips. I kissed him back, not considering the consequences or deliberating the reasons why it was a bad idea. I just knew that I wanted to kiss him more than anything. We were all over each other, my hands slipping down in the waist of his shorts, his grabbing onto my ass and pulling me into him, when the front door opened.

"Michael, you left your door unlocked," his father said, walking in. "Your mother and I are—"

He froze in the doorway, and Mike and I pulled apart and turned to face him.

"I didn't realize I was interrupting," Dr. Riccardi said. "Detective, I wish I could say it was good to see you again."

"I'm thirty-five years old, Dad," Mike said. "Get a grip. Blame anything you want on me, but leave Kimo out of it."

"You may be thirty-five, but you're still my son," Dr. Riccardi said. "You expect me to stand aside while you ruin your life?"

Maybe that walk down to Aiea Park really had been the better idea. "I'll leave you guys alone," I said, starting toward the door. Kissing Mike had been an impetuous act, and one I knew was only going to lead me into trouble.

"Stay where you are," Mike said, reaching out to take my arm. "Dad, I'll talk to you later. You can go."

"Don't take that tone with me, Michael," his father said. "Have you been drinking again? My God, boy, do you ever stop?"

"Out. Now," Mike said.

His father turned and walked out the door, closing it gently behind him. "He won't even slam the fucking door," Mike said. He shook his head. "Jesus, to think I'm the product of his sperm."

He looked at me and tried to smile. "How about that beer now?"

"I'll take one."

He went into the kitchen and returned with two Bud Lights. "At least you're watching your weight," I said dryly.

"Sorry about that," he said, popping the top on his beer and waving it toward the front door. "My dad still thinks I'm about twelve."

"Maybe if you acted like you were thirty-five he'd think you were."

"Don't you start." He knocked a dirty T-shirt off a chair and sat down, then motioned me to the sofa. "Make yourself comfortable."

I looked at the sofa. One end was piled with rumpled newspapers, the other with dirty jeans, socks, and T-shirts. Feeling like I was channeling my mother, I piled the papers neatly on the floor and then sat down.

"I don't remember you being such a priss," Mike said.

"We going to do this all afternoon?" I asked. "Snipe at each other?"

"What do you want to talk about?"

I sipped my beer and considered. "You ever hear of MenSay-Hi?" I asked.

He shrugged. "Yeah. Hookup site. What about it?"

"I put a profile on there a few weeks after we broke up."

"You mean, after you dumped me."

I ignored that. "I said that I was pretty much into anything. And men started contacting me. There are some kinky guys out there, I'll tell you."

I drank a little more beer. "I've always been a romantic about sex," I said, settling back against the sofa. "But after . . . you know . . . I just wanted to get laid. Now that I think about it, I guess I was punishing myself."

"Getting laid as punishment? That's a new one."

"It wasn't just the sex. It was like I wanted guys to treat me badly. I was angry at myself for not giving you the chance to explain, for throwing away a relationship that had real potential. I felt like I was a loser. And when guys treated me badly that just reinforced that idea."

I drank some beer. We sat there.

Mike said, "I treated you pretty badly, too. I shouldn't have cheated on you. And I should have fessed up, instead of infecting you."

"We were both at fault," I said. "And I think we've both been beating ourselves up over it."

Mike looked at the beer can in his hand. "I used to drink a lot in college, I ever tell you that?"

I shook my head.

"I'd go to these frat parties, and guys would be hooking up with girls, and I knew I didn't want that, so I just drank. I'd pass out and wake up the next morning on some strange floor, massive hangover. A couple of times I was lucky I didn't choke on my own vomit. Sounds a lot like the other night, huh? Except you were nicer to me than the guys in those frats."

"When we were going out, you weren't drinking, were you?" I asked. "I mean, did I miss something?"

He shook his head. "I cleaned up my act when I came back from college. Partly, it was fear of my dad. I was living at home, after all. He wanted me to do something stable, something with a future, and I started taking these fire management courses at the community college. Right away, it was like, I don't know, I fell in love."

He looked at me, and I could see the old Mike coming through, his eyes shining, his mustache curving up at the ends with his smile. I got chicken skin just looking at him—what mainlanders call goose bumps.

"I wanted to be the best damn fireman I could be. I started taking these one- and two-week courses at the National Fire Academy in Maryland, so that I could get promoted and move into fire inspection. That was all I thought about. I shoved being gay back into the closet. I didn't see any way I could be gay in that environment, so I just wasn't."

"I did the same thing with the police," I said. "Until I couldn't anymore."

"It's like I was asleep," Mike said. "Then you came out, and you were all over the papers and the TV. The gay cop. I had such a major crush on you, and I thought, well, maybe if you could do it, I could."

He smiled wryly. "You know the next part. I wasn't so together as I thought. I started to resent you, that you could be out, that you could go places and tell the truth to people and not be ashamed. And I couldn't."

"That takes time, you know," I said.

"Yeah. I've had a lot of time to think about it. The stupid thing is, I got drunk in San Francisco, because I was so pissed off at the way things had worked out—that I was too much of a pansy to face up to the guys at the conference and bring you along. When this guy made a play for me at the bar, I just went along with it."

"I don't blame you, you know," I said. "I mean, yeah, you hurt my feelings, and I was totally pissed off that you gave me gonorrhea. But I should have listened to your side of the story. I shouldn't have been so quick to kick you out of my life."

"You think we can be friends again?" Mike asked.

"I don't know." What was friendship, after all? A warm feeling for someone else? Harry and Terri were my friends, had been since high school. I knew I could count on them, and I'd walk over broken glass for them. But Mike? Could I be just a friend, when every time he touched me electric charges shot to my dick and I wanted to kiss him and rub my body against his?

He looked at me, his eyes wide like a child's, his mouth set in a straight line beneath his mustache. I sighed. "I still have major hots for you," I said. "But there's a part of me that's pissed off, too, and doesn't know if I can trust you. Especially not . . ." I waved my hand around his house. "I mean, you're kind of a loser now."

"Man, you know how to dish out the tough love," Mike said, but the ends of his lips snuck upward into a smile. He was quiet for a minute, then said, "So where do we go from here?"

I looked around the living room. "I am absolutely not going to start up with you again until you get your shit together," I said, and I knew I was saying that as much for my own benefit as his. "But it took my brothers and Harry to give me a hand to get over my own problems. Maybe I can do the same for you."

"I'm up for it," Mike said.

"Are you?" I stood up. "Let's get started, then. First thing, pick up your dirty clothes and run a load of wash. I'll help you clean up this place."

He smiled. "I wish I had one of those French maid costumes you could wear."

"Don't fuck with me, brah. I'm serious here. And you've got to go to a meeting or something."

"A meeting?"

"AA. Face it, Mike, you've got a problem with alcohol. You're not going to get over it on your own."

"I can stop drinking," he said. "Right now."

I just looked at him, resisting the urge to cross my arms. Finally, he said, "I'll go to a meeting."

"You got recycling?" I asked, starting to gather the papers.

"Bin's in the kitchen." He stood up and began collecting the dirty clothes.

It felt like we'd already ventured too far into emotional territory, so I started talking about the case, and Mike seemed grateful to go along with me. "We're stalled on the arson homicide," I said. "Ray and I have been focusing on identifying the kid who died. We handed the sketch out to all the beat cops, and we canvassed the stores and offices in the area. It's like he was hiding under a rock or something."

"I checked out all those other clinics you gave me," Mike said, as he put a load of clothes in the washing machine. "No suspicious fires at any of them."

We worked together for nearly two hours, sometimes in silence, sometimes tossing ideas around. "Any leads on the arsonist?" I asked, as I scrubbed caked-on food off the dishes in the sink and loaded the dishwasher.

He shook his head. "Whoever he is, the guy's a pro. There wasn't much evidence beyond what we found that morning. I've been looking for other cases using the same MO but I haven't found any that fit."

He took the vacuum from a cabinet and dragged it to his bedroom. As he ran it there, in the hall, and the living room, I mopped the kitchen floor.

"We've looked at the boy, and we've looked at the arsonist, and we're looking at gambling," I said, as I helped him make his bed with fresh sheets, though I knew I wasn't getting in it myself, at least not for a while. "What aren't we looking at?"

"The owners of the center have no motive. None of the other tenants do, either," he said, tucking in the sheet at the foot of the bed. For a minute, I thought about what it would be like to be nestled under those sheets with Mike.

"If I can get a line on Norma Ching from my aunt, that'll give us a new direction," I said.

"We could use one of those." He laid a pair of decorative pillows at the head of the bed, then stood back, looking satisfied. We walked back out to the living room, where Mike lit a vanilla candle someone had given him, and between it and the furniture polish and the kitchen cleanser, the house started to smell better. "You never did tell me what you came over here for," he said.

I collapsed on the sofa. "My truck wouldn't start." I told him about lunch with Arleen and Harry and seeing their new house.

"So they'll be my neighbors." He looked over at me. "You think you'll be coming by to visit them now and then?"

"I might. I might have other reasons to come up here, too. You never know."

"You want me to drive you home?" he asked.

"That'd be cool. But I've got to call the tow truck first."

I called and arranged to meet the truck down in front of Arleen and Harry's new house. We walked out to his truck and Mike said, "My parents are still out. My dad's going to freak when he sees how clean my house is."

"I thought your dad didn't freak," I said.

"He doesn't appear to. But I'm an expert at knowing what to look for."

We hung out and talked while we waited for the tow truck to arrive, and for a few minutes I forgot all that had happened over the past year. I remembered how much I'd enjoyed just being with

Mike, and wondered if we'd ever get over our problems. I still wasn't sure of the future, but I felt better that he was starting to get his act together.

After the tow left, Mike drove me down to Waikīkī. "Hey, did you forget?" I asked, as we passed Lili'uokalani Street. "That was my turn."

"I wanted to check something out first," he said. He cruised another couple of blocks down Kalākaua to the big A-frame church. He slowed down and peered out at the sign out front. "Thought so," he said. "I'm on time."

As he turned I saw the sign myself. The AA meeting was about to start. "I can run you back home, if you want."

"I can walk from here," I said, as he pulled into a parking spot. "Maybe we'll get together Monday, compare notes?" I asked, as I got out of the truck.

"It's a date."

Chapter 12

MEMORIES OF A CASUAL ENCOUNTER

SUNDAY MORNING I slept late, made raspberry chocolate chip pancakes, and tried to recharge my batteries for the week ahead. Late in the afternoon, Aunt Mei-Mei called to give me Norma Ching's address and phone number.

"She no happy," Aunt Mei-Mei said. "Norma. I no talk to her myself, you know, not since very long time. But my friend say Norma mad about something."

That was good, I thought. Angry people often made the best sources of information, because they had scores to settle.

"Thanks, Aunt Mei-Mei. You doing OK?"

"Ai ya, very busy," she said. "Jimmy and his friends come again tonight. Lot of food to cook!"

"You're not running a restaurant there, Auntie. Don't you let Jimmy take advantage of you."

She laughed and her voice sounded like a young woman's. "Jimmy nice boy."

I called Ray and told him that I had an address for Norma Ching—but that my truck was in the shop. "I'll drive Julie up to UH first thing tomorrow," he said. "I'll swing past your place, pick you up, and we'll go see this woman."

Around noon, I got a text message on my cell phone. Thinking it was from Mike, I bounded over to the phone. Instead, though, it was from a number I didn't recognize. It read "Know u from house in Black Pt. Need ur help. Meet me?"

Alarm bells started to go off in my head. When I'd been at my lowest, emotionally, I'd met a man I only knew as Mr. Hu. He owned a house in Black Point, a very fancy neighborhood just outside Waikīkī where I'd gone many times. He had arranged various sexual escapades for me, sometimes with him, but sometimes with other guys. If this guy had met me through Mr. Hu, was he trying to hold that over me? Or had he been on the same kind of desperate dive I'd been on, and gotten himself into deeper trouble?

I texted back, asking him who he was and what he wanted. He didn't want to tell me, though, and for a minute I wondered if he was just being coy about a hookup. I didn't want to mess around with a casual trick, though, because my head was so caught up in considering getting back together with Mike.

But after a couple of messages back and forth it seemed that he needed police help rather than a quick blow job, and I agreed to meet him at the Starbucks at the Royal Hawai'ian shopping center, which was only a few blocks from my apartment. He assured me that I'd recognize him.

I'd just gotten myself a raspberry mocha when a guy behind me said, "I'm glad you came." I turned around and recognized him. He was a middle-aged guy, part Japanese and part *haole*, wearing expensive jeans and a silk aloha shirt. Oh, and a wedding ring.

We'd had sex once, though I couldn't remember his name, if I'd ever known it. Just like the law student. How many nameless men had I slept with? The thought creeped me out. "Can we walk?" he asked.

"Sure." I put a sleeve over my coffee cup and we went outside. It was a nice, sunny Sunday afternoon, and the shopping center was busy with well-heeled tourists clustering under the palm trees, gazing in the windows of the fancy stores, and toting lots of shopping bags with marquee names.

The guy steered us toward the grounds of the hotel, where we could have privacy. "Do you remember me?" he asked.

"I do," I said. "But look, I'm in a different place now than I was. I'm not looking to hook up with anybody."

"That's not why I need to talk to you," he said. "I know you're a detective, yeah? And I might need help from the police. But if I tell you something in confidence, will you promise not to tell anyone else?"

I stopped him. "Look, it doesn't work that way. If you need a cop, then I'll do what I can to help you. But I can't make any promises until I know what's going on."

There was a look of pure anguish on his face, which was eventually replaced with one of resignation. "I guess I don't have much choice."

We found a bench in the shade of a couple of palm trees and sat down. "Let's start from the beginning," I said. "I'm sorry, but I don't remember your name."

"Brian."

OK, no last name. "And what's up, Brian? I assume from that ring on your finger you're married, yeah? Some guy you slept with threatening to tell your wife?"

He nodded. "Not just that," he said. "My boss, too."

"Blackmail? They ask you for money?"

He pulled an envelope out of his pocket, opened it, and handed me a sheet of paper. At the top of the page was a color picture of Brian, naked, with his legs up over his shoulders. A naked man was plowing his butt.

Below the picture were the words "There's video, too. If you don't want the world to see it, transfer $50,000 to this account." Below it was an account number, at a Singapore bank.

My mind was running a mile a minute. From Brian's dress and manner, I had the feeling he had the money—and whoever was blackmailing him knew that. I recognized the setting; it was the master bedroom at Mr. Hu's mansion in Black Point. And the naked back? That was mine. I wasn't sure Brian knew that, though.

I blew a big breath out through my lips. "When did you get this?"

"Friday morning. It was delivered to my office by messenger."

"Have you had any other contact with whoever sent it?" He shook his head. "How about the police? You report this to anyone?"

Again he shook his head. "I couldn't. But I recognized you, the time we got together, and I knew you were a cop. I was hoping I could trust you."

"Did you think I got one of these, too?"

He looked at me strangely. "You think they would send a copy to the police?"

"Not the police. Me, personally."

I could see his eyes widen as the wheels turned. "That's you?" he asked.

"You didn't know?"

He shrugged. "You weren't the only guy Mr. Hu fixed me up with."

I honestly didn't know what to do. It should have been a no-brainer. Take the guy into Vice, show them the note, have them decide how to proceed. But would anyone else recognize me? Would the whole squad, and then the whole department, know that I'd been caught on video, banging the shit out of a random middle-aged stranger?

I slumped back against the bench. "I need to think about this for a minute." It took a while, but my brain finally engaged.

The first thing was to see if I could be easily recognized. I called Gunter, who was close at hand, enjoying a post-coital mimosa at the Rod and Reel Club with his latest overnight guest.

Assuming I wasn't recognizable, I could present the evidence to Vice on Monday morning. Since I came out, I've been the department's go-to guy when gay men and lesbians are involved in crimes, usually as victims, though occasionally as perpetrators as well. I'd given a couple of talks about domestic violence in same-sex households, and I'd helped out a couple of prominent johns who'd been picked up in prostitution sweeps and didn't want the world to know they'd been picking up guys, or guys dressed as women.

So it was reasonable that Brian could contact me, even if he didn't know me personally, for help navigating his situation. If Gunter recognized my naked back and butt, though, and felt that the rest of the department might, too, I'd have to reconsider my story.

While we waited for Gunter to extricate himself from the bar, I said, "These guys don't look like the most sophisticated blackmailers." Brian looked interested.

"How can you tell?"

"Well, there's no deadline. No 'send us the money by Tuesday morning or else.' And maybe they score a couple of points by delivering to your office—but there's no guarantee you've seen this. It could be sitting on your secretary's desk."

"But if I don't respond . . ."

"We'll get to that. Plus, these aren't anonymous photos. There's a connection to Mr. Hu and to the place where the video they clipped this still from was taken."

Brian didn't look particularly reassured, and then I spotted Gunter. "I need to show my friend the picture."

"He'll recognize me," Brian said.

"You slept with him, too?"

He shook his head. "I don't want anyone to see that picture."

"No way around it," I said. "You can trust Gunter." I waved him over, and pointedly didn't introduce Brian. "Recognize the guy?" I asked.

He looked from the picture to Brian. "Is this a trick question?"

"Not him, dimwit. The other guy."

"The top? Cute." He peered at the picture, then shrugged. "You'd think with my wide experience of the homosexual population of Honolulu, I might, but I don't."

I gave out a sigh of relief. "Thanks, brah. That's what I needed to know."

"This the guy wanting the money?" he asked, pointing at my naked back.

I shook my head. "I get paid enough by the city and county of Honolulu," I said. "I don't need to extort money from tricks."

Brian didn't particularly like being called a trick. Gunter whistled. "That's you?" He took a closer look at the picture. "You've got a mole on your left shoulder," he said. He pointed to the picture. "It's fuzzy, like they weren't focusing on you. I suppose if you know what to look for you can see it."

Gunter left a few minutes later and I laid out the plan for Brian. "I'm going to talk to the lieutenant in Vice tomorrow morning. I'll show him the note and see what he wants to do. How can I reach you?"

"Will you have to give him my name?"

I nodded. "But they'll be discreet. You're the victim here."

"But what about testifying? I'll lose everything if this gets out."

"Let's work one step at a time, OK?" I put my hand on his shoulder. "I'll do whatever I can to take care of you."

Finally, he opened his wallet and pulled out a business card. "You have my cell number," he said. "Text messages are best."

His full name was Brian Izumigawa, and he was an executive vice president at one of the bigger banks in the islands. "Let me know if you hear anything more from these guys," I said.

He was reluctant to leave, as if just staying around me would make his problems go away, but finally I reassured him enough. I wished I felt as good as I pretended; I was still worried that someone in the police department would recognize me, or that Lieutenant Kee in Vice would insist on knowing the identity of the guy with his back to the camera.

And if my name didn't come out that way, would the investigation lead to Mr. Hu? Would he have a little black book of men? If he did, my name was sure to be there—perhaps with annotations as to my experience and tastes.

That was something I didn't want in the police department rumor mill.

Chapter 13

WHAT NORMA KNOWS

RAY SHOWED UP at my apartment at six thirty Monday morning, too early to spring a visit on Norma Ching. "I've got something to talk about downstairs in Vice," I said as we drove. "While I'm down there, I'll see if they know anything about this clinic, or about Norma."

Ray didn't ask about my other business with Vice, and I didn't volunteer any details. I had to see how things worked out first, and how much involvement I would have in Brian Izumigawa's case.

While Ray parked, I went down to the B1 level, the first of two levels below ground. The photo lab, narcotics, and the special investigations section, where they do research on evidence, are also down there. It's my favorite part of the building, and I'm always willing to hang around the labs and talk to the techs.

Lieutenant Kee's secretary, Juanita Lum, is a heavyset, no-nonsense Filipina, with lustrous black hair and skin so smooth she could do soap ads. From her wedding picture, which sat in a heart-shaped frame on her desk, you could see she'd been a real looker when she was younger.

"Hey, Kimo, howzit?" she asked.

"Pretty good, Juanita. The lieutenant have a minute?"

"He's on the phone. And then he's got a meeting. But let me see if he can squeeze you in."

She kept an eye on the red light on Kee's line while she chatted with me and kept on typing some kind of report. The multitasking made my head spin, but it was all in a day's work for Juanita.

When she saw the light go off, she buzzed the lieutenant. "I'm busy, woman," I heard him say through the intercom.

"And next week you'll want something from Homicide," Juanita said. "You scratch Kimo's back, he'll scratch yours. And your back itches a lot."

"Fine, send him in," Kee said.

In the four years or so that he'd been in charge of Vice, Kee had been perpetually grumpy. He had a long, sad face like a Bassett hound, and brush-cut black hair going gray at the sideburns.

"Thanks for giving me a minute," I said, walking into his office. "You hear about the arson homicide up in St. Louis Heights last Sunday?"

"Shopping center up on Waialae Avenue?" he asked. "What about it?"

"That address ever come up in your investigations?" I asked. "'Cause there was an acupuncture clinic there that sounds pretty shady, and they closed down and moved out a couple of days before the fire."

"I've heard the address," he said. "But I've been shorthanded since the last round of budget cuts. I haven't had a chance to get anybody up there."

"You know the name Norma Ching?"

He shook his head. "Doesn't ring a bell."

I paused, and Kee said, "That all?"

I took a deep breath. "Nope." I told him about Brian Izumigawa, how he'd contacted me, making it sound like he recognized my name from the media. I showed Kee the note Brian had been sent. "You get this dusted for prints?" he asked.

"He was cagey about what was going on," I said. "I didn't realize it might be evidence until he'd already given it to me and I'd put my prints all over it. I can still get it tested, though."

"Do it." He looked at me. "What do you make of this?"

Inside, I breathed a little sigh of relief. There was no reason why Kee should recognize my naked back, but I was still glad that he didn't. I told him my theory that the blackmailers were amateurs, and explained about Brian's connection to Mr. Hu and the mansion in Black Point.

"He told you all this?" Kee asked.

"We met up yesterday afternoon and I got him to open up."

"This needs some delicacy," Kee said. "You want to run this? Keep it quiet that way."

"If you want," I said. Good. There was little chance that the story would spread around the department if I was in charge.

"I'll clear it with your boss. Get back in touch with this guy. Tell him not to do anything until they contact him again. In the meantime, see what you can run down on this Hu guy."

I dropped the note off for fingerprint processing, taking a photocopy back upstairs with me, and filled Ray in on the case, leaving out my personal involvement. I checked the property records for the mansion in Black Point where Brian and I had been fixed up. It was owned by a corporation, of course. I put in another call to Ricky Koele.

"You're turning into my new best friend," he said. "Pretty soon we'll be surfing together."

"You get a lead on some good waves, you let me know." I gave him the name of the corporation that owned the mansion, and a few minutes later he was back on the line.

"It's a shell," he said. "The stockholders are another corporation out of Hong Kong. Wah Shing Limited."

"Why does that name sound familiar?" I asked him.

"Hold on. Let me do a cross-reference search."

He was back on the line a couple of minutes later. "You won't believe it. Remember that acupuncture clinic you called me about last week? Golden Needles? Wah Shing was their corporate parent."

"No shit?" I said. "Or should I say no Shing?"

"Call if you need anything else," Ricky said.

After I hung up, I sat there staring into space. It was too weird that this random trick and his blackmail case had somehow become connected to our arson homicide. A million things were running through my head, not the least of which was how I was going to come out of all this with my secrets intact.

I didn't realize Ray had been talking to me until he was waving his hand in my face and saying, "Earth to Kimo."

I told Ray that the same corporation was behind the lease on the acupuncture clinic and the house in Black Point where Brian Izumigawa had been filmed having sex.

"Whoa. What do you think that means?"

I looked at Ray. I liked him, and we worked well together. We'd shared bits and pieces of our personal lives as we got to know each other better. I knew about the money problems he and Julie were having, the way they argued sometimes about them. He knew about my complicated history with Mike Riccardi. But this was bigger. It was time to see if I could trust my partner.

"Let's head over to Norma's," I said. "I've got some stuff to tell you."

As detectives, Ray and I can either use personal vehicles for police business, or sign out an unmarked Crown Vic from the Vehicle Maintenance Section. Call me fussy, but if I'm going to feel something sticky on the seat or the dash, I want to have a general idea what it is. If there's a funny smell in the car, I want it to be one of my funny smells. And I don't want to have to worry about whether the last guy to drive it did something that's going to cause me a problem.

So I was reluctant to take a car out, and Ray was willing to drive us into Chinatown in Julie's Mini Cooper. Which put us on the road in a vehicle that didn't say, "We are the police. Fear us." But it had to do in a pinch.

There were big, puffy clouds outside, and a restless wind shook the kukui trees along South Beretania Avenue as Ray drove us. "I told you about how I broke up with Mike, right? About a year ago? After that, I started getting into this Web site called MenSayHi.com, a hookup site. Through it, I met this older guy, Chinese. I always called him Mr. Hu. He got off on choreographing these scenarios for me. He'd pair me up with guys, for whatever reason in his head, and then sometimes he'd watch, and sometimes he'd participate."

"Did you meet him up at that house?" Ray asked. "The one where the blackmail guy went?"

"Yup."

Ray looked over at me. "Shit. Is that you in the picture with him?"

"Yup."

"And you complain about me and one-word answers," Ray said. He pulled the car over a couple of blocks from Norma's. "Tell me the whole story."

I took a deep breath. "There isn't much more to say. I didn't know who Brian Izumigawa was, and I didn't know we were being filmed."

"You cannot tell anyone else that's you in the picture, Kimo." He looked back at the street ahead of him. "You do, and they pull you off the case, and your name goes down the drain. I've seen that happen. You're too good a cop to lose that way."

"Thanks." I felt a little better, knowing Ray was on my side. "But I have to say, I don't know what to do."

Ray looked out at the street, then turned back into traffic. "Right now, we go see Norma. If she worked for your Mr. Hu, maybe she can help us find him. Then we get both cases wrapped up fast."

Norma Ching lived in a run-down high-rise just off Hotel Street, which had once been the center of Honolulu's red light district. I'd heard stories about the brothels there during the second world war, when there were nearly 150 of them within a few blocks, servicing the servicemen.

Now, though, it's just another neighborhood. A lei stall was already open across the street, the beautiful colors and pungent scents a dramatic contrast to the shuttered storefronts around it. The only other business open was a Chinese grocery, and as we passed I looked in the window and saw a familiar face.

"Hey, Melvin, how you doing?" I asked, walking inside to the aroma of barbecued pork and roast duck. The shelves were lined with canisters of salty dried plums and apricots, tapioca pearls, and shrink-wrapped mushrooms. Chinese characters decorated bottles of vinegar and soy sauce. A couple of dusty red paper lanterns hung from the ceiling.

"Detective."

Melvin Ah Wong was Jimmy's father, if you could still call him that. He'd kicked the boy out at sixteen, when he discovered his son was gay. I introduced him to Ray, then said, "You seen your son lately?"

"My son is dead."

"Your son is very much alive, Melvin. He's at UH now, you know that? Looks happy, got lots of friends. You'd be proud of him."

"My son is dead, detective," Melvin said, and he walked past us.

"I always admire your people skills," Ray said, as he paid the shopkeeper for a package of salty dried plums.

"The guy's lucky I don't knock him out," I grumbled.

We walked over to Norma's building and took the elevator up to the tenth floor. We knocked on the door of 10-F and a moment later Norma opened it.

I wasn't sure I'd have recognized her on the street. Her white hair was wild and uncombed, and she wore a black cotton dressing gown hastily tied. I introduced myself and Ray.

"I'm not dressed for gentlemen callers," she said, smiling coyly. She was missing her front teeth and her smile reminded me of a Halloween pumpkin.

There was just a trace of a Chinese accent. She smiled flirtatiously at Ray. "Will you come in and give me a few minutes to fix myself up?"

We sat in her black lacquer living room, and all the hothouse plants reminded me of Uncle Chin's lanai, where he had spent much of his last years surrounded by flowers and birds. A glass étagère along one wall was cluttered with dragon figurines, bonsai trees, and a pile of round coins with a square cut out of the center— I Ching charms. A rice paper scroll hung on the wall with a bunch of characters signifying good fortune. I recognized love, peace, and harmony, among others. Through the doorway into the kitchen I saw a Buddha kitchen god and a Chinese calendar.

Ten minutes passed, and when Norma reappeared from the bedroom she was a different person. She'd put her teeth in, and donned an elegantly coiffed white wig. There was red powder on her cheeks, and she wore a smart black business suit with a white blouse, open at the neck.

"Now, how can I help you, detectives?" she asked.

"We wanted to ask you about the Golden Needles Acupuncture Clinic," I said. "You know it burned last week?"

She nodded. "We had already closed a few days before the fire."

"Why did you close?" I asked. "Not enough people needing acupuncture?"

She laughed. "Oh, detective. We didn't do acupuncture there, despite the sign out front. Since I am no longer employed there I feel free to tell you that personal services were provided to discreet gentlemen."

"Prostitution," Ray said. He and I looked at each other. So we'd been on the wrong track; it wasn't gambling that the other tenants had been hinting about.

"What an awful word," Norma said. "So unsavory, isn't it? Not that I participated myself, you understand. I am a little past my prime."

"Why did you close?"

"It was a business decision made by my ex-employer."

"Mr. Hu?" I asked.

Norma looked surprised. "Yes, that is the name I knew him by. But I doubt that is the name he was born with."

"You and I first met about two years ago, isn't that right?" I asked. "You were working at a lingerie shop. Just a few blocks from here, wasn't it?" She nodded. "That building burned, too," I said. "Interesting, isn't it? You worked at two places that both burned under fishy circumstances."

"I had nothing to do with either fire."

I pulled out Mike's list of suspicious fires. "A massage parlor in Waikele, a quick mart in Kaneohe, a coffee shop near the airport, and a Christian religious shop downtown," I said. "All of them burned. If I check your employment records, will I find that you worked at any of those places?"

Norma sat up very straight. "You can accuse me all you want, detective. But I am an innocent woman."

"I know that you know something, Norma," I said. "And I want to know what it is. What happened after Tommy Pang died? Who took over the lingerie shop?"

I saw Norma consider her options for a minute. I knew from Aunt Mei-Mei that Norma was angry; I figured if I just asked the right questions, she'd open up.

"For a long time, I didn't know who the new owner was," she said, having made her decision. "Everything went along. Then Mr. Hu called one day. He informed me that we were closing down, and that I should move everything to Waikele."

"I'm sorry, but I'm not following," Ray said. "This lingerie shop—did you provide the same kind of services there that you did at the acupuncture clinic?"

Norma looked at Ray the way a teacher might smile at a prized pupil. "You are following everything just fine, detective."

"Did Mr. Hu give you any reason for the move?" I asked.

"He said something about his arrangements with the police changing," Norma said. "I resisted, because I didn't want to go all the way to Waikele. I am an old woman, you know, and I do not drive. It was very inconvenient for me."

"And what did Mr. Hu say?"

"He told me that I was welcome to stay in the shop, if I wished. But it might get very warm for me."

"So you found your way to Waikele," I said.

"A car and driver is expensive," Norma said. "But better than the alternative."

"Why did the massage parlor close?" I asked.

She shrugged. "I am just an old woman. I do what I am told."

"From Waikele, you went to St. Louis Heights?" I asked.

"That is true."

"Did you know why the acupuncture clinic closed?" Ray asked.

"Mr. Hu did not say. But I had my suspicions."

"What were they?" I asked.

"A young boy," she said. "One of our employees. He ran away, and Mr. Hu was afraid he would compromise our operation."

"Jingtao?" I asked, and Norma looked surprised.

"So he did go to the police," she said.

I shook my head. "He was hiding at the far end of the center, in the back of the beauty salon," I said. "He never spoke to the police. He was killed in the fire."

Norma looked sad. "He was a beautiful boy," she said. "Very much in demand. But very unhappy inside."

"You have a new location?" Ray asked.

"As I told you earlier, I have been informed that my services are no longer needed."

"How can we get in touch with Mr. Hu?" I asked.

She shook her head. "I do not know. The number I had for him has been disconnected." But she smiled slyly. "But I know someone who might be able to help you. Her name is Treasure Chen."

I made the connection. Treasure had been Tommy Pang's girlfriend, and she had worked with Norma at the lingerie shop.

"The girl the pharmacist spoke about," Ray said.

I grimaced. If I'd only made the connection to the name the pharmacist had given us, we could have moved a lot faster.

"He did more than speak," Norma said. "Though he was always worried that his wife would find out."

"Where can we find Treasure Chen?" I asked.

"I do not know. But when you find her, I have a message for her."

"Yes?"

Norma spit, more sound than saliva, and wiped her hands briskly. "That is my message for Treasure Chen."

Chapter 14

ANGRY LOBSTERS

WE LEFT NORMA a few minutes later, after she told us that Treasure's phone number was unlisted and she didn't know where the girl lived. "We can check payroll tax records," Ray suggested. "There might be an address for Treasure Chen there. You know anything about this Mr. Hu besides his address and last name?"

I shook my head. "That was part of the deal. Control. He contacted me, I never knew how to reach him. But I might have another way to get to Treasure." It was almost lunchtime, and I told Ray to drive over to Ward Warehouse, a complex of shops between downtown and Waikīkī. "After she left the lingerie shop, her boyfriend got Treasure a job as the hostess at a restaurant called the Lobster Garden. Maybe somebody there has kept in touch with her, or has an old address we can start with."

The Ward Warehouse was a mini-mall, two long lines of stores facing each other on two levels with parking in the middle. To me, it's one of the least attractive shopping centers on the island. It looks like a child's play set—girders bolted together, corrugated metal sheets painted clashing colors.

The Lobster Garden was a touristy Chinese restaurant on the upper level. It was a festive place, decorated with framed Chinese calligraphy and red paper lanterns, and it was usually full of tourist families resting after a day's trek to Pearl Harbor, Diamond Head, or Hilo Hattie's aloha shirt factory. The centerpiece of the restaurant was a huge fish tank filled with live lobsters, their claws banded together. I empathized with them; I felt like this case had my hands tied in the same way.

The woman behind the podium was in her mid-forties, and her frown contrasted sharply with the smiley-face name tag which read HI, I'M MAE.

I showed Mae my badge and asked if she remembered a girl who'd worked at the restaurant a few years before. "Her name is Treasure Chen."

If possible, Mae's frown deepened. "Bad girl," she said. "Hard to get good staff today. Pretty girls, they only want flirt with customers. Ugly girls, they work for while, then get better jobs."

I resisted suggesting that the Lobster Garden improve their pay, and waited for Mae to continue. "I work here many years," she said. "Nine years soon. Year ago, my husband buy, when owner go jail."

A sunburned *haole* family came in, the youngest boy dragged along by his arm like a recalcitrant puppy, and Mae seated them. When she returned, she said, "Treasure work here long time ago. She mixed up with bad man, friend of owner, and he get her job." She pursed her lips together as if she was smelling something bad. "But this job not good enough for Treasure. She stay maybe six months, then quit. One day. No notice. Just no come back to work."

"You have any address information on her?" I asked.

Mae shrugged. "Maybe in office." She called a waitress over and asked her to watch the front, and then led us past the big tank full of lobsters waving their antennae and crawling over one another.

The office was a tiny room, barely enough space for a desk, a file cabinet, and a time clock on the wall with extra rolls of toilet paper stacked under it. Mae looked through a couple of drawers of the cabinet before she pulled out Treasure's employment application.

I wrote down the address, noticing that her only previous work experience had been at the lingerie shop that Norma Ching managed. I wondered if Treasure had left the Lobster Garden to return to work for Norma—and in what capacity.

The address Treasure had put on her application was a cheap rental near downtown, and as we drove over there I called Karen Gold, a woman I knew over at Social Security, and asked her to see what she had on Treasure.

The apartment manager told us that no one of Treasure's name or description lived there. He was new, and didn't remember her or have any forwarding information. "Another dead end," Ray said, as we drove away.

"I say we pass by the pharmacy one more time," I said. "See if Louis Cruz is willing to tell us anything more about Treasure. Norma says he was a customer."

"You think he's kept in touch?"

"I think if Treasure's set up shop somewhere new, she might be contacting her old friends to let them know."

"Good idea as any," he said, and turned on the engine.

Luck was with us: Lorna Cruz was running an errand, leaving Louis alone in the pharmacy. As soon as he finished dealing with his client, a heavyset Hawai'ian woman buying diabetes testing strips, I asked if he'd been in touch with Treasure since the fire.

He looked alarmed. "No, no touch."

"Come on, Louis, we know you were a client at the acupuncture clinic," Ray said. "And not for shots, either. We're not looking to jam you up, tell your wife or anything. We're just trying to find Treasure Chen."

"I swear, detective," Cruz said, putting his hand on the ornate gold cross around his neck. "I haven't spoken to her."

I handed him my card. "If you do, will you find out where she is?" I asked. "And then let us know?"

He nodded, pocketing the card quickly. When we got back to the station, I called the garage to see what was wrong with my truck. When the mechanic told me, and then quoted me the price to repair, my mind went blank.

"I gotta tell you, detective, I wouldn't fix this if I was you," the mechanic said. "You can get a grand, maybe, if you junk it. I'd just buy something else."

I thought about the money my parents had promised as the advance on my inheritance. "You may be right."

I hung up and called my parents. My father answered and I told him the situation with the truck. "So I was wondering . . . you said you'd be giving us each some money. When were you thinking of doing that?"

"I can write you a check today," my father said. "The law says we can give you each eleven thousand dollars tax free. What kind of car you want to buy?"

"I'm thinking maybe a Jeep," I said, surprising myself. I'd always had a thing for the Wrangler, with those flaps you could roll up when the weather was good—which was pretty often in Hawai'i. I could throw a surfboard in the back, or any other kind of athletic gear. I liked the picture of myself, tooling around Honolulu like that.

"You want me to go with you?" my father asked.

I'd never bought a car before. Everything I'd driven had been owned by my father first, then handed down. I was nearly thirty-five, and I ought to be able to handle buying a car—but it would be fun to hang out with my dad.

"Sure. Can you pick me up after work?"

He agreed he would, and I turned back to Ray, who asked, "You got any other ideas on how to track your Mr. Hu?"

I shrugged. "We have a last name, which Norma thinks wasn't his real name anyway. The only address we have, for the mansion in Black Point, leads us back to Wah Shing."

"Hold on. I've got an idea." He turned to his computer and started typing. A moment later, though, he said, "I thought I could see if we have anything in the system on a guy named Hu. Turns out there's a lot more than I expected."

"It's a common name," I said. "Without a first name you're screwed."

"Though not by him," Ray said, and laughed.

"Ouch," I said, but I laughed along with him. "I wish we knew more about the boy," I said. "I mean, we don't even know if Jingtao was his real name."

"I think the boy was just collateral damage," Ray said. "He happened to be in the back of the salon when they were burning the acupuncture clinic. Just bad luck."

"Yeah, but what if he ran away from the clinic, and that made the owners want to burn it? Did he threaten somebody? Did he know something? And how did he get here, anyway?"

"Good questions. You think up any answers, you let me know."

I thought that if Norma or Treasure could tell us when Jingtao arrived in the United States we might be able to track him through ICE, Immigration and Customs Enforcement, and I made a couple of notes. A few minutes later, Lieutenant Sampson called me into his office.

"Have a seat, Kimo," he said.

My mind was racing through my recent cases. Was there a problem with one of them? I remembered my visit to Dr. Riccardi at the STD clinic. Maybe he'd complained? But that was foolish—because I'd simply reveal why I had gone there, and Mike would be the one to suffer.

"I've had a request for your services," Sampson said. Today's polo shirt was a light blue, with a penguin crest. "From Vice."

I nodded. "I spoke to Lieutenant Kee this morning."

"I'm worried that Kee is not telling you the whole story. I don't like anybody holding out on my detectives—not even another lieutenant."

My heart started racing again. Had Kee recognized me from the photo and just not told me?

"Do you know what it is?"

He shook his head. "I didn't want to know. But I told him that if he didn't give you everything he's got, then I'll pull you off the assignment." He smiled. "He'd like to see you downstairs as soon as you're free."

I stopped at Ray's desk to tell him I was going back to Vice. "What do you think he's holding back?" Ray asked.

I shrugged. "I'll know soon enough."

Down at Vice, Juanita was at her desk. "Back again," she said. "You just can't stay away from us, can you?" She smiled. "The Lieutenant is expecting you. Let me tell him you're here."

When I sat across from Lieutenant Kee, he said, "Your lieutenant is a very persuasive guy." He pursed his lips in a frown. "What I'm going to tell you is confidential." I was baffled, but I kept my mouth shut. "A hustler used your name," he said. "We were running a sting in Ala Moana Beach Park, and he offered a blow job to one of my guys. He was jonesing for his next fix, and he was so strung out he didn't realize that he already had a rock until we searched him."

He sat back in his chair and steepled his fingers. "He bragged that he'd had sex with a lot of important guys. He gave us a couple of names, among them yours. We weren't sure whether to believe him or not; could have been the ice talking. He bonded out, and one of my guys made an appointment to meet with him the next day to get more details. He didn't show for the meeting."

I could feel the sweat dripping down my back, pooling under my arms. I was right; one of the hookers Mr. Hu had hired had recognized me. But that had been part of the power Mr. Hu held over me—the danger that what he forced me to do not only humiliated and degraded me, but could bring down my career.

The last time I went to Mr. Hu's mansion at Black Point, the night that drove Gunter to take me to the emergency room, Mr. Hu had told me after the fact that he'd paid the man who had fucked me so brutally. But did taking part in the act make me as guilty as either of them?

"I wouldn't dignify his allegation except that after you left this morning I was trying to remember where I'd heard that name before, the one your blackmail victim mentioned, Mr. Hu. This hustler also mentioned him."

"Can you tell me the hustler's name?"

Kee turned to his computer and punched in a couple of keys,

two-finger typing. After a moment he said, "The guy went by the name Lucas."

That was the name Mr. Hu had called him. Kee turned back to me. "Recognize the name?"

I nodded.

"How did you come in contact with him?"

I sat there for a moment, collecting my thoughts, considering how much to say. "I met a guy through a gay hookup Web site, and I met Lucas through him." I took a deep breath. I had to make it clear that I was not a guilty party. "I did have sex with Lucas—but I didn't pay him for it."

He nodded. "I have no evidence to the contrary, detective. If I had, we wouldn't be having this conversation."

Chapter 15

DATING DRAMA

MY FATHER PICKED me up just after four and we drove out toward the airport. Gray rain clouds clustered over the tops of the Ko'olau Mountains, but down on the Nimitz Highway it was sunny and breezy. "I made a couple of calls for you. We need to ask for Jerry Kaneali'i," my father said, pulling into a used car dealership.

"You know him?"

"Better. The boss and I, we went to UH together. Long time ago."

As we were getting out of his truck, my cell phone rang. I didn't recognize the number but I answered anyway. It was Dr. Phil.

"I've got a late shift tomorrow," he said. "Want to catch an early dinner?"

I'd almost forgotten about Dr. Phil—our one date had been so long ago. But I didn't want to get into all my romantic complications on the phone, and certainly not in front of my father. "Sure. Tomorrow would be great." He had to be at The Queen's Medical Center after dinner, so we made plans to meet at a steak house near the Aloha Tower.

The dealership was playing KINE, Hawai'ian 105, in the background, and the two receptionists at the front desk wore fragrant leis of red carnations. Jerry Kaneali'i was a big Hawai'ian guy in his late fifties, and he seemed pleased to see us. "The boss said to take good care of you," he said, shaking my hand vigorously.

He led us around the lot, showing us the Wranglers he had, and he was just explaining the horsepower on a dark blue one when my phone rang again.

The display said the call was coming from Haoa's office. "Hey, brah," I said.

"Hey to you, too," Sergei said. "How've you been? I had a great time with you last week—but you still owe me a tour of the bars of Waikīkī."

"Sure," I said. "When did you want to meet up?"

My dad was listening earnestly to Jerry explain about cylinders and torque. I was trying to understand, but I'd always just taken what I'd been given when it came to vehicles and I'd never paid much attention to what was under the hood.

Oops, I guess I was gay all along.

"I'm thinking Friday," Sergei said. "You and me, having some fun."

His voice was so loud that my father looked up. "Sure, that would be great," I said. "I'll talk to you Friday, OK?"

I hung up and said, "This one looks good. I'll take it."

"Kimo!" my father scolded. "We haven't even gotten a price yet."

"Don't you worry," Jerry said. "Like I said, the boss told me to take good care of you. Give you the special UH price."

Yeah, I wanted to say, tell me another one. But I'd seen the sticker price on the Jeep's window, and the figure Jerry quoted us when we went inside was a grand less. I guess there's something to be said for that old boys' network after all.

There were a million pieces of paper to sign. My dad pulled out a check already made out to me in the amount of eleven thousand dollars, and I endorsed it over to the dealership as my deposit. I was in the middle of filling out the loan papers for the rest when my phone rang a third time.

"Sorry," I said, seeing it was Mike. "I need to take this."

I turned away from the two of them and said hello. Mike said, "Hey there, handsome. We said we'd get together and catch up. You free tonight?"

His voice boomed around the small room. I had to figure out

how to lower the volume on the damn phone. I looked at my watch. "Sure. Say seven o'clock?"

"I'll bring dinner," Mike said. "See you."

I hung up, feeling red faced. We finished the paperwork and Jerry went off to get the keys. "Busy social life," my father said.

"It's not like that," I said. "Mike and I are working on the arson at the shopping center."

He raised his eyebrows. "I have three sons, remember? Your brother Haoa, he dated two, sometimes three girls at the same time, until he met Tatiana. Then, no more. Just her." He looked at me. "Is it like that with you and Mike?"

My immediate impulse was to protest. "Mike? No, not at all. I hadn't seen him for a year before the fire."

"He's a nice guy," my father said.

Fortunately, Jerry came back with the keys to the almost-new Jeep before I was tempted to reveal anything uncomfortable about my relationship with Mike.

Jerry had rolled up the flaps so the Jeep was completely open, and I hugged my dad and thanked him again before jumping in. Cruising down the Nimitz Highway was so cool—my first new car, even if it had been gently pre-owned for a year or so before I got it. The sun was just setting, but the air was still warm and the breeze whipped around the inside, bringing the smell of salt water that I always associated with my best days.

I took my time driving back to Waikīkī, enjoying the ride. I kept the radio on Hawai'ian 105, not minding the traffic, the fan-tail palms swaying in the light breeze, the hills glowing with the reflected light. A wild bougainvillea by the side of the road was a bright purple accent in an otherwise green landscape, highlighted by the last rays of the setting sun. I pulled into my parking space just as Mike stopped on the street in front of my building. "New wheels?" he asked.

"Yup. My dad drove me down to the dealership to pick it out."

"Pretty sharp. Give me a hand with the food."

He'd brought takeout from Raimundo's, the Italian restaurant where we'd had our first date—a family-size platter of chicken parmigiana, garlic knots, a vat of salad drenched in oil and vinegar. We carried it all upstairs and laid it out on my kitchen table, then dug in.

I remembered when we'd eaten at the restaurant, and how we'd shared a bottle of red wine. Would we never be able to do that again? Would he have to avoid wine and beer, and would I always be watching to see that he did?

"So what have you got?" I asked him, spearing some of the lettuce and a couple of croutons.

"Nothing much," he said. "Like I said before, the guy was a pro, whoever he was. No trace evidence, just that piece of potato chip bag you found." He ate some salad and then broke apart one of the garlic knots. "Unfortunately, a lot of guys use chips that way. So it's not much of a lead."

I told him about the UH student, and he pulled out his battered steno pad and made a couple of notes. "Think the guy could pull someone out of a lineup?"

I shook my head. "It was dark, and his mind was on getting back to his wife without getting caught. I don't think he got much of a look at the guy. Couldn't say more about the car other than it looked like a BMW or a Mercedes."

"So we have nothing?"

"Well, we might have something." I told him about Norma Ching, and that the prostitution at the acupuncture clinic was connected both to the lingerie store in Chinatown and the massage parlor in Waikele.

Mike whistled. "That is a lead. I'll look at those fires again. Maybe there's something in one of them that would tie us to a particular arsonist." He started cutting into the chicken. "You ought to talk to Vice, too."

"Well, actually . . ." I hesitated. Mike and I were delicately moving toward starting something up again, and I didn't want my past mistakes to screw that up.

I sighed. "This guy came to me yesterday. A guy I had sex with, a few months ago. We didn't know it, but we were videotaped, and he's being blackmailed. I went down to talk to Vice about it, and Ray and I did a little investigating. Turns out the house where I went for sex is owned by the company that leased the acupuncture clinic."

"Hold on," Mike said. "You were videotaped? Have you seen the tape?" He smiled. "Can I?"

I kicked him under the table. "I haven't seen the tape. The blackmailers sent the guy a still from the video. All you can see is my back." I paused. "There's more."

"More?"

"Remember what I told you yesterday afternoon? About some of the stuff I got into?" He nodded. "One of the guys Mr. Hu hooked me up with was a hustler. He cuffed me to the wall and paid the guy to fuck me until I bled."

"Ow."

"Yeah, that's a good word for it. But that was the last straw. I stopped going up there after that. The hustler got picked up on a drug bust, though, and gave my name to Vice."

"What does that mean for you?"

I shrugged. "I told the lieutenant that I'd had sex with the guy, but I hadn't paid for it. The guy disappeared, so they never got anything more out of him. But I have to look for him, see if he has a way to get to Mr. Hu."

"I don't think you should be on this case," Mike said, putting down his fork. "You're too connected. From your dad once owning the shopping center, to having sex with all these different guys. You need to tell your lieutenant and let someone else handle it."

"Yeah, and then the whole department finds out what I was up to," I said. "No way. Listen, it's not a big deal. I'll work it all out."

It was clear that Mike thought it was a big deal, though, and I thought that was both sweet and a little too forward. Yeah, maybe we'd get together again at some point—but he had no say over my life until then.

My cell phone rang, and from the display I saw that it was Terri. Our friendship, strong since high school, had faded a bit as I got caught up in my problems and she recovered from her husband's death and took over her family's foundation, the Sandwich Islands Trust. She'd been in Philadelphia all summer with her sister, and it seemed that all we did was talk on the phone once in a while.

"I need to answer this," I said to Mike. "Sorry."

He held up a hand and went back to eating.

"I have somebody I want you to meet," Terri said. "His name's Levi. I'm hoping you can have dinner with us on Saturday night."

"Dinner Saturday night?" I said. Mike looked up. "Gosh, let me check my social calendar." I pretended to page through a book, and Mike smiled. "Looks like Saturday is free."

I don't know why, but I asked, "Can I bring someone?"

Terri said, "Of course."

"You want to come to dinner on Saturday with Terri and meet her new boyfriend?" I asked Mike.

A grin spread across his face. "That'd be nice."

"Count us both in," I said. "Me and Mike. Call me Friday and tell me where and when." I hung up before she could pepper me with a million questions.

Mike said, "We could make a habit of this dinner thing."

"We could. We'll see how things go."

He looked at his watch. "I've got to make a meeting at eight thirty."

"What, no dessert?"

"We could both do without dessert," Mike said, patting my stomach.

"Hey, watch it, bud," I said, standing up and pulling up my shirt to expose my abs. Looking down, though, I could see they weren't quite as good as they'd been in the past, and I let the shirt drop.

"Exactly," Mike said.

"You saw mine. Let me see yours."

He stood up, a sly grin on his face. He was wearing a light

blue chambray button-down shirt, and he began unbuttoning the buttons one at a time, swaying ever so slightly to an unheard rhythm. I laughed and said, "You can skip the striptease," but he wouldn't stop.

When he had the shirt completely unbuttoned, he flipped open one side, then the other, tantalizing me with glimpses of his erect nipples, his hairy chest, the waistband of his shorts. "Just want you to see what you've been missing," he said.

I reached over and poked him in the stomach. "I see where all that beer's been going," I said. And it was true; there was a band of fat just above his waist that hadn't been there the year before.

He grabbed my hand and pulled me toward him. We kissed, and there was so much passion between us that my dick got hard and my pulse began racing.

Then Mike pulled away. "Like I said, got a meeting. You get to clean up."

He walked to the door, his shirt still open. "See you later, handsome," he said, and then the door closed behind him.

I took a deep breath. It was the same story for me, my hormones getting ahead of my brain. When I was I going to be able to change that behavior?

I slid a slack key guitar CD in the stereo as I cleaned up the dishes and turned on my computer. I'd first come across Mr. Hu on MenSayHi.com; maybe I could still find him through there.

After my brothers and Harry took me surfing, I put my MenSayHi account on hold, but I reactivated it now and started looking through the profiles, trying to see if Mr. Hu was listed, or if there was anyone online who might know him.

It didn't take long for the messages to start coming in. I sat there in my boxers, drinking the Longboard Lager I hadn't been willing to open when Mike was there, and tried to figure out which of the offers might be from Mr. Hu.

It was exercise in both eroticism and frustration. I didn't want to get my rocks off—I wanted to catch a criminal. But I couldn't help getting turned on by some of the messages. Nothing came in from Mr. Hu. Just a lot of horny guys looking for cybersex or a real-time hookup. Feeling no closer to finding Jingtao's killer, or whoever was blackmailing Brian Izumigawa, I gave up around eleven, turned the computer off, and went to sleep.

Chapter 16

CLEANING HOUSE

RAY AND I caught a double homicide in Makiki as soon as our shift began—two Asian women killed while they slept in a cheap one-bedroom—and we spent most of the morning at the crime scene. There was suspiciously little in the apartment to identify the women—no family pictures, no wallets or driver's licenses, though each woman had a tiny purse with cosmetics and cigarettes.

The front door showed pry marks, indicating that whoever got in did so without the women's knowledge. The crime scene techs dusted for fingerprints and found a couple of pieces of hair and fiber that might be evidence. But there wasn't much else.

It must have been a slow day at the morgue, because Doc Takayama, the medical examiner, was there himself. Or maybe it was the presence of Lidia Portuondo, who had responded to the 911 call. I had the feeling they were carrying on a sub-rosa relationship; something about the flirtatious way they talked over dead bodies, I guess.

Doc had turned thirty a few weeks before. Prior to that he'd never actually said how old he was. He'd been a prodigy in college and medical school, and he'd chosen pathology because he got tired of patients calling him Doogie Howser and asking if he'd gone directly to medical school from kindergarten.

"What do you think, Doc?" I asked.

"Preliminary? Both women were killed by a single gunshot to the head. My guess is that the killer used a silencer, because the position of the bodies indicates that both appear to have been killed in their sleep."

"Don't forget the stippling," Lidia said. She was looking fine that morning, her dark hair pulled into a French braid, her uniform crisp. There was a light blush on her cheeks, as if she'd been in the sun—or put on makeup just before Doc's arrival.

"Of course," Doc said, smiling at her. Stippling was a fancy word for a pattern of dots around the wound that indicated the gun was fired at close range.

"Time of death?" Ray asked.

"Four to six hours ago," Doc said. "I'll be more precise after the autopsy."

The building looked like it had once been a motel—two stories with a staircase at one end. Eight small apartments on each floor. A tired middle-aged Japanese woman was taking care of a couple of *keikis* in an apartment down the hall from the murder scene, but the kids were making such a racket I could barely hear her tell me she didn't know anything.

An elderly Hawai'ian man in a wheelchair was in one of the first-floor units, but he was disoriented and the room smelled of urine. He thought we were from the water department about his leaky faucet, and nothing we said could convince him otherwise. The rest of the neighbors were gone.

There was no superintendent on the property; the building was one of many owned by a small-time operator, and when I called over there the manager, whose name was Ed Millner, said that the lease was in the name of a corporation. "You don't know the names of the tenants?" I asked.

"Sorry," Millner said. "They paid the rent on time, they didn't tear the place up, and they didn't bother the other tenants. That's all we care about."

Doc had the bodies taken away and Lidia followed him outside. I saw them conferring before they parted and wondered if they were comparing forensic notes, or making a date.

"Let's recap what we have," Ray said, looking at his notepad. "Two unidentified Asian females, killed in the middle of the night by an unknown assailant. Anonymous 911 call. This case has 'solved immediately' written all over it."

"Now, now," I said. "We have the name of the corporation that signed the lease. Why does it sound familiar, though?"

Ray paged through his notes. "The house in Black Point," he said. "Lease in the name of the same corporation."

He looked up at me. "Well, the clinic was a front for prostitution," he said. "You think somebody's cleaning house?"

"I think we need to go back and see Norma Ching again," I said. On our way to Chinatown, we stopped and picked up chili at Zippy's.

"Who do you think made the 911 call?" Ray asked, as we sat in the restaurant and ate. I wasn't about to get my new ride crapped up with fast food wrappers in my first twenty-four hours of ownership.

"Why?"

"These women were killed in the middle of the night. With a silencer. And we know they were working girls, so it wouldn't be unusual for somebody to see men coming and going at night. So who discovered the bodies?"

"You think maybe Norma?"

He shrugged. "It's a question we can ask her."

There was no answer at Norma's door, though we knocked several times, and the pry marks on the outside looked fresh. The lady next door came out in the hall. She looked about a hundred years old, no more than four feet tall, her hair a wild white tangle. "You look for Norma?" she asked.

"Yes," I said. "You seen her today?"

The old lady shook her head. "She always bring me coffee first thing. But not today. I worried."

I looked at Ray, then back at the old lady. "You wouldn't happen to have a key to her apartment, would you?"

She ducked back into her apartment and returned a moment later with a security key on a red ribbon. I took the key from her and opened the door, calling, "Norma? Norma? You here?"

Ray and I walked into the apartment, already dreading what we'd find. Sure enough, Norma Ching was dead in her bed, a single bullet wound to her head. At a glance, it looked like the same caliber that had killed the two women in Makiki.

I called the medical examiner's office and asked Doc to come out himself. I asked that the same two techs, Larry Solas and Ryan Kainoa, come out, even though they should have been back in the lab processing the evidence from Makiki. I figured if the crimes were related, it was best to have all the evidence in the same hands.

We looked the place over while we waited, noting that the pry marks on the front door looked like they might match the ones on the door in Makiki. We found a bunch of gold rings, bracelets, and chains in a jewelry box on Norma's dresser and a few thousand dollars in cash in her freezer, so it was unlikely that her killer had broken in with the intent to steal.

Ray and I were both beat by the time we made it back to the station, as our shift was ending. I yawned and looked at the clock. I was thinking about heading home for a nice nap when I realized that I had to meet Dr. Phil for an early dinner.

"You want to go back and canvass that apartment building?" Ray asked. "People might start to come home soon."

"Can you do it? I've got a date." I explained about Dr. Phil's schedule. "It's his only night off this week."

"The things I do for my partner," Ray said. "If you can drop me up there, I'll get Julie to pick me up on her way home."

"You're a prince among men. This makes up for, oh, at least two times I've chauffeured you around."

Before we left, I tried Karen at Social Security, to see if she'd found anything on Treasure, but she'd already left for the day.

"I'm worried about Treasure," I said to Ray, as we walked to the elevator. "If the same person killed the two women and Norma, she may already be dead."

"Or maybe Treasure's our killer. Or maybe she was the one who called 911 about the girls."

"At this point, anything's possible."

I drove Ray up to the apartment building in Makiki. There were a couple of cars in the parking lot, which meant somebody was home. "Good luck. How about I pick you up tomorrow morning on my way in? Save Julie the trip."

"Have fun on your date. I'll try and get the case solved for you."

I realized on walking in to the steak house that I wasn't dressed well enough; an aloha shirt and black jeans are fine for homicide, but the men around me were all wearing business suits. Mel Tormé was on the sound system, and even the waiters wore ties. It was like I'd stumbled into my brother Lui's world.

Dr. Phil was waiting for me at the bar with a glass of fizzy water in his hand. "Alcohol doesn't mix well with medicine," he said, apologetically. "But you go ahead and have a drink if you want."

"I think I will," I said, imagining that if I did start dating Mike again this was how our relationship might play out. I ordered a cosmopolitan.

"Not the drink I'd expect of you," Dr. Phil said. "You seem more like a beer-and-a-shot kind of guy."

I wasn't sure how to take that, but I chalked it up to those getting-to-know-you jitters. "I do like a beer now and then," I said. "What's the matter, you not masculine enough for a fruity drink?" I wanted it to sound like a joke, but I don't think Dr. Phil thought of it that way. Another date off to a rocky start.

The hostess came over and showed us to a booth of dark wood, with a single spotlight hanging high above us and shining on the glossy table top. The menu and wine list were bound together in a leather-covered book, and the prices were a lot higher than I'd expected. I was cranky with Dr. Phil for picking such an expensive place, and for not telling me about the dress code, either.

But then he said, "Now, this was my invitation, so it's my treat. This is my favorite place and I don't get over here often enough. The filet is amazing."

I followed his lead and ordered the filet, with a baked potato and a Caesar salad. The food was excellent; the potato was as big as my foot, and the beef was tender enough to cut with a butter knife.

"What's up?" Dr. Phil said, as we were eating our main course. "You've been kind of distracted. Bad case?"

"Three murders in one day." I told him, briefly, about Norma and the two Chinese girls, and their connection to prostitution at the acupuncture clinic.

"I can't tell you how many prostitutes we treat at the ER," he said. "Not just STDs, either. Girls who get beat up, or cut, who don't have medical insurance, so anything that happens to them gets very bad before they come to us. Not just girls—boys, too. A couple of weeks ago, I saw this Chinese boy who somebody had used pretty badly. Rectal bleeding, anal fissures, and a bad infection. He didn't speak a word of English, and he had this older man with him who was supposed to be his translator, but I think he was more like a guard."

"Did you call anyone?"

Dr. Phil shook his head. "Not my job. The older man said that the boy was over eighteen, that he'd been attacked in an alley by some guys who got away."

Immediately I thought of Jingtao. "You remember a name for this boy?"

He shook his head. "And whatever name they gave, I'm sure it wasn't his real one." He drank his fizzy water. "Prostitution's a victimless crime. We ought to decriminalize it, regulate it, make sure the girls—and guys—get regular checkups."

I was tempted to tell him about Jingtao, how he'd escaped from the acupuncture clinic and then died in the fire. But I couldn't find a way to make it sound like I wasn't accusing Dr. Phil in his death, and neither of us said anything else for a while; we just sat listening to Dean Martin and the rest of the Rat Pack singing about the past. I didn't have the energy to court Dr. Phil when my mind was on Mike, and I'm sure he figured out something was up.

I yawned when the waiter asked if we'd like dessert, and Dr. Phil said, "No, I've got to get to work, and I think my friend here needs a nap."

"Sorry," I said. "I'm normally more animated on a date."

"It's OK. With schedules like ours, we've got to fit dates in whenever we can."

He paid the bill and said, "I'll see what my schedule's like for next week and I'll call you." I had a feeling that he wouldn't. He did let me leave the tip—which was more than I'd have spent on dinner with a date at a restaurant of my choice. It made me feel a little better about the way things were ending—but only a little.

Chapter 17

TREASURE HUNT

WEDNESDAY MORNING, AS promised, I picked Ray up on my way to work. "Any hope you guys are getting a second car?" I asked, cranky after my failed date with Dr. Phil, and after battling early morning traffic to get over to Ray's place.

"I've got a line on a used Toyota," he said. "I do a couple more special duty gigs, I can put a down payment on it."

"You learn anything last night?"

He shrugged. "Next door neighbor lady didn't like the girls—they dressed like tramps. Nobody I talked to heard or saw anything."

"We could track down the doctor whose license was used for the clinic," I said. "Maybe he knows something."

Dr. Hsing-Wah Hsiao was easy to find, considering he'd been dead for five years. The first hit I got on Google was his obituary. "Another dead end," Ray said. "This case has a million of 'em." I e-mailed the obit to Ricky Koele so that he could follow up on the clinics licensed in the good doctor's name.

We put in a couple of hours getting the autopsy results for all three homicides, reviewing arrest reports for prostitution and so on. I checked Doc Takayama's report on Jingtao; he cited some anal fissures, but no semen in the rectum. That didn't mean he was the boy Dr. Phil had treated, but it did make it likely that he'd been involved in the sex trade.

Just after nine, Karen Gold at Social Security called with an address on Treasure in Hawai'i Kai, and we drove out there. It was a nice apartment building with a lobby and a locked front door, and we had to call the management company and ask them to send someone over with a key to Treasure's apartment.

While we waited, we got coffee from the Starbucks in the Hawai'i Kai Town Center, where the Disney version of *Aloha 'Oe* was playing, and Tia Carrere was singing the song Queen Lili'uokalani had written. I couldn't help but think of the lyrics: *aloha 'oe* means "farewell to you," and we'd said that to too many people on this case already.

"Gonna have to put the medical examiner on speed dial, this keeps up," Ray said.

"I can't remember the last time we had a case with four dead bodies and almost nothing to go on," I said, looking out the window at the mountains across from the center. Clouds were massing at the tops, casting strange shadows down the valley. "Maybe Treasure knows something. That is, if she's still alive."

We drove back to Treasure's building, where a pleasant-faced *haole* with flyaway light brown hair met us. "I'm Stephen Viens," he said. "You guys the detectives?"

We introduced ourselves, and he let us in the front and took us up to the second floor. "Miss Chen?" he said, knocking on the door. "Miss Chen, you in there?"

There was no answer—which didn't necessarily mean that Treasure Chen was in the apartment and unable to answer. At least there were no visible pry marks. Viens opened the door and we walked in.

"Not much of a housekeeper, is she?" Ray asked. The living/dining room looked like somebody had gone through it in a hurry—papers, newspapers, cosmetics, and clothes scattered everywhere. The good news was that the place smelled like lilacs, courtesy of one of those plug-in air fresheners, rather than like a dead body.

Treasure's bed was empty, and the bedroom and bathroom bore similar signs of a quick exit. "I'll leave you to your business," Viens said, and Ray and I spent the next hour or so going through what

Treasure had left behind, looking for anything that might tell us where she'd gone.

There was precious little. I found the envelope from a greeting card in the bedroom wastebasket. The return address was "E. Chen," with an address in Waikīkī. "Maybe a relative?" I asked Ray.

"Could be."

Treasure's wardrobe was a lot like that of the girls in Makiki—slinky dresses and high-heeled shoes—though her underwear was much higher class. "Fancy stuff," Ray said. "You know how much panties like this cost?"

He held up a pair trimmed in lace, with a pattern of roses. "I bet you're going to tell me," I said.

"Hundred bucks, easy," he said. "Julie likes this brand, but it's not like she's got a drawer full of it."

"Too much information."

"Hey, you've got your area of expertise, I've got mine," Ray said. "That's why we make such a good partnership."

We swung past E. Chen's address in Waikīkī on our way back to the station. It was a nondescript high-rise on Ala Wai Boulevard, just down the street from Harry's. The doorman told us that E stood for Emerald, a very nice Chinese woman who worked in a bank, he thought. "Hold on," he said. "I might have one of her cards here."

He pulled a big book from underneath his desk. "Sometimes I have to get hold of a tenant at work," he said, as he paged through it. "You know, leaky pipe, special delivery, that kind of thing. Yeah, here it is."

He handed me a card. Emerald Chen was an executive vice president with China Trade Bank, with an address a couple of blocks from the Aloha Tower. At the luxurious building, we had to show our badges to a security guard in the marble lobby, who called upstairs and then directed us to the twenty-first floor.

The elevator doors opened to magnificent vista of Honolulu harbor, the autumn sunshine glistening off the water. A barge was navigating the Sand Point Channel, and a jet was landing on the reef runway at Honolulu International. Jake Shimabukuro was playing the ukulele softly over the sound system. A young Chinese man in a business suit approached us. "You're here to see Ms. Chen?"

"That's true," I said. "Is she available?"

"Let me take you to her office." We followed him down a hallway to a corner office with the same expansive view. Emerald Chen was somewhat older than I remembered Treasure, and not nearly as attractive. She was short and a little stocky, but her hair and makeup were immaculate and she wore a woman's Rolex with diamond accents.

"How can I help you, detectives?" she asked, after we sat down across from her massive teak desk.

"Do you recognize this envelope?" I showed her the one I'd picked up in Treasure's apartment.

"I thought you might be here about my sister," she said, sighing. "She's not in trouble again, is she?"

"I think she might be. Four of her business associates have been murdered in the last week, and we're worried Treasure might be in danger."

"What a charming euphemism," Emerald said. "Business associates. I know what my sister did for a living, detective."

"And what is that?" Ray asked.

"When Treasure graduated from high school, I offered to pay her tuition at any college, but she declined. She became a lingerie model, and for that you can read 'high-class prostitute.'" She frowned. "After about six months, she found herself a rich criminal."

"Tommy Pang," I said.

"You knew him?"

I nodded. "I investigated his murder."

"So you met my sister. She's a beautiful woman, and smart enough to know how to use that beauty to get what she wants."

"What happened to Treasure after Tommy Pang died?"

"She tried a few legitimate jobs. She was a restaurant hostess for a while, and she worked behind the makeup counter at Clark's, then at a real estate company, selling time-shares. But she ran into a woman she'd known at the lingerie store and got drawn back into that business."

"Norma Ching," I said.

"You've done your homework, detective."

"Someone shot and killed Norma Monday night," I said. "As well as two women who worked at the clinic with her and Treasure. We're worried Treasure is either dead or on the run. Have you heard from her?"

Emerald Chen looked deflated, like she'd always expected the worst from her sister but still hoped for the best. "No, I haven't. As you might guess, we're not close. I've never approved of her lifestyle, and she's rejected my efforts to help her."

"She may not be in a position to reject you anymore," I said. "If she contacts you, will you let us know?"

"Do you think my sister killed these women?"

I shook my head. "I think she discovered the two victims in Makiki, and she called 911. As you said, she's a smart woman. She must have realized she was a target, and she took off. Do you have a current picture of Treasure? We could use one to help us look for her."

She reached around behind her to a photo in a silver frame. "This was taken last year, at my grandfather's birthday," she said, handing it to me.

Treasure truly was a beautiful woman, a head taller than her older sister. There was a faint family resemblance between them—but in the photo they looked like a beauty queen and her chaperone. Treasure had a slim face, rounding to a narrow chin. Her cheeks were flat planes, and her eyebrows were carefully plucked. Her black hair was glossy and curled around her face.

"May we take this with us?" I asked.

Emerald nodded, and I slipped the photo out of its frame. Ray and I stood up. "Be careful, Miss Chen," I said. "If someone wants to kill Treasure, you don't want to be in the way." We gave Emerald our cards and the young guy showed us back to the elevator.

Back at the station, the autopsy results were in. Norma had been killed first, at least an hour before the two women. Doc's report said that the women's physical condition, including their dental work, implied that they had grown up in mainland China.

Ballistics results showed that the same gun had been used on all three women. "How do we connect these murders to Jingtao and the arson at the acupuncture clinic?" I asked. "There's a circumstantial connection, but arson and homicide are two very different crimes. What if we have more than one bad guy?"

Ray shrugged. "Beats me," he said.

Chapter 18

REMEMBERING LUCAS

BILLY KIM FROM the ballistics lab called a little later. "You guys want to come down here?" he asked. "I've got a match on the gun used in your shootings."

Ray and I went down to B1, passing Vice on the way, and I wondered how Brian Izumigawa was holding up. I hadn't heard from him, which I took as a good sign. Maybe Mr. Hu was too busy with other problems to chase down Brian.

"What have you got?" I asked Billy. He was a skinny Korean guy who knew everything there was to know about ballistics.

"A cold case. A John Doe." He pulled up the results on his computer monitor and showed us how the bullets matched.

"What do you know about this victim?" I asked.

Billy shook his head. "Not much. Steve Hart caught the case." Steve was another detective in our squad. I'd had a run-in with him early, when I took away one of his first big cases. It was nothing to do with him; a bomb had gone off at an event I was attending, resulting in a high-profile death, and because of my personal connections I was determined to be the guy to break the case open.

Steve Hart still held a grudge against me, though I'd tried my best to be a good guy since then. Sometimes our shifts overlapped, sometimes not. That day, he came in a couple of hours later, and Ray and I waited until he'd settled in at his desk to ask him about the dead John Doe.

"No leads," he said. He was a tall, rangy *haole*, a California transplant with a chip on his shoulder. "You think you can do something with it, be my guest."

He dug around and found the folder, which Ray and I took back to my desk. The first thing we saw was a photo of the dead guy, and I knew that I'd seen him before. But where? His eyes were closed, but otherwise his handsome face was untouched. He had the slimness and pale skin that I'd come to associate with those addicted to ice, the smokable form of crystal meth. Had I arrested him? Seen him hanging around Waikīkī?

I closed my eyes and focused—and then I realized he was the hustler Mr. Hu had paid to fuck me, who had tried to use me to bargain with Vice.

My first few encounters with Mr. Hu were pretty vanilla, but quickly the stakes escalated. It seemed that he had made it his personal mission to break me. Each time I went to the mansion, he had constructed a new scenario to debase or degrade me, and each time I couldn't help but go through with what he asked. I had toyed with the occasional bondage or sadomasochism fantasy in the past, and I think my sense of self-worth had been so knocked down after breaking up with Mike that I relished the chance to indulge in some of those darker sexual passions.

The last time I saw him, we were in the living room of the mansion in Black Point and he asked me if I'd ever been with a prostitute. I'd laughed and said, "I don't need to pay for sex."

"But when you pay, you get what you want," Mr. Hu said. He was handsome in his way—tall, a little stocky, always beautifully dressed in expensive suits, Egyptian cotton shirts, silk ties, diamond cufflinks. Most of the time he stayed fully clothed; when he did strip down, I saw silk bikini briefs that retailed for a hundred bucks or more.

"I get what I want," I said.

"Yes, but what about what I want?"

I slipped my right foot out of my deck shoe and raised my leg so I could stroke the inside of Mr. Hu's thigh through his suit pants. "What is it that you want?"

"I want to see you naked."

"You do, do you?" I said, beginning to unbutton my aloha shirt. I was proud of my body, though by that point in my relationship with Mr. Hu I'd been skipping most of my athletic pursuits in favor of visiting the mansion in Black Point. I stood up to shuck my shirt and step out of my pants, and I was uncomfortably aware that I'd put on a few pounds around my waist.

Mr. Hu saw it, too. "Not so sexy, are you?" he said.

"I can leave if you want." I stood there in my boxers, my stiff dick already poking its head through the slit. Of course, I wasn't going anywhere, but I couldn't help trying to be assertive.

"No, you will do," he said. "The boxers, please."

I pulled them down and stood there before him, as if I were on display for his purchase. "There is something about you, Kimo," he said, appraising me. "I don't know quite what it is. You are a handsome man, but I see many, many handsome men. I appreciate your enjoyment of sex—your willingness to transcend your own boundaries."

"And you like the fact that I'm a cop," I said. "That turn you on, Mr. Hu? You have cop fantasies?"

He smiled tightly. "I have had my own experiences with the police," he said. "For the most part, not erotic at all. No, it is something inside you, something I am trying to bring out. Appetites you have repressed."

That was scary. If I'd been repressing appetites, it was with good reason. We don't need to act on our every desire, after all. "Please step over to the wall, face it, and place your hands against it," Mr. Hu said.

"Assume the position," I said, as I placed my hands in the cuffs mounted there, and he locked them shut. "You going to pat me down? Think I might be carrying a concealed weapon?"

"Your weapon is clearly evident." He took a silk handkerchief from his pocket and tied it around my eyes as a blindfold. "We will try something new tonight."

With my eyes covered, I felt my other senses heightened. I thought someone else had entered the room, though whoever it was walked very quietly. He came up behind me, and Mr. Hu said, in a voice underlaid with desire, "Eat his ass."

I felt the man's hot breath against my butt, then his tongue, poking and probing me. "Yes, fuck him with your tongue," Mr. Hu said. "He likes being fucked."

He kept up a steady flow of instructions to the unknown man behind me, the soundtrack to his personal porn flick. The guy sure knew how to use his tongue. He licked the tender spot between my ass and my balls, he tongue-fucked me, then when my ass was loose and juicy he finger-fucked me, first with one, then two, then three fingers.

I was moaning with desire by the time Mr. Hu told the guy behind me to fuck my ass. "He has a very large dick, Kimo," Mr. Hu said. "I hope it is not painful."

"No, you hope it is painful. You hope he splits my ass in two and fucks me so hard I can't sit down for a week."

"You know me so well. And I know you, too. I know that what you think of me is what you want for yourself."

I heard the telltale tear of a condom package, the squirt of a lube bottle that sounded like a fart. The guy was hung like a donkey, or so it seemed. Even with generous amounts of spit and lube, he could barely wedge the rubber-covered head of his dick in my ass. He stood behind me, grabbing my shoulders and trying to piston in and out of me, and the blindfold magnified the sensations. I began crying and moaning, begging him to give up. "You're killing me. Mr. Hu, please, please, make him stop."

"I can't do that, Kimo," Mr. Hu said gently. "Once something is begun it must be finished."

I thought I heard his pants unzip and his breathing quicken. Finally, donkey dick pushed one more time up my ass and whimpered, and I realized it was the first time I'd heard his voice—the soundtrack had been exclusively Mr. Hu's.

"You may finish the detective off," Mr. Hu said, and a warm hand encircled my dick. It took just a few strokes and I was creaming—but without pleasure, just a release from pain.

Mr. Hu unsnapped the handcuffs, and as I rubbed my wrists he said, "You may remove your blindfold, Kimo." The guy behind me moved away, and it was all I could do not to slump against the wall. I untied the silk and turned around, expecting donkey dick to be butt ugly.

But he wasn't. He was incredibly handsome, with sandy blond hair and one of the best bodies I'd ever seen, the kind that took hours in the gym to sculpt. Bulging biceps, a six-pack at the waist, thick thighs. He could have stepped out of the pages of a gay porn magazine.

"This is Lucas," Mr. Hu said. "I paid him two hundred fifty dollars to fuck your ass. I hope you enjoyed it."

I shifted on my feet. My ass hurt, felt distended and uncomfortably liquid. "I hope you enjoyed watching it."

Lucas pulled the soggy condom off his dick and took a washcloth from Mr. Hu to clean up. I could see the effects the drugs were having on Lucas, in the paleness of his face, the way he looked a little skinnier than his frame should have allowed. My dick had deflated, and though on an average day I could have stared at Lucas for hours, jerking myself over and over again, all I wanted to do was put my clothes on and get out of that place.

By the time I got home I knew there was something wrong. My ass was bleeding and the pain was worse than anything I'd experienced before. I called Gunter's cell phone and dragged him away from a hot boy at the Rod and Reel Club. He made me pull my pants down and bend over, and as soon as I did, he said, "This is beyond anything I can do for you, pal. You're going to the ER."

"No," I said. "No way."

"Yes way. Give me your keys. I'm driving." He smiled. "Don't worry, I know a very discreet ER on the road to Kailua. Nobody's going to know anything."

He picked up my keys and jingled them in his hand. "But you are going to tell me every detail."

Of course I didn't. I told him Mr. Hu had used a huge dildo on me. It seemed better than telling the truth, that a gay prostitute with a donkey dick had fucked me into oblivion while Mr. Hu watched and jerked himself off. I don't know why I didn't just tell Gunter the truth; but then when he told Harry and my brothers I was glad I'd made up the story.

Looking at the photo of Lucas, I worried once more that this investigation was coming uncomfortably close to my personal life.

Chapter 19

WHERE ALL ROADS LEAD

"YOU RECOGNIZE THIS guy?" Ray asked.

I nodded. "He was a hustler. I heard him called Lucas. He's the guy who gave my name to Vice."

"Anything in the folder?"

I looked. Steve Hart hadn't found much. He didn't have an ID on the victim—but then he hadn't had the inside information I had. And I could empathize with him; I had two dead Chinese girls on my sheet who didn't have names, either.

The autopsy results showed that Lucas had died from a single bullet to the head, in the same way that Norma Ching and the two Chinese girls had been killed. Tox screens revealed that he was an ice user, high at the time of death. He had also tested positive for syphilis.

"Shit," I said. That was all I needed. I remembered that Lucas had used a condom that night, but he'd also tongue-fucked me and jerked me off. Had he had syphilis then? I'd had enough experience with STDs thanks to Mike and the gonorrhea he had passed me. I didn't need syphilis on top of it.

"What's the matter?" Ray asked.

I didn't want to tell him. But I'd already lied too much, to myself, my family, and friends. "This is not a story I want to tell in the middle of the station," I said. "Come on, let's take a ride."

Ray shrugged and said, "Sure." We didn't talk much as I drove us up toward Black Point. We rolled up all the flaps to enjoy the fresh air from some trade winds blowing in off the ocean with the promise of a bright, sunny winter.

"Fancy neighborhood," Ray said, as we started up the street where Mr. Hu's mansion was located.

"All lava underneath here," I said. "Hence the name. They say when King Kamehameha arrived from the big island, his war canoes stretched all the way from here to Hawai'i Kai."

"The homicide department doesn't work out for you, you could always get a gig as a tour guide."

"You like this neighborhood? 'Cause I'm happy to let you out."

"No, no, continue the tour," he said, holding up his hand.

Whenever my personal life spilled over into my job, I got irritable. I'd been cautioned by Lieutenant Sampson about finding the appropriate balance between my work and my sex life, and I could see another warning on the horizon.

"Neighborhood first developed in the thirties," I said, trying for a lighter tone. "Some of the most expensive houses on the island. We're talking ten to fifteen million bucks."

I pulled up in front of Mr. Hu's house and shut the Jeep off. There was a for sale sign on the lawn, and the wrought-iron gates were closed. The place looked deserted, but the grass grows so fast in the islands that it could have just been a couple of weeks since the lawn service had been by.

"This is where you came to meet Mr. Hu?" Ray asked.

"I want to say, I appreciate how cool you are," I said, looking not at Ray but out the window. "Most guys, they'd freak out at some of the stuff I've told you."

"I ever tell you about this human sexuality course I took in college?"

I looked over at him. "Nope."

"Very interesting. I mean, I took it in part because of that cousin I told you about, Joey, the gay one. I wanted to understand what was up with him. But I got into it. I was thinking maybe of majoring in sociology then. You know, save the world from all its problems."

"I can see that in you." Ray cared about people, especially those in trouble, victims, even bad guys who'd been turned bad by circumstance.

"We read all this graphic stuff," Ray said. "Some of the guys were grossed out. I think a couple of my buddies signed up because they thought we'd be studying the Kama Sutra or something, learning exotic sexual positions. But between the course, and my cousin, and some of the other shit I've seen, the bottom line is, you can tell me anything. I'm not going to get grossed out, I'm not going to tell the rest of the squad, and it's not going to change my opinion of you."

"I appreciate that, partner." Looking up at the shuttered mansion, I told him about the night Lucas fucked me so badly Gunter had to take me to the ER.

Ray squirmed a little in his seat, but I could see he was trying not to show it. "So Steve Hart's John Doe was your donkey dick?"

"Think so. Course, I could always ask Doc Takayama for corroboration."

Ray laughed. "I want to be there for that."

Back at the station, we kept pulling at the threads of the investigation, hoping some new clue would unravel. Just before the end of our shift, Brian Izumigawa called. "How are you holding up?" I asked.

"I'm scared, I can't sleep, I can't eat," he said. "I picked up the phone a dozen times to call you but I was afraid of what you'd say. Please, tell me you have some good news. I can't take much more of this."

"We're working on chasing down Mr. Hu." Listening to a victim without getting upset yourself is a skill that takes a long time to master. I was still working on it, especially when a case like this hit so close to home, but I focused on keeping my voice quiet to calm Brian down. "He's in the middle of something much bigger than your blackmail, and if he hasn't contacted you about the money again, it's because he's got a lot on his plate right now. Just hold on."

"Easy for you to say," he said.

We talked for a while longer, edging around the question of whether he should just give up and tell his wife. "Brian, you're the only one who can make that decision," I said. "But if I were you, I'd hold off for a few days, at least. Let me see what I can do with Mr. Hu. If we can remove the immediate threat, you'll have a clearer head to think through what's best."

I had been dragged out of the closet myself, without the chance to present my own case to my family and friends, and it had been a terrible experience. If I could, I wanted to help Brian avoid that kind of pain—for himself, his wife, and everyone around him.

When we wrapped up the call he was feeling less anxious, and I left for the Gay Teen Center and the relaunch of my self-defense/ self-empowerment group. When I'd run the group in the past, several of the kids had been occasional prostitutes, hanging around places like Ala Moana Beach Park, and I hoped that one of them might know something about Lucas.

Chapter 20

PREMIUM MEMBERS

I WAS SITTING on the wooden floor of the church social hall when a tough girl named Pua, which is Hawai'ian for flower, led the first couple of kids in. I jumped up and greeted her with a big hug. Hanging a little behind her was chubby Frankie, with sleek black hair pulled into a ponytail. He wore mascara around his eyes, which made him look like a raccoon, and I hugged him, too.

"Like old times," I said. "All we need is Jimmy and Lolo." I hadn't expected Jimmy Ah Wong, now that he was comfortably settled at UH, but I wondered about Lolo, a tough boy who used to hang out with Frankie and Pua.

"Lolo's dead," Pua said. She reached over and squeezed Frankie's hand. "He got into ice about a year ago, and then he OD'd."

"What a shame," I said. "Poor guy."

About a dozen kids showed up, and I had everybody lie down on the floor on their backs. I led them through some relaxation exercises and then a couple of yoga postures, to get them in touch with their bodies and into a good space mentally. Then I got Frankie to help me demonstrate a couple of self-defense moves, and after that we sat around in a circle and talked.

"Where have you been?" Frankie asked me. "We missed you a lot."

"I'm sorry. I went through some tough times and I just didn't feel like being out among people." Kids have built-in shit detectors, and I could see that neither Frankie nor Pua was buying that.

It was to be my day for confessions. "You guys remember the fireman I was dating for a while?"

Frankie nodded. "He was hot!"

Pua laughed and punched him.

"Yeah, he was," I said. "He was also deep in the closet, and you know being in the closet can make you do dumb things. He cheated on me and we broke up, and I was in a pretty bad place for a while." I smiled at them. "But I'm back, and I'm sorry that I bailed on you guys. I want you to know that I'll try not to do that again, and any time any of you have a problem, I hope you'll come and talk to me."

As Pua and Frankie were getting ready to leave, I said, "Hey, guys, can I ask you something about a case?"

"Sure, Kimo," Frankie said.

"Frankie thinks he might want to be a policeman," Pua said.

"That's great," I said. "We need more gay cops. You've got to finish high school first, though."

"I'm a senior," Frankie said. "Me and Pua, both. Sometimes it's tough, but I'm not letting anybody keep me from getting educated."

"Good for you." I hesitated, hating to bring up bad memories, especially when Frankie was so proud of his achievements, but I had to ask. "Listen, I know you and Lolo used to hang out at Ala Moana Beach Park, and I'm looking for information on a guy who hung there, too." I pulled out the picture of Lucas.

He looked peaceful, though clearly dead. There was no blood or gore, but there'd been some settling of those handsome features. The cosmetologist at the morgue had done a nice job with him, trimming and styling his hair. If you tried, you could imagine he was just asleep—but you had to try pretty hard.

"You know him?" I asked.

"Lucas," Frankie said, nearly spitting the name. Tears welled up in his eyes, and he turned away.

"Lucas is the guy who turned Lolo on to ice," Pua said, putting her arm around Frankie's shoulders. "He was a real bastard."

"I'm sorry," I said. "Somebody shot him about a month ago."

"He was older than us, like maybe twenty-two or twenty-three, but he liked hanging around with kids," Pua said. "Like it made him feel superior to be able to lord things over us."

She squeezed Frankie's shoulders, and he wiped his eyes with the back of his hand. "He always bragged about the guys he fucked," she continued. "He'd talk about guys who were supposed to be important or powerful, like bank presidents and shit, and when we didn't recognize their names he'd get all pissy."

I felt like I'd gotten a shot of adrenaline to the heart. Had Lucas bragged about me? I knew he'd given my name to Vice. What if he'd told other tricks?

"I didn't believe him most of the time," Frankie said. "I mean, he had a huge dick, and I guess he was kind of cute. But towards the end, he was just this skanky ice whore. I didn't see how any rich guy would want to fuck him."

"You don't know anything more about him? Like where he lived, or other guys he hung around with?"

Pua and Frankie looked at each other. Pua said, "Maybe Jimmy would know."

"Jimmy Ah Wong?" I said. "I thought he wasn't . . . you know . . . hanging around the park anymore."

Jimmy had been a hustler for a short while, after his dad found out he was gay and kicked him out of the house. But when I'd seen him at Aunt Mei-Mei's house, he'd seemed happy, and I knew she paid his tuition and gave him spending money. "He's not hustling," Frankie said. "He's, like, helping guys."

Pua said, "He belongs to this gay-straight alliance at UH. They collect condoms and safe sex literature up at the campus, and then they take it down to the park and hand it out. After Lolo died, Jimmy was trying to help Lucas."

I thanked them, told them I'd see them in two weeks, and started back to my apartment. I needed to get tested again—something I'd been putting off. I had always tried to be careful, but sometimes my guard slipped, especially when Mr. Hu was involved. Discovering that Lucas had syphilis gave me a new incentive.

A flock of orange-billed myna birds startled me, swooping down from the trees and right over the heads of a clutch of Japanese tourists crossing Kuhio Avenue. Once again, my dick had gotten me into trouble. Was I ever going to learn from my mistakes? Had I gotten syphilis, or something else, from Lucas or one of the other semi-anonymous tricks I'd fooled around with while Mike and I were apart? What if word got around the station that I had been involved with a dead ice whore?

Cops and firemen love to give each other shit. I knew cops who teased other straight guys with jokes about ass-fucking and dick size. Just a few days ago I'd heard one cop ask another, "What island you from, brah? Ho-Molokai?"

I was sure guys talked stink about me behind my back. But I have a short temper and a strong right jab, so most guys knew not to go too far. I'd once kneed another cop in the groin when he suggested a gay man who had been beaten by a trick had been asking for it, and I'd head-butted a lard ass who told me I wasn't fit to wear a badge because I sucked dick.

Since I came out, I've worked hard to be just another cop, reining in any behavior that might seem flamboyant, laughing at the fag jokes, even teasing a few guys myself when I caught them in over-bright aloha shirts or very fresh haircuts. Most of the time, I felt like other cops were able to look beyond my sexual orientation and see me, Kimo.

I admired Jimmy Ah Wong for turning his life around, and more for his outreach to the hustlers who congregated around Ala Moana Beach Park, gay and straight. He was going back to the place where he'd been at his lowest, and using his experience to help others.

While I'd tried to do the same thing, I wasn't always successful. But all you can do is keep trying, right? I called Jimmy's cell phone and offered to buy him lunch the next day. "I've got a test tomorrow afternoon," he said. "I've got to cram. Can we make it Friday?"

"Sure," I said. "But while I have you on the phone—I understand you've been going down to Ala Moana Beach Park with kids from the GSA."

"Yeah."

"You ever run into a hustler named Lucas there?"

"Is he in trouble?"

"He's dead. I'm trying to track what he's been up to. He ever say anything about who he worked for, how he got his clients, that sort of thing?"

"There was some private Web site where he posted his pictures, and you needed a password to get on and contact him. It was all like a big secret. He said he had these important clients, very discreet."

"You remember the name of the Web site?"

"It was something funny," he said. "Like a pun on the name Hawai'i."

"MenSayHi? That's a public site."

"Yeah, that's it. He said there was some kind of private part you needed a password for."

"Thanks, Jimmy. I'll look into the Web site. And I'll pick you up in front of Hamilton Library at noon on Friday."

I logged on to MenSayHi when I got home. I'd spent a long time on the site during the year after my breakup with Mike, but I'd never signed up for the full membership. For free, they let you chat and send and receive messages, and that had been enough for me.

But after talking to Jimmy, I clicked on the link that read "Members Only." A box popped up which read, "You are entering the premium area of MenSayHi. Please enter your premium user ID or click here to set up premium access."

I followed the instructions. For your $9.95 a month, you got full-length videos, extensive photo galleries, webcams, and the ability to private message the actors in the webcams. I filled in my credit card information and clicked Submit.

The button reminded me of my experiences with Mr. Hu, where

I'd definitely submitted to his will. I wondered if he was behind the Web site, or was simply one of its primary users.

A window popped up asking me to wait while my information was verified, and then when it closed the screen behind it read "Welcome, Premium Member." My dick stiffened as I saw the cornucopia of sex spread out before me. The screen was broken up into three categories: Galleries, Videos, and Webcams.

There were a dozen still shots of handsome men, of all types, under the Galleries heading. You could click on each guy to see a series of shots of him in various positions. The stocky black guy with close-cropped hair was jerking off in frame after frame, getting closer to orgasm in each one. The dude with greasy black hair and a football jersey was stripping, getting down eventually to a white jockstrap, showing his ass and then his dick.

The photos were better quality and more explicit than what was available for free. They were posed photo sessions with professional photographers, not some horny dude with a digital camera shooting himself getting off.

The last gallery I clicked on surprised the shit out of me. Not only did I know the guy, I'd fucked him. It was Sergei Baranov, my sister-in-law Tatiana's brother.

I was so shocked that I jumped out of the galleries and went back to the home page. Was Sergei a video star, too? I clicked on the first video, and once again I was surprised and titillated. The quality was good and the guys were sexy and built. Two blond dudes got it on next to a swimming pool, the one in the pool occasionally taking a mouthful of water and shooting it into his partner's ass.

Two jocks were fucking in the locker room when the coach walked in, first yelling, then joining in the fun. Two skiers traipsed into a living room with a roaring fire, stripping down and massaging each other's tired muscles. A guy with a stopped-up sink volunteered to suck off the plumber who was flat on his kitchen floor.

I didn't find any videos featuring Sergei, and I had to remind myself that I was looking for clues in my case. How had Lucas participated in this site? I went back to the photo galleries and found a series of shots of him in action.

His photo set displayed his chief attraction, that ten-inch donkey dick. I'd only seen it briefly in person, though of course I'd felt it shearing me in two. I opened up one picture in Photoshop and zoomed in. Man, he was big, and thick. No wonder he'd hurt me so much.

I went back to the photo set. There were more shots of Lucas in action, though in all cases you couldn't see the face of the guy working on him. Some of the men sucking him were clearly older, from the occasional gray hairs I spotted and the lined jowls of a mouth spread wide open.

The last shots were of Lucas fucking guys. Some men were on all fours on beds, others lying next to him with one leg raised. The last few were men cuffed against a wall as Lucas fucked them. The scene looked familiar, and I realized that these photos had been taken in the living room of the mansion at Black Point.

It's difficult to recognize yourself from behind, especially when half your body is obscured by another man, and the camera is focused on the sight of his huge dick getting ready to slam into your butt. But the guy in shot 34 had a small half-moon scar behind his right calf, just like the one I had from a wipeout when I was a teenager. Add in my general body type, and my black hair, grown a little shaggy at that time, and you had a definite match.

My erection wilted, and I went back to the home page. At the bottom of the screen were a half dozen windows that represented live webcams of naked guys. Below each window was a chat frame where I could initiate a conversation with the blond twink who looked like he hadn't started shaving yet, the hefty Asian who was a few calories away from sumo wrestler, the brunet with tribal tattoos, or the black guy whose body was as ripped as a Mr. World contestant.

I wondered if they were all in Hawai'i, or if these cams were linked to dozens of sites around the country—maybe around the world. Was there a night shift of guys in Australia, a morning shift in Europe? Had Lucas been one of these guys? Could you chat one of them up and then make arrangements to meet in person?

I didn't have the enthusiasm to pursue the site anymore, so I clicked off, then sat there on my bed wondering what I'd gotten myself into.

Chapter 21

TOO HANDSOME

I HAD TROUBLE getting to sleep. I couldn't stop thinking of my picture on MenSayHi, and of Lucas, and how far he'd fallen, from gorgeous high-end hustler to, in Frankie's words, a skanky ice whore. It reminded me of how tenuous our grip is on our lives. All it takes is a couple of body blows to knock you completely off course.

In my case, it was breaking up with Mike, and Mike had been kicked around by the breakup, too. I'd seen it in criminals and victims alike. Losing a job, or an apartment, or the death of a loved one, or a serious illness, could knock the shit out of your life. The lucky ones, like Mike and me, had family and friends to fall back on.

The unlucky ones ended up like Lucas.

The next morning I surfed for an hour at first light, and it felt good to be regaining the skills I'd lost. Every wave I caught, no matter how small, was a step forward in my rehabilitation. I forgot about Lucas, Norma, Jingtao, and the two unnamed hookers, and focused on the water. There was a welcome pain in my arms and legs by the time I was done, and I walked slowly back to my apartment, savoring the sunlight that was just beginning to gild the beach and the tops of the palm trees.

At work I told Ray what I'd learned from Frankie and Pua, and about my lunch plans with Jimmy on Friday. I didn't say anything about what I'd found on MenSayHi; I wanted to think about it for a while, and see what else came up.

The lieutenant had pulled us out of the rotation so we could focus on the murders of Jingtao, Lucas, Norma, and the two Chinese hookers. "I want to do some research on this Wah Shing Corporation," Ray said. "I'm thinking they might have some more real estate here in town, or some leases out there. Why don't I work the phones for a while?"

"I'll help." I called Ricky Koele, and a little later he faxed over a list of all the corporations with ties to Wah Shing. Ray started calling the big real estate companies, to see if any of them had dealings with the company. He didn't learn anything new, though, and I spent too much time staring into space and wondering what kind of photos of me were out there.

I checked the file and saw that Steve Hart hadn't put Lucas's fingerprints into the national database. The guy was a victim, after all, so that was a reason, but it was still sloppy police work. I went downstairs to the Special Investigations Section and found Thanh Nguyen, a fingerprint tech I knew who worked in Records and Identification. He was a wiry guy in his early sixties, and word around the building was that he'd been in the South Vietnamese army.

He pulled the records up and ran a search. The results came back a few minutes later; there was a match to a Lucas Tyler, who had a record for solicitation, petty theft, and criminal mischief in Seattle.

I was surprised; I'd always assumed that hookers took on new names, but maybe Lucas Tyler hadn't been imaginative enough. And Lucas was a sexy name; it's not like his real name was Fred or Harvey.

I went back upstairs and called the Seattle PD. The detective who took the call was friendly but couldn't provide much information. All the charges had been dropped except a felony theft charge, for which Tyler had served six months in the county jail. He did get me the information on Lucas's bond; a woman named Elizabeth Tyler had put up the money for him. He gave me her phone number.

Ray got on the extension when I called her. I introduced myself and explained I was a homicide detective in Honolulu. "Is this about Lucas?" she asked.

"Do you know him?"

"He's my brother. What kind of trouble is he in now?"

"I'm afraid he's dead." I explained what we knew of the circumstances.

"I'm not surprised," she said, with a chill in her tone. "The last time I talked to him, he was nuts. He said he had all these photos of men having sex with him, that somebody was blackmailing these guys and giving him a cut of the profits. I told him he had to get out of Honolulu. I even offered to pay his plane fare home."

"Did he give you any details about these men—names, occupations?"

"To be honest, detective, I didn't want to know. Lucas was always too handsome for his own good. Everything came easy to him. Our parents spoiled him like crazy, teachers passed him along when he didn't do the homework. He started taking money for sex when he was sixteen."

Once she got started, she didn't seem to want to stop. "He seduced the principal of his high school and got the man fired. He had sex with the quarterback of the football team and the boy was so mortified to be exposed that he dropped out of school and joined the Army. He was killed in Iraq."

When she finally ran out of Lucas stories, I asked, "If you think of anything that might be relevant, will you contact me?" I spelled my name, and gave her my phone number at the station.

"He broke our parents' hearts," Elizabeth Tyler said. "Not because he was gay. They were very liberal people. But they believed that everyone was good at heart, and Lucas wasn't."

"Seduced the principal, huh?" Ray said, when I hung up. "And the quarterback. Sounds like my cousin Joey's fantasies come to life."

"Not mine," I said. "Our principal was seventy-five if he was a day, and the quarterback was a real jerk."

Despite all our work, I didn't think we'd made much progress, and that worried me as I drove out to a different STD clinic, this one in Aiea. Once again, I received a number and submitted to various indignities. The nurse on duty was a young guy, with a scar on his right cheek that looked like it had been caused by a knife. "What brings you in? Just being careful?"

I was beyond being bashful at that point. "I had sex with a guy a couple of months ago. I think everything was safe, but I can't be sure, because I did experience some bleeding. Later on I learned that he had syphilis. I just wanted to make sure I didn't pick anything up from him."

"Do you know if he's notified his other partners?"

"He's dead," I said. "Gunshot, not syphilis."

His eyebrows rose, but he just nodded. "Have a seat back in the waiting room, and we'll call you."

I didn't bother to pick up a magazine and pretend to read. My brain was whirling with all the little facts I knew about the murder victims. I was glad that we'd put a last name and a history to Lucas; I hate it when someone dies unknown and unmourned. Even somebody with as many issues as Lucas Tyler.

An hour passed. After my encounter with Lucas, and the subsequent intervention by my brothers and Harry, I'd been celibate, relying on cybersex and Internet porn, until I'd fooled around with Gunter, and then Sergei. If I turned out to have anything, I'd have to tell both of them. And then Sergei would tell his sister, who'd tell my brother. The whole drama of it made me tired.

Fortunately, when the duty nurse called my number he handed me a piece of paper which certified that I had a clean bill of health. I felt better—but just a little.

Chapter 22

69 IN 609

AFTER ANOTHER HARD surfing session Friday morning, I sat in front of the computer and stared into space, hoping for an inspiration that would help us solve the case, but came up with nothing.

Around eleven-thirty, I drove up to Mānoa and picked up Jimmy in front of the library. His hair was no longer in a Mohawk, and he was letting the black roots grow in. His skinny frame was filling out, the results of gym workouts and Aunt Mei-Mei's cooking and care packages. We went to a plate lunch place near the campus, and after we'd ordered, he said, "I'm glad you called me, Kimo. But I know you. You want to talk about Lucas, don't you?"

I pretended to be offended, and in truth I was, just a little. "What, I can't call up my friend Jimmy and hang out with him?"

He looked at me with the same built-in shit detector I'd seen in Frankie and Pua. I shrugged and showed him the photo of Lucas, and the corners of his mouth turned down. "Poor guy," he said. "I haven't seen him for a while. I was afraid something like this would have happened to him."

"You knew him?"

He told me about how he and some kids from the GSA at UH had been going down to Ala Moana Beach Park. "I met Lucas for the first time a long time ago," he said. "Back when—you know."

I nodded. "He was nice to me. He was making a ton of money, and he liked to hand it around. He bought me this pair of two-hundred-dollar sunglasses. And whenever he'd see me, he'd buy me food."

"I'm glad he was nice to you." And I was; I wanted to see Lucas as a victim rather than a villain, and knowing he'd been kind to Jimmy helped.

"I didn't see him for a long time. And then when I started going down to the park with the GSA, I recognized him, and I felt terrible."

"Did he tell you anything about his life? Anything that might help me find out who killed him?"

"He was living in this apartment in Kaka'ako, but he got kicked out." The waitress brought our food, and Jimmy said, "I went there once. I could show you."

"That'd be great." We ate for a few minutes. "You mentioned when I talked to you that he'd been getting customers through MenSayHi," I said. "You know anything more about that?"

"There was this Chinese guy," he said, spearing some macaroni-potato salad. "He's the one who got Lucas involved. Lucas wanted to hook me up with him, but I said no."

"Good for you."

He ate for a minute. "I'm not sure, but I think he said something about being videotaped. Like it was some kind of insurance policy for him, maybe. That when he got too old to turn tricks he'd be able to get money from these rich guys."

That tied in with the pictures I'd seen on the MenSayHi site, and with what Elizabeth Tyler had said. I wondered if one of the blackmail victims was behind the killings. A stronger guy than Brian Izumigawa might have decided to take matters into his own hands. He might have traced Lucas to the acupuncture clinic, and was trying to eliminate anyone who might have knowledge of his actions or clients.

After lunch, Jimmy and I drove down to Kaka'ako, an industrial neighborhood across from the port of Honolulu, out past the Kewalo basin, with its assemblage of small boats. Jimmy pointed out a high-rise tower where he thought Lucas had lived.

"I wish I could remember the apartment number," Jimmy said.

"There was something funny about it. Lucas liked to make jokes, you know. Like about the Web site name." He thought for a minute. "I think the apartment number was 69," he said. "I remember something about him doing sixty-nine there."

I dropped him back at the campus and drove to the station. There was a message from Brian Izumigawa, with his cell phone number. When I reached him, he didn't have any news, just wanted to see if I'd made any progress.

I hated to admit that we weren't much farther ahead than we had been the last time he and I talked. So I said encouraging things, that it was all going to work out, and after I'd listened to his fears for a while I managed to get him off the line.

While I talked to Brian, Ray checked the address Jimmy had shown me. By the time I was done, he'd finished his call. "It's a condo, not a rental. There's no apartment sixty-nine, but there's a six-*oh*-nine," he said. "And the deed is in the name of a corporation. Wah Shing."

I shook my head. "Man, these guys got around, didn't they? Anybody living there now?"

"Building manager didn't know. The corporation's been paying the maintenance, though. Want to go over there and take a look?"

Kaka'ako was in the middle of a transformation. The high-rise tower Jimmy had pointed out dominated the neighborhood; on one side was Restaurant Row, a collection of twenty-some restaurants and a multiplex cinema, but on the other side was a derelict empty lot. There were low warehouses and parking lots all around. We parked at a meter on a side street and walked up to the building.

Ray whistled as we entered the marble lobby. "Some people know how to live," he said. Fresh flowers in Venetian glass vases decorated the reception desk, and a koa wood bowl my mother would have loved sat on a low table by the door. A couple of over-stuffed couches clustered in a corner, and the walls that weren't mirrored were paneled in dark wood.

I wasn't that impressed, but Ray was loving every detail. I could see him promising Julie that one day they'd live in a place like that.

The concierge was a beautiful Filipina in her late twenties, wearing a tailored navy suit. "Good afternoon, gentlemen," she said. "How may I help you?"

We showed her our badges. "We're interested in apartment six-oh-nine," I said. "You guys have a key to that unit?"

"Let me see." She went into a back room, and came out a few minutes later with a tall, muscular guy with black hair tending toward salt-and-pepper, wearing a similar suit—though I liked it better on him than on her. "I'm Sean Hackbarth," he said. "The manager. You're the detective I spoke to about unit six-oh-nine?"

"That was me," Ray said. "The corporation that owns the unit has come up in one of our investigations, and we're just curious to see if anyone's living there."

"So you don't have a warrant?"

Ray shook his head. "Nope. And to be honest with you, we don't have grounds for a warrant. This is just curiosity."

"Four employees of this corporation have turned up dead in the last week," I said. "Three of them shot execution style while they slept. One of the employees is missing." I showed them both the picture of Treasure Chen. "A Chinese woman in her late twenties, very beautiful."

Hackbarth looked at the concierge and she shrugged. "If you have a parking card, you can enter the building directly from the garage," she said. "Some of the residents we never see unless they have a package delivered."

"Can you show us the apartment?" Ray asked Hackbarth. "We want to see if Ms. Chen's body is there. If it's not, we're good to go."

"I'll take you up," he said.

We followed him to an elevator bank. "Residents have key cards they use for the elevator," he said. "You slide it in, and then choose your floor."

"Cards coded to a particular floor?" Ray asked as we stepped inside.

Hackbarth slipped his card into the reader and pressed six. "No. Once you've swiped your card, you can go to any floor. If you're a guest, the concierge calls your party. Once you've been approved, she punches a code in the system that calls the elevator for you, with your floor preprogrammed."

Ray nodded. "Good security."

"There are flaws," Hackbarth admitted, as the elevator door opened on six. "A visitor who enters the elevator with a resident can punch any floor once the resident has swiped a card."

He held the door as we stepped out, then pointed up at a security camera. "We do monitor the cameras, but we don't chase someone who gets out on the wrong floor. We don't have the manpower."

"Still, it's a place Treasure could feel pretty safe," I said to Ray.

"A lot safer than Norma Ching's place, or that apartment in Makiki," he said.

Hackbarth led us to apartment 609 and knocked on the door. When there was no answer, he unlocked both locks.

There was a security chain but it wasn't engaged. We walked into the apartment, a one-bedroom with a view toward the airport and a small, half-round balcony off the living room.

"Somebody's been living here," Ray said. There were dirty dishes in the dishwasher, and a pint of milk in the fridge that hadn't expired yet. In the bedroom, we found some women's clothes, the kind of slinky dresses and expensive underwear that we'd found at Treasure's apartment in Hawai'i Kai.

"So if Treasure's been staying here, where is she now?" I asked.

"Great question," Ray said. "Get back to me when you figure it out."

Chapter 23

TREASURE AND THE TAPES

WE THANKED SEAN Hackbarth and walked out in the hallway, where I saw a security camera. "You keep the tapes?" I asked, pointing toward it.

"It's all digital," he said. "Every day, the system overwrites the data from a week before."

"So you've got a week's worth of data from this camera?"

"Come on down to the office. I'll show you."

We started working backward, and didn't have far to go. At ten o'clock that morning, a tall, attractive Chinese woman left apartment 609 and walked to the elevator. She got in and disappeared from the frame.

"That her?" Ray asked.

I compared the photo we had of Treasure to the digital image, and the match was close enough for me. "How about cameras in the garage?" I asked.

Hackbarth punched in some buttons on the keyboard, but the cameras in the garage were no help. We saw Treasure exit the elevator, then walk out of the frame.

By then it was the end of our shift. "You want to call Sampson, get him to authorize the overtime for a stakeout?" Ray asked.

"Suppose we have to." I was to meet Sergei Baranov that night at eleven at the Rod and Reel Club, but if we were running late I could always call him. He was a big boy; he could occupy himself at the club on his own.

I walked outside and called Sampson, reaching him on his cell phone. "You aren't sure that this is the girl?" he asked.

"We're looking for a beautiful Chinese girl who works for the company that owns the apartment and ran the acupuncture clinic that employed Norma Ching and the two dead girls. Logic says the girl we saw is Treasure Chen."

He authorized us, and then I called the detectives' area and asked the receptionist to put me through to whoever was on duty.

"Hart."

Great. Steve Hart was already unhappy that we'd made some progress on his cold case—the death of Lucas Tyler. But I needed his cooperation. "Can you pull up a motor vehicle registration for me?" I asked. "I'm out in Kaka'ako for a stakeout and I need to know what I'm looking for."

"Got a name or address?"

I gave him Treasure's name and the address in Hawai'i Kai. He was gone for a while. "I've got a license in that name and address, but no vehicle."

"Can you check a corporate?" I gave him Golden Needles and Wah Shing, and he sighed loudly. "Hold on."

"Yeah, you're a prince," I muttered. He came back a couple of minutes later. "Three vehicles under the Wah Shing name. A Mercedes, a BMW, and a Lexus."

"Can you read me the data?"

Another big sigh. But he did, and I copied it all down. "Thanks, Steve. I owe you one." He hung up without saying anything else. Ray came outside and I showed him what I had.

"What kind of car did that guy see?" he asked. "The guy from UH who saw the arsonist?"

I struggled to remember. "BMW or Mercedes, I think. Dark color."

"So could have been any of these three cars," Ray said.

"Could have been. Maybe Treasure's our ninja, and our shooter too. We could wrap this case up tonight."

"Chance would be a fine thing," he said.

There was a coffee shop across from the entrance to the condo's garage, and we agreed that I'd sit there scanning license plates of suspect cars, and Ray would stay in the control room with Sean Hackbarth, whose shift didn't end until eleven. If I got a hit, I'd call Ray, and he'd pull up the camera in the garage and see if a woman who matched Treasure's description rode up to the sixth floor. Once she did, we'd go up and pay her a visit.

It got dark after six, and when a parking space opened up in front of the coffee shop I moved the Wrangler and took up position there, where it would be easier to see license plates as the cars paused and waited for the garage grille to rise. Around seven o'clock, a black BMW pulled up with a plate that matched one we were waiting for, and I called Ray.

By the time I got to the control room, the woman had parked and gotten into the elevator, and Ray and Hackbarth were watching the sixth floor camera. The woman got out of the elevator and walked to the door of apartment 609. We watched her go inside. "You'll call if she goes out before we get up there?" I asked Hackbarth.

"You got it."

The concierge programmed the elevator to stop on six. At the door to 609, I knocked, and said, "Miss Chen? Honolulu PD. We'd like to talk to you."

I was just about to knock again when the door opened.

Treasure Chen didn't look as beautiful as she did in the photo with her sister, but seeing everyone around you get murdered has a general effect on your looks. I showed her my badge, and she said, "I remember you, detective."

"May we come in?"

She shrugged. "I guess so."

I realized as we sat down in the living room that until that evening I'd never considered Treasure as a suspect in the murders. I wasn't sure why; was it because she was beautiful? And yet, Lucas Tyler had been handsome, and cruel as well.

"Where were you on Tuesday morning?" I asked.

She looked wary.

"I didn't kill them," she said. "I called 911. Why would I do that if I'd killed them?"

"So you know what we're talking about," I said. "Why don't we start from the beginning. Last I saw you were working at the Lobster Garden. What happened?"

"After Tommy died, I got fired. That bitch Mae never liked me. Her husband liked to flirt with the hostesses, so they never lasted long. A while later, Norma offered me my job back at the lingerie shop."

"As a prostitute?"

"If that's what you want to call it. I modeled lingerie, and sometimes the men wanted more." She made a sour face. "I didn't like giving massages. But at least I made money. No one wanted Norma, so she hated it. The only money she made was from managing us. But what else could an old woman like her do?"

"There were more of you?"

"Always three or four girls," she said. "And usually a boy, too."

"Did you ever meet the man who owned the shop?"

"Eventually. One day he came to Waikele." She pursed her lips together. "I offered to give him a massage, but he didn't want me. Only the boy."

"Was that Jingtao?"

She shook her head. "No, he only came a few months ago. This was another boy, one who left."

Ray, who'd been taking all the notes, continued the questioning. "Did you know about the fires?"

"What do you mean?"

"The lingerie store burned shortly after you moved to Waikele. And then after you left that place, it burned, too."

She looked surprised, and I saw the wheels in motion in her head. "And then the acupuncture clinic burned, too."

He sat back on the sofa and crossed his legs. "You know anything about it?"

"No. I didn't realize that the first two locations had burned down."

"Why did you move from Waikele to St. Louis Heights?" he asked.

"No one told us. One day Mr. Hu showed up, said we had to move. So we moved."

I glanced around the living room. It looked as if someone had walked into a showroom and bought the whole room, from the cream-colored sofa to the glass coffee table, even the mass-produced artwork on the walls.

Ray was still asking questions and taking notes. "Did he pick the new location, or did you or Norma?"

"He did. But when we moved, he made me comanager, with Norma. He wanted to get rid of her, but he had to train me first. He promised me that one day she would be gone, and I would be in charge."

"How did you contact Mr. Hu?" I asked, hoping she had better information than I did.

"We didn't. He always called us. When the boy ran away, we didn't know what to do. We had to wait a couple of days until he called. He came to the clinic a few hours later and told us that we had to move out."

I leaned forward. "Where were you supposed to go?"

"He didn't have a new location yet," she said. "He was very angry that we'd let Jingtao get away. He said that if Jingtao went to the police, he could compromise our whole operation."

"So what happened after that?" Ray asked.

"We packed up everything," Treasure said. "We were short on staff, so Meiying and Meizhen and I did most of the work, with Norma supervising." The way she said the word it was clear what she thought of Norma. "She sent the three of us home and said she'd be in touch. I was supposed to keep tabs on Meiying and Meizhen, and I called them every day to make sure they didn't go anywhere."

Ray asked how to spell their names, and if Treasure knew their last names. "The last name on their paperwork was Wang," she said. "But they weren't related. So it could be their real name, or not."

"When was the last time you spoke to them?" I asked.

"Monday afternoon. I was supposed to pick them up on Tuesday morning and take them grocery shopping, since they didn't have a car. But when I got there, there was no answer at the door."

"Did you have a key to the apartment?"

"The lock was broken. I was worried that they'd run away, like Jingtao, but then I went into the bedroom."

She started to cry, but I wasn't sure if the tears were just for our benefit or not. "I was so frightened. I thought someone had killed them to . . ."

"To what?" I asked.

She took a deep breath. "We had cameras in the clinic," she said. "We would take movies of what happened in the rooms, and then Mr. Hu would look at them. If he recognized a man, he would take the tapes away." She began to cry in earnest. "I thought one of those men—came and killed the girls—because of the tapes."

Ray got up and got her a paper towel from the kitchen, which she used to wipe her eyes. "You have any idea who those men might be?" I asked.

She shook her head. "I didn't recognize them. And Mr. Hu took all the tapes."

"Even the ones from Friday?" I asked.

"Yes. When he came, he took everything. Even the cameras."

I wasn't sure what to do next. Treasure didn't know how to get hold of Mr. Hu. That meant that I was the only person who might be able to find him. And if I didn't soon, then both Treasure and Brian Izumigawa could be at risk.

Chapter 24

WHO AMONG US IS INNOCENT?

I LOOKED OUT the window and saw a jet coming in for a landing at Honolulu International. Another planeload of tourists coming to spend a week in paradise. "Who else knows about this apartment?" I asked Treasure.

"Mr. Hu bought this place so that a guy who worked for him could meet with high-profile clients." She lowered her voice, as if Mr. Hu was listening in. "There are cameras in the bedroom. But this guy, Lucas, was always locking himself out, so Mr. Hu gave me a spare key. Then Lucas disappeared a few weeks ago, and I knew the apartment was empty. You see how good the security is. I thought I'd be safe here."

"Did you know that Lucas was dead?"

Treasure shrugged. "I'm not surprised. He was using way too much ice. Men didn't want him anymore, and Mr. Hu wasn't happy."

"Does Mr. Hu have a key to the apartment?"

"I'm sure he does."

We waited for Treasure to make the connections on her own. "You don't think that Mr. Hu . . ."

I shrugged. "I don't know what to think yet. But somebody's tying up loose ends. Lucas, Jingtao, Norma, the two girls. Logic says Mr. Hu could be behind it. Or somebody who wants to take over Mr. Hu's operation. Which is pretty much the same thing when it comes to you."

"Where can I go?" she asked.

Ray and I looked at each other. I didn't think there was much chance we could get Treasure into any kind of protected witness program; there wasn't a case against anyone yet. And I had a feeling she knew more than she was telling us, so I wanted her someplace where I could keep tabs on her.

"Did Mr. Hu know you and Norma didn't get along?" Ray asked.

"I think he agitated it," she said. "He would tell me things about Norma, and then he would tell her things about me."

"So he'd never think you'd hide out at Norma's, would he?"

"That shithole in Chinatown?" Treasure asked.

"You have a better idea?" I asked. "A sugar daddy who might put you up?"

Treasure sighed. "I guess I could stay at Norma's for a few days, until you find Mr. Hu and lock him up."

I wasn't sure that Mr. Hu was behind the murders yet. But if Treasure believed it, she'd be willing to hide out for a while.

We waited while Treasure packed up. By the time we were ready to leave she'd camouflaged herself, darkening her skin a few shades, pulling her shoulder-length black hair into a ponytail, and donning a UH T-shirt, a pair of shorts, and rubber slippers. Instead of a high-class madam, she looked like a college student.

We walked out of the building, Ray first, scanning the street. It was dark, and we both had our weapons ready, not knowing what to expect. But the only people we saw were a middle-aged couple heading to Restaurant Row and a group of teens who'd just come from a movie.

Ray climbed in the back with Treasure's rolling suitcase, and she sat up front with me for the drive to Norma's building in Chinatown. "Where were you today?" I asked as we drove.

Treasure looked out the window. We were passing the Aloha Tower, all lit up like a beacon welcoming tourists to our beautiful islands. "There was an office," she said. "I thought maybe Mr. Hu kept the information he was using to blackmail people there. I thought if I could get hold of the tapes, I could use them to protect myself."

"Where was the office?" I asked.

"Across the street from the shopping center," she said. "But there was nothing there."

"Define nothing," I said. "Cleared out like the acupuncture clinic?"

She nodded.

"You had a key?"

"No key. A combination lock. I found the combination one day on a piece of paper and I memorized it. You never know." She gave us the address and the number, and Ray wrote it all down.

When we got to Chinatown, Ray remained in the Wrangler with Treasure, while I headed to Norma's building. I didn't know what to expect, so I moved carefully, looking left and right, my hand on my gun and ready to draw if I had to.

A black cat scrambled across in front of me and my pulse raced. But there was no one around except a young Chinese couple hurrying home in the dark, and I got into Norma's building unmolested. The crime scene tape was still stretched across her door, and I was glad I'd kept the key Norma's neighbor had given us Tuesday morning.

I unlocked the door and slid under the tape. The apartment had a lingering smell of death, but I lit a couple of sticks of incense. It didn't look like anyone had been there since the medical examiner's office had taken away Norma's body.

"Everything looks fine," I said, when I got back to the Wrangler. "I think we should leave the crime scene tape up, though. Makes the place look uninhabited."

"I'd better get some food," Treasure said. "I hope Norma had cable."

We took her to the Foodland on Ala Moana and stocked her fridge. On our way back, Ray called Julie and arranged for her to pick him up at Norma's. I parked across the street, checked the area one more time, and then we got out of the Wrangler, Ray and I carrying her bags of groceries like loyal vassals. At least she was pulling her own rolling suitcase.

Ray saw Julie sitting in their car, and he waved. Just then Treasure tripped and sprawled to the ground. Her suitcase fell over and the zipper burst, and her clothing started spilling out. She began to cry.

Julie got out of the car and hurried over. I'd met her a couple of times, when I was picking up or dropping off Ray. She was Italian, with dark, curly hair pulled back into a ponytail, wearing a polo shirt and shorts. "Can I help you?" she said, kneeling down to Treasure. "I'm Julie, Ray's wife."

Treasure let Julie stand her up, and then Ray held her while Julie stuffed the lacy lingerie back into the suitcase. Between the three of us, we got Treasure, her clothes, and her groceries up to Norma Ching's apartment.

Julie went into the bedroom and stripped the bed, making it up with new sheets and waving around the incense smoke. Treasure sat on the living room sofa like a lost child as I made tea and helped Ray put away the groceries. Ray saw me looking at my watch and said, "Why don't you head out? Julie and I will stay with Treasure for a while."

"Thanks. I'm beat." I walked out to the hallway where there were no signs of life, not even the nosy woman who'd been Norma's friend. It was about ten thirty and I was due to meet Sergei at eleven. It had been a long day, and the last thing I wanted to do was spend the next couple of hours with Sergei cruising the bars, hoping one or both of us would get lucky.

But I'd promised, and there was always the chance that we'd end up together. Our first romp had been a lot of fun, and though I was tired, my dick stiffened at the thought of a second round.

When I walked into the Rod and Reel Club, Sergei was already at the bar making conversation with Fred, the bartender. Fred's handsome but brainless, a sexy dude with a buff chest, a diamond stud in his left ear, and enough charm to pave the length of the Kamehameha Highway. I felt a little jealous, wondering if Sergei would go home with Fred rather than with me at the end of the evening.

But Sergei was glad to see me, enveloping me in a big bear hug, kissing me on the lips, and squeezing my butt. I felt a second wind and ordered a Longboard Lager. When it arrived, Sergei and I went outside to the patio.

The moon moved in and out behind clouds above us. The ground light was too strong to see any stars, but the music wasn't loud and I could smell plumeria blossoms from a tourist's lei behind me. I started to relax.

"How's life in Honolulu treating you?" I asked.

"Way different from Anchorage, I'll tell you that," he said. "I don't think I've stopped sweating since I got off the plane."

"Haoa working you too hard?"

He shrugged. "I do the payroll, and I interview and hire guys. That's the toughest part. Americans don't want to work that hard for that money. So most of the guys these days are from someplace else. Chinese, Okinawan, Filipino, Malay, Samoan. I could run a Pacific branch of the UN if I wanted."

He took a swig of his beer and leaned forward. "I shouldn't tell you this, you being a cop, but sometimes you have to look the other way when a guy doesn't have the right paperwork. I mean, you have no idea what the government wants these days. Some guys, they just don't have the stuff."

"You think they might be illegal?"

"I don't ask, I don't tell."

I'd always thought my brothers were scrupulously honest—but who among us can pass every test? I'd lied to my family for years about my sexual orientation. Lui had sent TV reporters to chase me when I came out, making a news story out of my life. Even Haoa had reacted badly, beating up Tatiana's friend Tico when he went on a gay-bashing spree with some of his workmen because he couldn't deal with the fact that his little brother was a *māhū*.

For the next couple of hours, Sergei and I drank, played some pool, and danced. I kept thinking about Mike, though, and when a big Samoan guy asked Sergei to dance, and they locked lips on the dance floor, I was happy to turn Sergei over to him.

Chapter 25

MAJOR CONVERSATIONAL SHIFTS

SATURDAY MORNING I slept in, catching up on sleep and letting my body recover from the stress of the week. I wasn't sure what to do with the knowledge that Sergei might be hiring illegals to work for Haoa's landscaping firm. Should I just keep quiet? Tell my father and let him decide what to do? If I told Haoa, he'd explode; Tatiana would have to mediate. Maybe I should just go to her? It was too confusing.

Around noon I drove out to Diamond Head and caught a few waves, stretching my body and clearing my head. On the way back, I rolled up the flaps on the Wrangler, turned the CD player up on some classic Bruddah Iz, and chilled out. It was the weekend, after all. I'd worry about what to do about Sergei on Monday.

Since Mike and I were meeting Terri and her new boyfriend for dinner out in Hawai'i Kai, it made the most sense for him to pick me up. It was a cool night, with a stiff breeze blowing in off the ocean, and I waited outside for him wearing a navy sports jacket over khaki slacks and a light-blue oxford cloth button-down shirt.

It was the way I'd dressed as a teenager for formal occasions, and I guess it stuck with me.

Punahou was a prep school, and like preppies around the country, we had our own uniform: polo shirts, khakis, oxford cloth button-downs, web belts, and deck shoes. Our only concession to island life was the addition of aloha shirts, and pukka shell necklaces, and leis on formal occasions.

"You look nice," Mike said, when I slid into the front seat of his truck.

There was something so déjà vu about the experience—almost by reflex I leaned across the seat and kissed his cheek, saying, "You do, too."

He still smelled the same, a lemon aftershave with tones of sandalwood. He must have shaved just before leaving his house, because his face was smooth. I remembered the texture of his cheek when he had a five o'clock shadow, the slight roughness that always reminded me I was kissing a man.

Mike was wearing a blue-and-white striped shirt and black pants, and I loved the way his short sleeves took hold of his upper arms and showcased his biceps.

"What have you been up to?" I asked. "Any progress on the shopping center investigation?"

"I had another case, took up most of the week," he said. "This twenty-eight-year-old guy was dumped by his girlfriend because of his drinking problem, so he poured gasoline on the furniture on her lanai and set it on fire. But he didn't realize that the wooden furniture with foam cushions would burn so fast. The stuff caught while he was standing out there yelling for her, and he ended up with third-degree burns."

"Bummer."

"It made me think about love and liquor," he said. "How when things go bad I turn to alcohol, just like this guy did. And I need to be aware of that." He turned onto Diamond Head Road and said, "Why did you invite me tonight?"

It was lame to say I didn't know why. So I thought about it, and I said, "Remember when I came to your house last Sunday?"

"It was memorable," Mike said dryly. "Your ears must have been burning that night when my dad and I had a conversation about you."

"I'm not his favorite person." I looked over at Mike. "Does he think I'm the one who made you gay?"

Mike laughed. "You mean are you the seducer who converted his innocent little boy into a cocksucker? No, he said to me one day that he knew I was gay back in high school."

"So what's he hate me for? Does he think I turned you into a drunk?"

"Ouch."

"Sorry."

"Do you think we're ever going to be able to have a conversation without one of us hurting the other?" he asked.

"Man, your brain is just popping neurons like crazy," I said. "I'm having trouble keeping up here. The answer to your first question is the answer to your second question."

"Now who's being obscure?"

We got onto the Kalaniana'ole Highway for the last part of the drive out to Hawai'i Kai. The mountains loomed up beside us, trapping us between them and the sea. "What I mean is that a month ago, if somebody had asked me if I still had feelings for you I would have denied it like crazy," I said. "And then I saw you at the fire, and I realized that was a total lie."

I looked over at him. "When you challenged me at your house and I said that I still loved you, that was the truth. I'm not sure I love you enough to start dating again and work through all your shit, but I can't deny there's still something between us." I took a deep breath. "And that's why I asked you to come to dinner, I guess. Because I want to either get you out of my system, or get you back in my life."

"My dad hates you because he thinks you broke my heart, and he thinks it's because of you that drinking became a problem for me again," Mike said, as he pulled into the parking lot of the restaurant. "And both of those things are true."

He got out of the truck then, forestalling any further discussion, and we saw Terri and a tall, handsome guy approaching us. Mike shrugged into a sports jacket and plastered a smile on his face.

Terri handled the introductions. Levi Hirsch seemed like a nice guy, and there was definite chemistry between him and Terri. The four of us walked into the restaurant, where a slack key piece by Hapa was playing. The ceiling arched above us in imitation of an old Hawai'ian *halau,* or meeting house, and the furniture was all dark wood with a floral print of hibiscus and red ginger on the cushions.

We sat at a table on the terrace overlooking the dark ocean, making small talk. When the waiter came by, Levi said, "Why don't we share a bottle of wine. White all right with everyone?"

I looked over at Mike, who said, "Fine with me." Levi surveyed the wine list, ordering a bottle of Alto Adige Sauvignon, which, according to its description, was an Italian white that was racy, with distinctive flavors of melon, grapefruit, and grass followed by spicy green peppers and gooseberry notes. I would have preferred a beer, but I went along with the crowd.

Dinner was delicious and convivial. I couldn't help noticing every time Mike sipped his wine, though he only had one glass and refused a refill. "No, it's great," he told Levi. "But I'm driving."

"Got to be careful when you've got a cop in the car with you," Levi said.

"I'm always careful around Kimo," Mike said with the hint of a smile.

Terri insisted on paying for dinner, which was a relief for me after getting myself into debt for the Wrangler. Back in Mike's truck, I said, "That was fun. I'm glad you came."

"I can drink, you know."

Man, I wished I could anticipate some of his mind jumps. "I thought you were going to AA meetings."

"I am. But I don't think I'm an alcoholic."

"OK."

"Don't look at me that way. I have a problem with alcohol. When I have emotional issues, I get drunk. I know that. I'm seeing a psychologist."

"Really?"

"EAP program. I went into it voluntarily. Nobody in the department knows."

The full moon hung over the ocean as we drove down the

Kalaniana'ole Highway. The night had gotten cooler, and I had the window rolled down just a couple of inches. The flat, straight road was a contrast to my mood; I felt like we should have been driving up the Pali Highway, with its twists and turns instead.

"I can't start to date you again until I work things out," Mike said. "Man, I want to. I want to kiss you so much. But my shrink says I need to take things slow. That if we start up again, and then you dump me, I'll end up in trouble again." He turned to look at me, and I thought I saw tears glinting off his cheeks in the moonlight. "I can't risk that yet."

"You're not the only one with problems," I said quietly. "I don't want to pick up with you again just because I think it'll make me feel better." I swallowed, my throat suddenly dry. "But I do want to see you again. Do you think you can do that?"

He looked over at me and smiled. "I can do that."

We sat there in silence for a while. As we turned back into Waikīkī, full of neon and tourist traffic, he said, "I did learn one thing about our case. The fires at the lingerie store in Chinatown, the massage parlor in Waikele, and the acupuncture clinic all showed evidence of accelerants. It isn't much, but it does show that they were all arsons, and there was nothing to indicate that a different guy was involved."

"We've got the girl staying in Chinatown. I think she knows more than she's telling us, but she's got to get good and scared before she's going to break down."

"Keep me in the loop."

When he pulled up in front of my apartment, I leaned over to kiss his cheek again, but he turned his face so that our lips met. My pulse quickened as I reached my arm around his back and pulled him close. We kissed, my lips remembering the familiar texture of his, my cheek against his, my nose inhaling that scent of lemon and sandalwood. My dick hardened and I wanted nothing more than to drag Mike upstairs, strip him down, and fuck him until we were both senseless, until all that existed was the physical and spiritual connection between us.

But we both knew we couldn't do that. "Like a couple of horny teenagers in a truck," Mike said. "Gotta love something that makes you feel like seventeen again."

"I don't know about you, but I wasn't making out with sexy men in cars when I was seventeen."

"Neither was I. Think of all we missed."

"Think of all we have to look forward to," I said.

"Yeah. Blue balls all the way home."

I laughed. "You're a goof. Drive carefully, and don't think of me again until you're home in bed, naked."

"If you don't get out of my truck right now . . ."

"I'm getting." I leaned over and kissed his cheek one last time, then scrambled out of the truck. I climbed the outside staircase to my apartment and watched the taillights of his truck until he reached Ala Wai Boulevard and turned.

Chapter 26

THE GANSU POSTER

SUNDAY I WENT over to see Treasure Chen and make sure she was OK. She was antsy, cooped up in Norma's apartment. "It's creepy here," she said. "I can't sleep in the bed. It's like her spirit is still there. And the police tape outside? Don't get me started."

I assured her we were making progress on the case, even though I didn't feel that way. "You're safe here," I said. "Think of it like Norma's spirit is protecting you."

She laughed harshly. "For real? If Norma's spirit is here she's trying to figure out how to get me killed, too." She rubbed her arms. "I got all chicken skin," she said. "You've got to get me out of here."

"Give me another couple of days. Meanwhile, nobody is going to look for you here."

"That's true. This shithole reminds me too much of where I grew up."

I sat down at the kitchen table and motioned her to join me. "How'd you recruit the people to work for you?" I asked. "That boy, Jingtao—it didn't seem like he spoke English at all. He answer some kind of ad?"

"Mr. Hu had somebody who recruited them in China, some back-ass place where there was no work. Promised them the Golden Land, come to America."

"Who did the visas? You?"

"You really don't know?" she asked.

"Wouldn't ask if I did."

"There were no visas. I mean, I guess they had tourist visas to get into the U.S., but whoever it was in China did all that."

"You mean those girls, and the boy, they were illegal?"

She laughed and smoothed back her hair. "Come on, detective. It's prostitution. That's the illegal part."

"What did you do when their visas were up? Send them back?"

"You're not listening. Mr. Hu picked them up at the airport and brought them to the clinic. They'd work, they'd get a little money, they'd give most of it to Mr. Hu to pay for their airfare, their apartment, everything. Sometimes Mr. Hu would sell a girl on to somebody else, especially if she got sick or lost her looks. The boys didn't last long. Usually they didn't like what they were doing, and they complained a lot."

She wrinkled her nose. "That boy, Jingtao, he was the worst. He wouldn't do anything. Then he ran away. What a pain in the ass." She laughed. "I guess I made a joke, huh? Pain in the ass?"

"Yeah, funny," I said, remembering the pain Lucas had given me.

Before I left, I made sure she was locked in safely. "Ray or I will call you tomorrow," I said, standing in the doorway of the apartment. "If anything happens, you have both our cell phones, yeah?"

"Just get me out of here fast," she said. "I have a limited shelf life, you know. If I'm not going to work for Mr. Hu anymore I've got to find a new gig."

"I'll introduce you to the guys in Vice. Maybe they can give you a lead."

"Big comedian." She made a shooing motion and I stepped out in the hall, then she locked and bolted the door behind me.

I thought about calling Mike to see if he wanted to hang out, but knew that was a bad idea. Instead I went surfing, then to bed early. Ray was already at his desk when I got to the station the next morning. "Hey, I've got some good news and some bad news for you," he said.

"I never like the sound of that. Give me the good news first."

"Over the weekend, Julie and I bought another car."

"Great. What's the bad news?"

"It's a Yaris."

"Oh, come on. As if the Mini Cooper wasn't goofy enough."

"Hey, it was cheap. And now I won't have to depend on you to pick me up and drive me around." I told Ray what I'd learned from Treasure, and we decided we'd check out the office she'd mentioned when we were driving her to Norma's, though she thought it had been cleared out. "But I'm driving," I said.

The wind waved the palm fronds and shreds of rain clouds scudded overhead as we drove up to St. Louis Heights. We had the flaps rolled down on the Wrangler, and I kept the intermittent wipers on. It was a cruddy day, and that matched the way I felt.

Across the street from the building Treasure had told us about, a demolition company was razing the remains of the shopping center, and I felt a pang of loss. It was my dad's first commercial project, and he'd recruited all of us to help. I was only six or seven, but on the weekends, I carried supplies around, bringing my dad and brothers water, taking away trash.

Lui and Haoa were teenagers and they complained about having to spend their weekends working, but even my mother helped, spackling holes in the drywall, painting, and washing the glass storefronts.

"Remember that law student?" Ray asked, bringing me out of my reverie.

"The one who called 911?"

"That's the one. He said he was having sex across the street, right? You think this is the place?"

I shrugged. "I can ask him."

The building was two stories tall, with a staircase at each end and a balcony that ran across the front. There was no lobby; each office opened to the street. Most of the doors advertised some kind of import or export business, though there was an insurance agency, an acupuncturist, and a law office on the ground floor.

We walked up to the second floor, where the salt air had pitted the concrete banisters along the front rail. Chunks were missing, showing the rebar underneath. We found the door marked WAH SHING, with a Realtor's box hanging from the lock. A combination lock through a hasp kept the box closed.

Just in case there was evidence somewhere, we both put on plastic gloves. I read Ray the combination Treasure had given us, and the lock dropped open. He pulled out the key and unlocked the office door.

I wasn't expecting much, and I wasn't disappointed. The place was nearly as barren as the acupuncture clinic. A beat-up, puke green couch sat along one wall, where I figured the law student had gotten his ass plowed the night of the fire. Across from it was a metal desk with a single drawer and a cheap swivel chair.

There wasn't a picture on the wall, or a piece of paper on the desk. The plastic wastebasket was empty. "We could always dust for prints," Ray said.

"To prove what?" I asked. "This isn't a crime scene."

The space had been divided in two by a wall with a door set in it, and I walked through to another barren room. At least there was a poster on the wall there, a photo of a Chinese landscape taken in Gansu Province, where the travel agent had said Jingtao was from.

Carefully I pried the poster from the wall. There was some Chinese writing on the back, which I couldn't decipher. Ray came in the room and I showed it to him. "You know anybody who can read that?"

"My godmother," I said. "She doesn't live far from here. We'll swing past her house on our way back to the station." I shrugged. "It probably doesn't mean shit, but there isn't anything else here."

There was a metal desk like the one in the outer office, a slightly more comfortable chair on casters, and an empty file cabinet. "Phone jack," Ray said, pointing to the wall. "Maybe we can get a number and trace the calls."

"That project has your name written all over it, partner."

We left a few minutes later, after satisfying ourselves that whoever had cleaned the place out had done a great job. I called Aunt Mei-Mei and asked if we could stop by, and she said, "You out early, Kimo. I make you breakfast."

"No, Aunt Mei-Mei. Don't go to any trouble."

"No trouble."

When she greeted us at her front door, wearing her apron once again, I introduced Ray to her, and she served us scrambled eggs with unidentifiable little bits in it, which were delicious. "I still make big meals," she said. "Lots of leftovers."

She ate like a bird, picking a small piece of egg with her chopsticks, then rolling it in sticky rice. "This is great," Ray said. After we finished, I put a fresh pair of gloves on and showed her the poster, which I unrolled on the kitchen table when the plates had been cleared.

"Is name and address," she said. "In China."

"Can you write it in English?" I asked.

She found a pad from a Chinese store, and wrote, in careful letters, the name Guo Yeng-Shen, with an address below it. "Gansu," I said. "That's the place where the picture was taken, yeah?"

"Yes." She looked at me with a keen interest in her dark eyes. "This help you find who burn down your father's shopping center?"

"I hope so." I kissed her cheek and thanked her for her help. As we drove back down to the station, Ray said, "That woman should open a restaurant."

"You guys need to get out more. Don't get me wrong, Aunt Mei-Mei's a great cook. But I can show you places in Chinatown that make her look like an amateur."

"Maybe we'll double date sometime," Ray said. "Me and Julie, and you and the fireman."

I remembered the double date Mike and I'd had with Terri and Levi Hirsch on Saturday night. It had been fun, despite all the angst over our relationship that had arisen in the truck on the way there and home.

"Yeah," I said. "We'll do that sometime."

Chapter 27

NOBODY DIES IN CHINATOWN

I E-MAILED THE law student and asked him about the office he'd visited. Then I called a guy I knew in Immigration, a freckled, red-headed *haole* from the mainland named Frank O'Connor, and arranged to meet him at the Starbucks near his office.

The first time I met Frank I mistook him for an intern, but I was assured he was a Stanford grad who'd distinguished himself in the San Francisco office before being posted to Honolulu. We had worked together a year before, when an illegal immigrant had turned up dead in the lobby of a downtown office building.

"What's up?" he asked, after I'd introduced Ray.

"You know anything about smuggling illegals in from China for prostitution?"

"Big topic. I know a few things." He sipped his cappuccino and sat back in one of the big armchairs in the window of the coffee shop.

"How do they get in?" I asked. "Boat?"

"Pretty long sail," he said. "Sometimes, yeah, they come up from the Marianas that way, but mostly they fly into Honolulu on tourist visas, then they disappear. There's a saying, you know. Nobody dies in Chinatown. Somebody dies, somebody new comes in and takes over the identity."

"One ring behind everything, or multiple?" Ray asked.

"Multiple. You guys are from Homicide. That leads me to believe you've got a dead girl."

"Two girls, two guys. Three of them might be from Gansu Province."

Frank nodded. "Somebody's been bringing people in from Gansu, promising them a better life in the U.S. But they're so much in debt from the travel that they don't have any choice but to work it off."

I gave Frank the information we had on the acupuncture clinic and the other places that had burned, and he said he'd see if they had any leads. Then I remembered the poster we'd found at the abandoned office. "You recognize this?" I asked, showing him the name and address as Aunt Mei-Mei had written it.

"Where'd you get this?" he asked, immediately on alert.

"It was on the back of a poster." I explained where we'd found it.

"I recognize the name—a guy we've been looking at, on the ground in Gansu. He recruits the prostitutes and sends them here."

He drained the last of his coffee. "The new China's a tough place," he said. "Especially in a province like Gansu, where there are few resources. Lots of girls, and some boys, too, get recruited to go into prostitution. Most of them end up in the big cities, Beijing, Shanghai. Prostitution's tolerated there. You have a lot of men who go to the cities to work on construction, leaving their wives and families back home, and they need a little love."

"So how do they get to the U.S.?" Ray asked. "Why not just stay in Beijing?"

Frank shrugged. "It's the old story. The streets of America are paved in gold. Guys like Guo Yeng-Shen convince these kids that they can do better over here. They get fake social security numbers, and they think they're working toward green cards. But when they've exhausted their usefulness they either disappear or get sent back home."

The talk about illegal aliens reminded me of my conversation with Sergei, and I knew I couldn't wait any longer to talk to Haoa. After we left Frank, Ray said he needed to swing past a pharmacy and I said I'd meet him at the station. As soon as he was gone, I pulled out my cell phone and called my brother.

"Hey, brah, howzit?" he said.

"I need to talk to you. Can I meet you somewhere?"

"Sounds serious. What's up?"

"I'll tell you when I see you. Where are you now?"

"Out by the airport." He gave me the name of a hotel. "I'm giving them a quote for landscaping. You want to meet me in half an hour? I'll buy you lunch."

I'd just walked into the hotel's restaurant when he came in, wearing pressed khakis and a white polo shirt with his landscaping business's logo embroidered on it. With his sunglasses on his head, he looked like the model of a prosperous island businessman.

He charmed the hostess, as he does with any woman from six to ninety-six, and she giggled as she seated us at a table overlooking the pool. "Look at that grass," he said, pointing out the window. "Looks like crap, because they're cutting it too short, and it burns."

I ordered a burger, and Haoa a chicken Caesar salad. "Tatiana's got me on a diet," he grumbled.

I told the waiter to change my order to a chicken Caesar as well. "Couldn't eat a burger in front of you," I said.

"You're a prince among men. So what's with all the urgency?"

"I was talking to Sergei on Friday night," I said. "I'm worried he might be hiring illegal aliens to work on your crews."

I've known my brother all my life, and I can read him pretty well. Unless he'd turned into a masterful liar, this was all news to him. He groaned. "Please do not tell me that my lame-ass brother-in-law is involved in something shady," he said. "Tatiana thinks he's gone totally straight."

We both laughed. "Well, in a manner of speaking," Haoa said.

"Was he in trouble in Alaska?"

The food arrived. Haoa looked at his salad and said, "I wish I'd ordered the burger." I waited. He said, "Yeah, Sergei's a general fuckup. Nothing major, you understand. But every other week he was in some kind of trouble. Getting drunk at a bar. Beating up a guy who made a crack at him. Pissing in the street where a cop could see him. Receiving stolen goods. Possession with intent to distribute."

"Whoa. And you hired this guy?"

"Tatiana swore up and down that she would keep him in line. Hell, I see the way she runs me and the kids. I figured she could do the same for him." He shrugged. "Everybody needs a second chance, Kimo. Sergei's a fun guy, Tatiana loves him, I thought I was doing a good deed."

"We don't actually know that he's doing anything shady."

Haoa frowned. "I know. A leopard doesn't change his spots." He ate some lettuce and then said, "I've had my suspicions. We've been expanding like crazy the last six months, and it's hard to hire good help for what I can afford to pay. But Sergei, it's like he found this pipeline of guys. And they're good workers, too."

"Chinese?"

"All kinds. Chinese, Filipino, Indonesian."

"You ever ask to see their papers?"

He shook his head. "That's what I have him for." He looked at me. "What am I gonna do, Kimo? I could lose my business over this. Hell, I could go to jail, couldn't I? Who'll take care of Tatiana and the kids?" He put his fork down on the table and it skittered away and fell to the floor. "Jesus, I'm fucked, aren't I?"

"You're not fucked yet," I said. "I was talking to a guy in Immigration today. Let me ask him what you should do. You cooperate, maybe all you get is a fine."

"Can you do that?"

I shrugged. "I don't know, Haoa. But you know I'll do everything I can to protect you. After everything you've done for me . . ."

"Thanks, brah." He shivered. "Shit, I've got to tell Tatiana about this."

"Who did all your paperwork before you hired Sergei?"

"Had another guy, but he quit. Tatiana was helping me out when she suggested we bring in Sergei."

"So get Tatiana to go in and look things over," I said. "Before we go all crazy. Meantime, I'll talk to my guy, but I won't use any names yet. See what he says."

"We've got to do this fast," Haoa said. He pushed the half-eaten salad away from him. "I've got no appetite anymore."

"Poor guy," I said. "You'll waste away to nothing in a few days."

"Get even skinnier on prison food," he grumbled.

I looked at my watch. "I've got to get back to work," I said. I reached over and clasped his shoulder. "Don't worry, brah. I'm going to take care of you."

Chapter 28

BURN VICTIM

RAY AND I spent the rest of the afternoon wading through information online. I had no idea there were so many different names for male prostitutes—from man-whores to program boys. Men had been selling sex to other men since ancient Greece and Rome, beginning in the United States in the late 1600s.

Guys who identified as straight and yet had sex with men for money were called gay for pay. Hustlers were guys, like Jimmy Ah Wong, Frankie, and Lolo, who solicited for sex on the street. Escorts, like Lucas, made contact with clients through personal ads, Web sites, and agencies. According to the research I found, most guys who sold sex supplemented their income in other ways: pornographic actor or model, go-go boy, or by performing in sex shows or on a Web site. That matched what I'd seen on MenSay-Hi. Another common trade was massage therapist, which connected to the businesses Norma Ching and Treasure Chen had been running.

When I got home, I found an e-mail from the law student, who needed to talk to me. Between him and Brian Izumigawa, I couldn't seem to get rid of past tricks. "Where are you?" the student asked when I called his cell. "I need your help."

"I'm at my apartment in Waikīkī. You want me to meet you up at UH again?"

"No, I'll come down there. Give me your address."

"You want to come to my apartment?"

"Please. I have to show you something. In private."

Reluctantly, I told him where I lived. It didn't sound like he wanted to hook up, and I didn't have the energy to argue with him. While I was cleaning up, Gunter called me. "I'm still at work, but I need to talk to you. Can I come over when my shift is done?"

What was up? Why were all these guys desperate to talk to me at my apartment? "Sure, Gunter. I'll be here."

About a half hour later, my doorbell rang. I looked out the peephole and recognized the South Asian guy. "Thank you, thank you," he said, bursting into the apartment. "I didn't know who else to talk to. I'm in terrible trouble."

"OK, slow down," I said, closing the door behind him. "Come sit down and tell me what's wrong."

"I can't," he said, and he burst into tears.

Awkwardly, I put my arms around his shoulders and hugged him, and he cried against me. "It's OK," I said. "You can tell me anything."

"I have to show you," he said, sniffling. He pulled away and turned his back to me. He undid his pants and pushed them and his white briefs to the floor, then leaned against my sofa.

"Holy shit," I said. "What happened?"

His hairless mocha buttocks were dotted with burns, and there was a white gauze patch awkwardly taped over his anus. "That fucker," he said, talking through tears. "He burned me."

I remembered the cream that Mike had used on my back when I'd been scorched at the Hawai'i Marriage Project fire. Unfortunately, I'd used it up and never replaced it. "I've got to make a call," I said. "Don't worry, I'm going to take care of you. Lie down on the sofa on your stomach."

He leaned down to pull up his pants, and I said, "You might as well leave those off." He stepped out of them and lay down on the couch.

I dialed Mike Riccardi on my cell. "You still have some of that burn cream?" I asked, as soon as he picked up.

"Hello to you, too," he said. "Yup. I've always got a tube in my truck."

"How quickly can you get over to my apartment?"

"You burned yourself?"

"Not me. Another guy."

"Give me a half hour," he said.

I sat down on the floor, so that my head was about the same level as the law student's. "OK, why don't you tell me what happened?" I asked. "My friend is on his way over with some cream to help you out."

"Nobody can know," he said. "I did not realize how bad it was until this morning. Fortunately my wife did not see me."

"Start at the beginning," I said. "Who did this to you?"

"The man I had sex with the night of the fire," he said. "He called me yesterday, when I was at the library. He told me that he wanted to see me."

He started crying again, and I patted his shoulder. "Take your time."

"I said that I did not want to," he said. "I am trying to be a good husband. But he said that he had taken pictures of me that night, and that he would send them to my wife if I did not do what he said. He told me to come to an apartment. He made me take all my clothes off and lie down on the bed."

He began sobbing again. "I am so ashamed. I should never have gone with him in the first place. Now my life will be ruined."

"Where was the apartment?" I asked.

"In Kaka'ako," he said. "A beautiful high-rise."

On a hunch, I told him the address of the building where Ray and I had found Treasure Chen hiding. With her moved to Norma's, anyone else could be using the place. "Apartment six-oh-nine?"

He looked up at me, tears streaking his face. He was quite handsome, and I could see that many men would find him attractive. "How did you know?"

"It's an address that has come up in our investigations."

That brought on a fresh round of tears. "He is a criminal. I knew it."

"What did he do once you were lying on the bed?"

"He tied my hands and feet to the bedposts. It was very uncomfortable, my legs stretched open so wide. He lit a cigar, and he began blowing the smoke into my bottom. I just wanted him to fuck me so that I could go, but he wouldn't."

I tried to remember the bed in the apartment. It had a wooden headboard and footboard, with posts at each corner. "I kept asking him to let me go, and he got angry. He said I could go when he said so. Then I felt something burning."

I had to get up to answer the door. Mike stepped in, then stopped when he saw the law student on the couch, naked from the waist down, his buttocks burned and bandaged. "What's up?"

"This is my friend Mike," I said to the law student. "He's a fireman. He's accustomed to dealing with burns."

"Man, somebody burned you good," Mike said, squatting down next to him. "What's your name?"

He sniffled. "Fouad," he said. "Fouad Khan."

I filled Mike in on what Fouad had said so far.

"Let me get a look at you," Mike said, and he began carefully peeling off the tape that held down the gauze. Fouad whimpered and squirmed.

"You were saying that you felt something burn you," I said to Fouad.

"He was tapping his cigar ash on me," he said. "And then he put the lit cigar right onto me. I cried out and begged him to stop, but he wouldn't."

Mike peeled off the bandage and said, in a low voice, "Man, that looks nasty."

Fouad's anus was red and inflamed. "He kept relighting the cigar and then putting it out on me." He was crying again. "I looked around and saw that he had taken off his pants, and I was relieved. I thought that at last he would finish and I could go home."

Mike squeezed some salve into his palm and began massaging it into Fouad's buttocks, slowly and carefully. "But he would not," Fouad said, wincing and crying. "I saw him stroking himself, and then when I thought he would finish, instead, he put the cigar in me."

I couldn't believe he had so many tears in him. I wasn't sure if it was the memory or Mike touching his burns. I grasped his hand and squeezed. "He ejaculated on me then," Fouad said. "And after that he said I could go, but that I would have to come whenever he asked, or he would show the pictures to my wife."

I exchanged a glance with Mike. "OK, buddy, I'm going to put some cream where you're burned the worst," he said to Fouad. "This might sting a little."

It appeared to sting a lot. Fouad grasped my hand and squeezed until I worried he might break a couple of bones. "You ought to go to the emergency room," Mike said. "These burns are nasty, and you don't know what kind of damage was done inside."

"No," Fouad insisted through his tears. "No hospital."

"Hold on a minute," I said. "Suppose we said that you were attacked. Last night, leaving the library. Two or three men attacked you. Maybe they thought you were Arabic, and they said anti-Arab things."

I saw Mike nodding. "They held you down, pulled your pants down, and burned you," he said.

"You were embarrassed to go to the police last night, but if you go to the emergency room now, they'll call the police for you. You can report the assault."

"But that is against the law," Fouad said. "To make a false report."

"Someone raped and burned you," I said. "That's the truth. You tell the officer that you didn't see anyone's face, and they won't be able to pursue the case. It's not right—but it will be something you can explain to your wife. And if we catch this guy, then you'll be safe."

Fouad nodded.

"I need you to describe this man to me, tell me anything you can about him."

While Mike continued to administer the burn cream, Fouad said, "He is about fifty years old. Caucasian. His hair is dark brown, going to gray, and his face is red, like a man who drinks a lot."

I took notes. "Anything else?"

"He has a very good body. Like he works out in the gym."

"How does he dress?"

"As if he has been in the military. Those shirts, with the little flaps."

"Epaulets," I said.

"Yes. Very nice black shoes, always shined."

The description sounded familiar, but I couldn't place it.

"This is the best I can do, buddy," Mike said. "You got some bandages, Kimo?"

I brought a roll of gauze to him from the bathroom. "Fouad, I want you to put this on yourself," Mike said. "You don't want them questioning you at the ER about who did this for you."

Fouad stood up and awkwardly wrapped the gauze around his butt. "You're going to the ER right now," I said. "Go to The Queen's Medical Center. It's near police headquarters downtown, and they'll send over a cop to ask you questions. I'll do my best to follow what happens."

"Thank you so much," Fouad said. He pulled up his briefs and his pants, and then embraced first me, and then Mike. "You are good men."

Since I'd just encouraged the victim of a crime to lie to the police, I wasn't that good, but it was the best solution to a bad problem. Mike and I followed him outside and watched him drive away.

"You think he's going to do it?" Mike asked.

"I don't see that he has any other choice. Otherwise his wife's going to have some very serious questions." I paused. "I didn't want to say anything, but I think his assault might tie into our investigation."

The streetlamp lit Mike's face, and I was reminded of how handsome he was and how much history there was between us. There was no hiding the fact that I was falling for him all over again. "Come on, Romeo," I said, refraining from taking his hand, "let's go back inside, and I'll tell you the whole story."

Chapter 29

PROPOSITIONING GUNTER

"HOW DOES HIS assault tie into our case?" Mike asked, as we climbed the stairs to my apartment.

"He's been around the edges for a while—he's the one who called 911 about the fire at the shopping center. He was having sex that night in an office across the street, the office of the Wah Shing Corporation, which is also the parent company for the acupuncture clinic. Plus Wah Shing owns the condo where he was attacked—the one where Ray and I found Treasure Chen hiding out. That means the guy who assaulted Fouad is tied to the prostitution, and maybe the arsons."

"But you said your guy was Chinese, yeah? The guy who burned Fouad was Caucasian."

The doorbell rang. Mike looked at me. "You think that's Fouad again? Or are you expecting someone else?"

"Only way to tell is to open the door."

It was Gunter. "Oh," he said. "I didn't realize you had company."

Mike and Gunter looked at each other, and I remembered that neither of them liked the other. Gunter was a little jealous, angry on my behalf about the way Mike had treated me. As for Mike, Gunter was the kind of gay man who made him uncomfortable— flamboyant, aggressive in his sexuality.

"I can come back," Gunter said.

"No, stay," Mike said. "I was just leaving."

Mike gave me a hug and quick kiss on the cheek. "Call me tomorrow," he said. "Nice to see you, Gunter."

"You, too," Gunter said. When Mike was out of the apartment, Gunter turned to me. "You're not getting back together with him, are you? Because you know that is a recipe for disaster."

"Things are complicated. We're working together on a case. And I needed his help with something tonight."

"I could have helped you with that," Gunter said.

"We did not have sex. A guy showed up here with burns and Mike brought over some burn cream."

"Right."

"It's true." I told him about Fouad.

Gunter shivered. "Kinky."

"You didn't come over to harass me about my love life. What's up?"

"I may be out of a job. That is, unless I do what Stan wants." He sat down in my easy chair and I sat across from him on the couch.

"What does Stan want?"

"He wants me to fuck around."

"And you're opposed to that?"

"I don't fuck for money," he said. "And I'm sure as hell not going to get caught on camera fucking somebody so Stan can blackmail him."

"Whoa! Where did that come from?" Immediately I thought of the blackmail attempt on Brian Izumigawa, and the *haole* who had pictures of himself having sex with Fouad Khan. How many gay blackmailers were out there?

"You know Stan's company took over the contract at the Kuhio Regent?"

I nodded.

"Well, he started replacing all the employees with his own people. Half of the maintenance guys don't speak English. I'll bet they don't have green cards either."

"How does that connect to Stan wanting to pimp you?"

"He pretty much told me that if I didn't, he'd replace me."

I got us a pair of beers from my refrigerator. I was working my way through a six-pack of Big Wave Golden Ales. "How did this happen?" I asked. "Over drinks at the Rod and Reel Club? In his office?"

"He's been hinting around for a while," Gunter said. "You know, talking to me about sex, flattering me, asking me if I liked to be photographed, that sort of thing. And at the same time he's been asking me all these questions about the people who live at the Regent."

"Any good targets there?"

He shook his head. "You know I have excellent gaydar. The only gay men in that building are a couple on the twenty-third floor, and a few younger guys who aren't rich enough for blackmail." He moved to the floor, leaning back against the chair.

"Today, he asked me to meet him at his office before my shift." He took a swig from his beer. "I was worried he was going to fire me, like the rest of the staff. But instead he said he had a proposition for me."

"Not the kind of proposition you usually get."

"All the way there, I was psyching myself up," he said. "I mean, thinking about where else I could work. I know a couple of guys at buildings, but what I've got at the Regent is sweet. The residents all know me, I have a great shift, I can walk to work from my house."

"What did he say?"

"He started out with all this bullshit, how happy he was with the job I was doing, how he only heard great things about me. But things were different with his organization, he said. He expected more from his employees."

He twisted around so he was looking at me. "He told me that he knew I wasn't making a lot of money, and he had a way I could have some fun and make some extra cash at the same time." He frowned. "I told him I was getting along fine on my salary, but he insisted."

I'd never seen Gunter looking so vulnerable, not even when he'd been hospitalized with burns after the Marriage Project fire. "I can quit, I suppose. Or I can wait for him to fire me, and then collect unemployment. But it sucks that he can just do this."

"Did he say he had a particular client in mind for you?"

He nodded. "This Japanese businessman. He likes tall blond guys, and Stan said he'd go crazy for me. That he had a place I could take the guy, this nice apartment, and that he would show me where the cameras were in advance, so I could make sure the guy's face would be photographed."

"Did you ever hear Stan mention a guy named Mr. Hu?" I asked.

"Mr. Who?"

"Hu. H-U. A Chinese guy. He's blackmailing that guy you met at the park. I wonder if Stan is connected to him."

"He hasn't given me any names," he said.

"But I can't imagine there are two separate gay blackmail operations going on at the same time," I said. "Stan has got to be connected to Mr. Hu somehow. I'm trying to crack this other case, and you can help."

"Me?" Gunter said, and his voice almost squeaked.

I looked at him. Gunter is tall, and though he's skinny, he's quite muscular. I've never seen him be afraid of anything—not even a couple of drunk frat boys who were calling guys names outside the Rod and Reel Club one night.

"It's the only way," I said. "Unless you just want to give up without a fight—quit your job and go find another one."

He took a swig of his beer. "What if Stan finds out?"

"The worst he can do is fire you."

"You haven't seen his temper," Gunter said. "We had this Filipino maintenance guy at the Regent, and one day Stan was doing an inspection and he didn't think the guy had done a good job cleaning. He knocked him out."

"Wow. And nobody reported him?"

"Reported him? The Flip was probably illegal. He left and never came back."

"All the more reason to take Stan down, Gunter."

"Will you watch my back?"

"I'll talk to my boss in the morning."

He drained the rest of the beer. "I'm going home," he said.

I raised an eyebrow. "Alone? Your bed will seem awfully empty."

"I do sleep alone on occasion," he said. "When I find there's nobody around who interests me."

He stared at me for a moment and then swept regally toward the door, like Bette Davis in full flight. Unfortunately he stumbled over one of my Rollerblades, which spoiled the effect.

I was just starting to enjoy having an empty apartment when my doorbell rang again. It was nearly nine o'clock, and I wondered who it could be. Fouad? Mike? Gunter?

Through the peephole, though, I saw Haoa and Tatiana. "I'm going to kill him," my sister-in-law said, when I opened the door. "Either that or ship him back to Alaska."

"Come on in," I said. I embraced them both. "Hey, brah," I said to Haoa.

"She insisted we come right over," he said. "After dinner we went to the office and she looked through the paperwork."

"I cannot believe my brother is such a fuckup," Tatiana said. "The files are mess. And I left everything in perfect condition for him."

"So you're saying that he hasn't been checking for working papers?"

"He's been smart about it," Haoa said. Tatiana glared at him, but he said, "It's true. He's messed up the files so much you can't tell at first glance what's going on. If Tatiana hadn't known what was supposed to be there, it might have taken us a couple of days to figure out what he was hiding."

"What do you want to do?" I asked Tatiana. "You want to talk to Sergei first? Send him back to Alaska?"

"I think the only thing that's going to wake my brother up is a stint in jail."

"Knowing Sergei, he'll have some new racket set up inside,"

Haoa said. Tatiana kicked him. "Hey, he's your brother. Kick him, not me."

"I'll call my guy in Immigration tomorrow," I said. "See what he says we should do."

Haoa and Tatiana left a few minutes later, still squabbling, but I knew it would take more than a criminal brother to break them apart. I finally was able to lie down and read for a while, a thriller about an ATF agent who gets himself in trouble by his single-minded pursuit of the truth, by a Florida cop named James O. Born. I wished I could be so single-minded; it seemed that there were always detours pulling me away from what I was supposed to be focused on.

Chapter 30

MAHALO MANPOWER

THE NEXT MORNING, I called Juanita Lum as soon as I got in, but Lieutenant Kee was at a meeting at Honolulu Hale, our city hall, and wouldn't be back till the afternoon. I hung up as Ray walked in, looking like he'd gotten too little sleep. "We were out pretty late with Treasure last night," he said. "That girl can drink."

"She have anything to say?"

"She had lots to say. About her father and her sister and what a bitch Norma Ching was. Unfortunately, nothing that was useful. And the more she drank, the more useless the information was." He massaged his temples.

"You OK?"

He shrugged. "I'm not accustomed to so much booze anymore. Got a little hangover. But I'll survive."

While Ray rounded up aspirin, I called Frank O'Connor at ICE and made plans to meet at his office at eleven. Ray had a trial to go to for a case we'd closed a few months before, so he left to nurse his hangover at the courthouse. While I waited for the meeting, I did some more online research, this time on illegal immigration.

There were two different terms: smuggling and trafficking. A smuggled migrant is one who goes voluntarily, in exchange for payment. It might be as simple as hiring someone to drive you across a border. It might be more elaborate, as in the cases of men who brought in boatloads of Haitian refugees. In general, though, the relationship between the migrant and the smuggler ended upon arrival in the United States.

The smuggled migrants were often dumped somewhere—off the coast of Florida, for example, and left to make their way by swimming or wading through shallow water. In other cases, the migrants arrived with the names and phone numbers of relatives, and disappeared into the immigrant underworld.

A migrant who was trafficked was often lured by false promises or misled about immigration policies. They could also be driven by fear of violence, as from Haiti, or economic despair, as appeared to be endemic in Gansu Province.

These individuals were bound to their transporter in many ways—through fear, economics, or lack of knowledge. They were much like slaves, in that they had no way to leave their situations, and often all the money they earned went to pay back their transporters or reimburse their employers for living expenses.

It sounded like the Chinese workers at the acupuncture clinic had been trafficked. When I met up with Frank O'Connor, he agreed with that idea. "You have something new?" he asked. "I'm working on the information you gave me—but it was only yesterday, after all."

"What would be the penalties for someone who hired illegals?" I asked. "Unknowingly. I'm talking about a company owner, and it's a guy who works for him who hired the guys."

He looked at me shrewdly. "Are we still talking about prostitution?"

"Nope. This is a guy I know, and I want to be honest with him about what might be involved."

Frank punched a couple of keys on his desktop keyboard and glanced at the screen. "You say he had no direct knowledge that the workers were illegal?"

"Nope. This has only been going on for about a month, we think, and he trusted the guy who was processing the papers."

"Is he willing to cooperate fully?"

"Of course."

"He could probably get away with a plea and a fine, depending on the circumstances. When he's ready to talk, bring him to me."

On my way back to the station, I called Haoa and let him know what Frank had said. "Tatiana's going back to the office tonight to make copies of everything," he said. "I swear, when this is over . . ."

"When this is over, Sergei's still going to be Tatiana's brother," I said. "You might as well accept that."

"That doesn't keep me from beating the crap out of him."

"I have a feeling there's going to be a line for that."

When I got back to the station it was time for our meeting with Lieutenant Kee, but Ray still hadn't returned from his trial so I went downstairs by myself.

"You're the Lone Ranger today?" Juanita asked. "Where's Tonto?"

"He go speak with big chief wearing robes," I said. "The LT around?"

"In a meeting. But it shouldn't last long. Have a seat."

Juanita was multitasking again, carrying on a conversation with me while she filed documents and bantered with passing detectives. After about fifteen minutes, a couple of guys left Kee's office and Juanita told him I was there.

"I might have a connection to that blackmail case I told you about the other day," I said. I sat down across from him and told him about Gunter.

"What's the boss's name?" Kee asked.

"Stan LoCicero."

"You know the name of his company?"

"Mahalo Manpower. They have the security and maintenance contracts for the Kuhio Regent."

He turned to his computer and started typing, two-fingered, cursing periodically as he must have hit the wrong key. "Goddammit, Juanita, get in here," he bellowed after a while.

"What's up, Lieutenant?" she asked, appearing in the doorway with a smile on her face.

"Come over here and type in my password."

He moved back from the computer, and she leaned over and

punched a few keys. "While you're there, find whatever you can on a guy named Stan LoCicero or a company called Mahalo Manpower," he said.

Juanita shot me a glance and I had to struggle not to laugh. Her fingers danced over the keyboard, and then with a flourish, she hit the last key. "It's printing," she said.

"Damned computers," Kee grumbled as she walked out. He pulled a page off the printer and scanned it, then handed it to me.

There was nothing on the company, and the information available on Stan LoCicero didn't fill a page. He had been mentioned a few times in the course of investigations—but then so had I. Nothing had stuck.

My brain buzzed, trying to fit together the pieces. Mr. Hu lived in a house owned by Wah Shing, which also owned the acupuncture clinic, which meant he was involved with the fire at the shopping center. He had hired Lucas Tyler to have sex with me. Lucas had told Vice that he was photographed or videotaped for blackmail purposes. And because he had set me up to have sex with Brian Izumigawa, I assumed he was the one behind the blackmail.

But was he connected to Stan LoCicero, Gunter's boss? Or was there more than one guy out there videotaping gay men and blackmailing them?

Was Stan the *haole* guy who had burned Fouad, the law student? If so, had Stan left Fouad and then set the fire across the street? A lot of facts floated around, but what was missing was a good theory to tie them all together.

"I want to know a lot more about Mr. LoCicero," Kee said, bringing me back to the present.

"So do I." I told him I thought his investigation might tie into the arson and homicide Mike, Ray, and I were pursuing.

"I want you to find out everything about LoCicero," Kee said. "Where he's from, what he's into, down to what kind of toilet paper he uses. I want you to know him as well as you know your best friend."

"I'm on it."

"Tell your friend to stall for a day or two. Say he's got a flu bug or something, call in sick. Once we know more about LoCicero, we'll know how to proceed."

When I got upstairs, I called Gunter and told him what Kee wanted. "Fine with me," he said. "I didn't want to go to work today anyway."

"I'll call you tonight. We'll do some brainstorming."

"I brainstorm best over alcohol," Gunter said. "Preferably in the presence of hot, handsome manflesh."

"No you don't," I said. "And I'd stay away from the Rod and Reel Club if I were you, since Stan knows that's your hangout."

"You sure know how to ruin the fun of a day off."

"Gunter, you have enough resources to entertain yourself for a month without breaking a sweat. I'll call you later."

By the time I hung up, Ray had returned from court. I briefed him on what I'd heard from Frank O'Connor and Lieutenant Kee. He asked, "What was the name of LoCicero's company?"

"Mahalo Manpower."

"That name sounds familiar." He flipped through his notes. "Mahalo Manpower was one of the other companies owned by Wah Shing."

"Well, that connects Mr. Hu and Mr. LoCicero." That was a relief; it meant that all our cases were linked. We looked LoCicero up and found that despite his appearance on Vice's radar, he had no criminal record. He owned a house in Hawai'i Kai, near where Treasure Chen had lived, and a Harley-Davidson VRSCDX, the Night Rod Special, was registered at his address. The corporate office for Mahalo Manpower was in a small building just on the other side of the H1 expressway.

"I say we find Mr. LoCicero and follow him around for a while," I said. "See where he goes and what he does." I thought for a minute. "And I think this is a good time to bring in our computer consultant."

"Your friend Harry?"

"The same. There must be something in cyberspace about Stan LoCicero."

"In the meantime, we can stake out his office, see where he goes, who he talks to," Ray said. "Maybe he'll lead us to Mr. Hu."

We roughed out a plan, and then got Lieutenant Sampson to buy into the program. "With your permission I'm also going to get my friend Harry to do some cybersearching on him," I said.

"Your friend still charging the same price?"

Harry had always worked for free, to help me out and because he loved poking around in places he wasn't supposed to be. "Sure."

"Then it's fine with me. You need any overtime, I'll authorize it."

Back at my desk, I put everything I knew about Stan LoCicero into an e-mail to Harry. "I sent you a message, brah," I said, when he picked up his cell.

"Just got it."

It sounded like he was in some public place, so I said, "Where are you?"

"Looking at wedding invitations with Arleen," he said.

"How'd you get the e-mail, then?"

"BlackBerry," he said. "Welcome to the twenty-first century, brah."

I was barely up to speed with my laptop. "You have time to look into it?"

He lowered his voice. "Arleen's got us booked all afternoon with wedding crap," he said. Back at normal volume, he said, "If you need this stuff ASAP, I'll get right on it." I heard him explaining to Arleen in the background. When he came back to me he said, "I owe you one, brah. Talk to you later."

I drove us over to the offices of Mahalo Manpower. A black Mercedes was parked in the lot, and the license plate corresponded to one of the three cars registered to Wah Shing. Who was driving it, though? Richard Hu? If it was Stan's car, it was one more thing that connected him to Mr. Hu.

My stomach grumbled. "Let's get something to eat, then come back here at the end of the day," I said. We drove up University to a Zippy's near UH and got some of their killer chili, and sat in the front window to consider what we knew.

Ray pulled out a steno pad and said, "I've been making some notes."

The pad reminded me of Mike Riccardi, and I remembered the electricity that had passed between us the night before, wondering what would have happened if Gunter hadn't shown up when he did.

But that, as they say, was another story entirely.

Chapter 31

MEN WHO SAY MORE THAN HI

RAY TURNED TO a clean page and wrote WAH SHING in the center, drawing a circle around it. Then he drew a line to MAHALO MANPOWER, and circled that, too. He did the same for each of the business names we knew about, including the acupuncture clinic, the massage parlor, and the lingerie store. The only name I didn't recognize was Island Internet. I called Harry and asked him to check it out.

"So who's behind Wah Shing?" Ray asked, when I'd hung up. "Mr. Hu?"

"Must be. He's the only guy who comes up over and over again. And the house he lived in is owned by Wah Shing."

"How'd you hook up with him, anyway?"

I closed my eyes and tried to remember. Had I answered his ad? Had he answered one of mine?

I'd joined MenSayHi about a month after I broke up with Mike, once the gonorrhea was completely gone. I'd been celibate since my diagnosis and the horniness was building up. The first guy I answered said his name was Lenny, and that he was a muscular top into dominating other well-built, well-hung men.

I flattered myself into thinking he'd believe I fit the bill, and e-mailed him a couple of digital photos, including one of me flexing with a hard-on. My face was always in shadow; because of my very public coming-out, I had a recognition factor in the gay community and I wasn't eager to reveal myself to a total stranger.

Lenny responded a day later and we met up at his house in

Mililani, where he had a variety of toys, including dildos, vibrators, and a sling. "I thought I recognized you from your photo," he said, when I showed up.

We had some fun together, and when we were done he said he had a friend I might like to meet. I was noncommittal, and over the next few weeks I answered a number of ads and had a lot of sex. Some of it was good, and some was bad. By the time I heard from Lenny again, I was ready for somebody who knew what he was doing, and I agreed to meet up with him and his friend.

My first impression of Mr. Hu was that he was very ordinary. A middle-aged Chinese guy wearing a business suit, he looked more like he was ready to interview me for a job than to fuck me.

But fuck me he did, after watching Lenny do the same.

I couldn't put my finger on it then—and even now, after months of encounters, it's hard to quantify—but there was something about him that I connected to. It was as if he got me, in some very basic way, and I reacted to that.

It was similar, in a way, to what I felt for Mike. I loved Mike, and I didn't love Mr. Hu at all, but I felt like they were able to see into me and accept what they saw.

I couldn't explain all that to Ray; I barely understood it myself. So I simply said that I'd met Lenny online and then he'd introduced me to Mr. Hu a little later.

"You know anything about this Lenny?" Ray asked. "Maybe he could give us a line on Mr. Hu."

I couldn't remember the address of the house in Mililani, but I thought I'd recognize it again if I saw it. "Let's take a drive," I said.

We'd just thrown away our lunch trash when my cell phone rang. "Hey, brah," Harry said. "Island Internet owns a couple of Web sites—looks like they're all gay porn, gay hookups. The big one is called MenSayHi.com."

"Thanks, brah. You have an address on them?"

"In Mililani." He read it to me and I wrote it down.

It was another gorgeous day in paradise, so we rolled up the flaps on the Wrangler and hit the H1. We were surrounded by rental cars full of vacationing tourists, going slow, changing lanes without warning. I blasted my horn a couple of times, but it was a losing proposition.

After the third time I'd tailgated some clueless vacationer, Ray said, "I know this must be weird for you, getting your sex life dragged into a case."

"Not so weird as you'd think," I said. "I mean, I wish it weren't this way, but I have a habit of letting my dick get me into trouble."

"Do tell."

"Remember I told you about that case that dragged me out of the closet? I stumbled into it because I went to the Rod and Reel Club one night and I found a body behind the club. And then when I was undercover up on the North Shore, I fooled around with a guy who ended up getting killed." I sighed. "Sampson gave me this big lecture then, how I had to learn to separate my personal life from my cases. But is it my fault that a guy I had sex with turns out to be a criminal?"

"Sampson might suggest you be more careful about who you have sex with."

"And how do I do that? Require a background check from every guy before I get naked with him?"

"Come on, Kimo," Ray said, grabbing onto the door frame as I took a fast curve merging onto the H2. "You knew there was something weird with Mr. Hu from day one. And then you said he admitted he paid that guy to fuck you. I'm not trying to bust your chops, you know, but those were red flags that you just ignored."

"I know. I ought to be a monk."

"No. You just need to find the right guy and settle down with him." He looked over at me. "You think the right guy is the fireman?"

I shrugged. "Maybe. If he gets his shit together."

I pulled off the H2 and started to navigate the local streets of

Mililani, trying to find my way back to Lenny's house. I spotted a car with a bumper sticker for MenSayHi and pulled up. "Here's our address. And I think this is Lenny's place."

The house was a nondescript ranch, painted beige, with a couple of scraggly hibiscus bushes with big red blossoms in the front yard. Ray and I walked up to the front door and I rang the bell. It sounded like he had a herd of dogs inside, barking like crazy. It took a couple of minutes until Lenny answered, a pair of small, furry white Pekingese yapping at his feet. "Kimo," Lenny said. "What's up?"

I introduced Ray. "You mind if we come in and talk?" I asked.

"Sure." He leaned down and picked up the two dogs. "This is Bette, and this is Greta," he said, showing them off. "I'll put them in the kitchen."

When he wasn't wearing his leather chaps, with studded black straps crisscrossing his chest, Lenny looked like an ordinary guy. He was about six feet tall, broad shouldered, with a bit of a gut. He was barefoot, and wore a UH T-shirt and sweats. We followed him into the living room, and when he came back we all sat down. The furniture was a mix of styles, as if he'd inherited half of it and picked up the rest at a thrift shop. If I hadn't had sex with him, I'd have doubted he was gay.

"What can you tell us about MenSayHi?" I asked. "What's your connection?"

"I'm the webmaster," Lenny said. "I've got a ProLiant DL380 G5 Server with quad-core processors and a smart array in my spare room, with a T1 fat pipe."

"OK, I didn't understand anything you said," I said. "But what I want to know is how you're connected to Wah Shing Corporation?"

Lenny looked wary. "Wah Shing is our corporate parent. They provided the start-up funding."

"Is Mr. Hu behind Wah Shing?"

"What's this all about, Kimo?"

"That's what we need you to tell us, Lenny. We've got this giant jigsaw puzzle, and we're trying to fit the pieces together."

Lenny looked from me to Ray and back. "I knew it was too good to last," he said. "I met Richard Hu about two years ago, online, through another site. We hooked up, and after sex we started talking. I had this idea for a Web site, and Richard provided the money."

He sat back against the sofa. "We launched about a year and a half ago. The main site is self-supporting through ads and basic memberships. Then there's the private site, for premium members. Streaming video, live chat, exclusive photo galleries. You know, Kimo, it's a class site."

"Except for the prostitution in the background," I said.

"Hey, I don't get involved in any of that," Lenny said, leaning forward. "Everything I do is completely legit. All I do is provide a venue for guys to hook up. What they do after they hook up is their business, and out of my control."

"We're not interested in you, Lenny," I said. "We're interested in Richard Hu. What do you know about him besides the money he provided?"

"Should I have a lawyer?" Lenny asked.

I shrugged. "That depends. If you broke the law, then yeah, you should have an attorney to protect your rights and broker a deal. But if you didn't, all you're doing is giving us information, and nobody ever went to jail for that."

Lenny shifted around uncomfortably on the sofa, then said, "I don't know much. I never let him put cameras in here. Hell, I'm not interested in being somebody's performing monkey. If I want to have sex, I want the only people watching to be people I invite."

"But he filmed other people?" I asked. Lenny nodded. "And then he gave you the pictures to post, didn't he?"

His face looked like he'd swallowed something nasty. "Come on, Lenny, I recognized myself." I saw Ray looking at me. "I know I didn't sign any release that said you could put naked pictures of me on your site."

"You can't see your face," Lenny said. "It could be anybody."

"I recognize my own ass."

"Maybe I should call my lawyer after all," Lenny said.

"Suppose I promise we won't prosecute you for posting the photos. In exchange for you telling us everything you know about Richard Hu."

Lenny said, "In writing?"

"In writing."

"I'll be back."

When Lenny walked out, Ray said, "He has pictures of you on his site?"

"From the back. Nothing anybody else could recognize."

"So Lieutenant Sampson wouldn't know it's you?"

"Unless he's seen my naked ass, which I know I'd remember."

Lenny returned, carrying a laptop. "Write it up," he said, handing me the computer. He'd already opened Microsoft Word.

I'm not the fastest typist in the world. While I was struggling, Ray asked, "You know a guy named Stan LoCicero?"

"Yeah. He works for Richard."

I looked up from the computer. "Doing what?"

Lenny shrugged. "Whatever Richard tells him. Richard funds a business for him, too. Some kind of temp agency."

"Mahalo Manpower," Ray said.

"That's it. I've only met him a couple of times. The dude's kinky."

I finished typing and handed the laptop back to Lenny. He read what I'd written, and nodded his head. "I'm printing it in the other room," he said.

"How kinky is Stan?"

"Dude's kind of a firebug," Lenny said. "Likes to smoke cigars, you know? And sometimes he likes to burn guys."

Lenny left us again, and I knew that we had our connection between Stan and the shopping center arson. If the law student could put Stan, a known firebug, across the street from the center at the time it burned, that meant there was a very good chance Stan was our arsonist, and responsible for Jingtao's death.

When Lenny returned, he was carrying a sheaf of papers. The first page was the note I'd written. I signed it.

"This is Richard's list of everything in the private member directory. It tells you who's who in the pictures."

I scanned the list. Lucas's name figured in many of the pictures, though there were different guys with him. I recognized some of the names—Brian Izumigawa, a dean at UH, and a member of the Honolulu City Council, among others.

"You know anything about blackmail?" I asked Lenny.

He shook his head. "If Richard's blackmailing anybody, he never told me."

"But you had to know something was up with all these pictures," Ray said.

"Richard said the guys got a thrill from seeing themselves online. Like you, Kimo, you can't see their faces. But they know it's them."

"Are there pictures where you can see their faces?" I asked.

"If there are, Richard never gave them to me."

"Where does Richard live?" I asked. "In that house in Black Point?"

"As far as I know. He also has an office in St. Louis Heights, and an apartment in Kaka'ako. Some of the pictures were taken there."

All addresses we knew. We quizzed Lenny for a while longer, but it was clear we'd gotten all we could out of him.

Chapter 32

ENCOUNTERS OF THE SEXUAL KIND

WE TOOK THE sheaf of papers back to the station, where we split the list in two and started googling the names. As it got close to four o'clock, we decided to table the research and get back to the offices of Mahalo Manpower. Ray wanted to show off his new two-door minicar, so we got into the Yaris and I kicked the seat as far back as it would go. It wasn't quite far enough for me, and my knees were knocking up against the glove compartment.

"Good thing we're not planning on arresting anybody," I said. "Have to put him in the trunk."

I twisted around to look behind. The backseat was there but small. "There is a trunk in this thing, isn't there?"

"You like this neighborhood?" Ray asked.

"Just saying, is all." Between construction on the H1 and a fender bender blocking one lane on North King Street, it took us longer than expected to get into position. I was pleased to see the black Mercedes still in the parking lot.

It was a ragged, industrial neighborhood, a lot of buildings with roll-down garage doors and little landscaping. Ray parked across from a little convenience store and we sat back to wait. We didn't have to wait long; Stan LoCicero came out about fifteen minutes later, got in his car, and drove off.

"Game on," Ray said.

Stan followed North King to North Beretania and headed toward Waikīkī. It was easy to keep him in sight in the rush-hour traffic, which was moving about as fast as a green sea turtle crawling on shore to lay her eggs.

When he turned onto Kalākaua, I said, "I'll bet I know where he's going. Drop me by the Rod and Reel Club. If he goes somewhere else, call me."

Fred, the handsome, brainless bartender who normally worked the late shift, was behind the bar, and I flirted with him for a few minutes, my cell phone on vibrate in my pocket. The sound system was playing some old *hapa-haole* music for the tourist crowd, and the lights twinkled in the trees that lined the outdoor patio. An elderly man wore an aloha shirt in a pattern of heart-shaped red anthurium flowers, and his wife wore a muumuu in matching fabric.

"Hello, detective," a voice said over my shoulder. "Can I buy you a drink?"

I turned to smile at Stan, holding up my Mehana Volcano Red Ale. "I've got one now, but maybe later," I said. "Who knows what the evening holds?"

"Who knows indeed," Stan said, taking the stool next to me. His left leg slid next to my right one as he did.

"What brings you here this evening?" I asked.

"I was hoping to run into your friend Gunter," Stan said. "He called out sick today. Wanted to see if that was true." He shrugged. "Guess it must be so."

Good thing I had told Gunter to lay low. I'd have to call him and let him know Stan was on the prowl. "You're quite the public figure," Stan said, taking a swig of the Longboard Lager Fred brought for him. "How is it for you, among your fellow officers? They accept you?"

"It's been a tough road," I said. "But you know, cops are people just like everybody else. Some are OK, some aren't."

"Still, you must need to keep your nose clean," Stan said. "Can't get into any scandal."

I looked at him innocently. "What do you mean?"

The elderly man in the anthurium shirt got up to do a little hula dance, and his wife laughed and filmed him for the folks back home.

"Let's say somebody had some intimate knowledge of you," Stan said. "And he was to go public. Might damage your reputation."

"Depends," I said, my blood pressure beginning to rise. "I'm your basic law-abiding citizen. Sex between men isn't illegal in Hawai'i." The first sodomy law had been enacted in 1850, though the last case had been prosecuted in 1958, and subsequent revisions to the criminal code had all but removed the penalties.

"It is when money's involved."

Stan took a long drink from his beer and I looked at him. I had a feeling I knew where he was going.

"I've never had to pay."

"But what if someone paid on your behalf?" he asked. "And what if there was videotaped evidence?"

A tour bus pulled up outside and honked its horn, and most of the sunburnt *haoles* in the bar got up to leave. I didn't think they had any idea that the Rod and Reel Club, a kitschy destination by day, turned into a steamy gay club after dark. When they'd all left, I turned to Stan. "If you're talking about Lucas, I have some bad news for you. First, he's dead. And second, before he died he told the Vice department what had gone on. So there's nothing there that could hurt me."

Stan's body language stiffened, and I could see a shadow of the temper that Gunter had seen when Stan hit the Filipino maintenance man. He was a guy who didn't like to be crossed.

"There's a difference between being told something, and seeing it in living color," he said. "I don't know that's a difference you'd be able to withstand."

The adrenaline was flowing, and I had to resist the impulse to punch Stan in his jowly red face. But showing him that I wasn't afraid wasn't necessarily the best course of action. I had to understand him before I acted. Why was he threatening me? Did he know that we were closing in on him? Or was I just the latest target of his blackmail ring?

"Suppose I was nervous," I said, choosing my words carefully. "Suppose I wanted to make sure that whatever evidence there was never came to light. What would I do?"

"For now, sit tight," Stan said. Then, leaning close to my ear, he said, "That is, if your ass has recovered from the battering it got from Lucas."

Fred came by to see if we wanted another round. "Maybe something with a fruity little umbrella?" he asked. Both of us declined.

Once Fred left, Stan said, "That's a very sexy little video, detective. I've watched it quite a few times myself and I always find it entertaining. You've missed a promising career in porn."

"I'll stick to police work."

Stan drained the last of his beer. "Then I'll be in touch." He dropped a twenty on the bar for Fred and walked out.

I called Ray to let him know that Stan was on the move. "He parked at the garage on Seaside Avenue," Ray said. "I'll wait for you by the side entrance."

I paid Fred, declined his offer of a quick step into one of the private rooms in the back of the building, and walked over to the garage. As I got into the Yaris, Ray said, "Stan just took off. Heading out toward Diamond Head."

"Maybe he's going home now."

I called Gunter and let him know that Stan had been checking out the bar. "I'm being good," he said. "Well, maybe not good, but I'm staying home." In the background I heard another man's voice, and Gunter laughed. "Gotta go, brah. Thanks for the warning."

Ray and I followed Stan, keeping a safe distance back in rush-hour traffic on the Kalaniana'ole Freeway. He turned into Hawai'i Kai, climbing up to the community of Kalama Valley, pulling into the driveway of a nicely kept ranch with a tall hibiscus hedge around the entire property. Behind the shield of red and yellow blossoms and green leaves stood two coconut palms. He went inside, coming back out a minute later with a Siberian Husky on an expandable leash.

He was smoking a cigar, letting the dog pull him along the curving street as it sniffed and peed. We slouched back in the Yaris, and Stan went in the opposite direction with the dog, so he didn't spot us.

The Ko'olau Mountains provided a lush backdrop to clean streets and manicured lawns. Every house had flowering plants in the yard, all shades and sizes of hibiscus and bougainvillea. "Ritzy area," Ray said. "Stan must be doing pretty well for himself."

A half hour after Stan returned with the dog, the garage door opened, and Stan, dressed in full leathers, roared out on his Harley, a red do-rag wrapped around his head. He went up the coast, stopping at a biker bar outside Waimanalo Beach.

The wind was whipping the waves to a white froth, spraying a fine layer of sand across the highway. We pulled up across the road and about a quarter of a mile away. "You think I ought to go in there?" Ray asked.

I looked at him. "You?"

"Well, the guy knows you," he said.

"Look at the lineup of bikes out there. Don't you think you'd stand out?"

"I can be tough when I have to."

"I don't doubt it. But to be effective you'd need some leathers and a bike, and we don't have either of those. I say we give up on surveillance tonight. We've got a lot of research to do tomorrow morning. I doubt Stan's going to pick up a guy tonight at this bar."

"You never know. He's a gay biker, after all."

"If there was such a thing as a gay biker bar on O'ahu, I'd know it," I said. "After all, I am the official homosexual of the Honolulu Police Department."

"As opposed to the unofficial ones," Ray said, putting the Yaris in gear.

"We don't talk about them."

On our way back downtown, I called Haoa and found out that

he and Tatiana were at the office, photocopying the records on every employee. "Remember, just because there's no paperwork, it doesn't mean the guy's illegal," I said. "It could just be that Sergei's sloppy."

"Yeah, go on thinking that," Haoa said.

We rolled the windows down and the trade winds swept in the cooling night air. Was Sergei just trying to satisfy Haoa's constant need for staff? Or was there something else? I'd seen the photos of him on MenSayHi, so I knew he had more than just a tangential connection to Mr. Hu and Stan.

Rather than making the turn onto Lili'uokalani, which would have put him in the wrong direction for home, Ray dropped me off on Kalākaua and I walked around for a few minutes, trying to work things out.

The constant parade of car headlights, combined with the neon and the store lighting, made it hard to see any stars, but a slice of moon hung above the ocean, clouds moving swiftly past it. There was a cacophony of noise around me—rap music, car horns, and loud laughter—but I felt cocooned from it all, my brain working through the case. But by the time I got home I hadn't come up with anything new. After I'd stripped off my shirt and fixed some dinner, I relaxed with a book for a while. Around nine I called Mike. "Hey, what's up?"

"Hanging out," he said. "Your burn guy from last night go to the ER?"

"I don't know. Didn't hear from him."

"Don't you have a buddy in the ER?"

That stumped me. Had I said something about Dr. Phil? I didn't think so. "How'd you know that?"

There was silence on Mike's end. Finally he said, "You went to Raimundo's."

I remembered back to my first date with Dr. Phil, the day I'd gotten my hair cut at Puerto Peinado and had my hair washed by Jingtao. "Yeah?"

"Raimundo remembered you from when we used to go there. I was in a couple of days later and he mentioned it to me."

That was interesting. I had occasionally obsessed about Mike myself during the time we'd been apart, once seeing his truck parked on Kalākaua and scouring the area looking for him. "We have a new lead," I said. I told him about going out to Mililani to see Lenny.

"You had sex with Lenny?" Mike asked. "Me, too."

"Really? Were you on MenSayHi?"

"Yup. That's how you met him?"

"You didn't have sex with Richard Hu, did you?"

"Don't recognize the name. He a friend of Lenny's?"

"You could say that."

"Lenny and I didn't click," Mike said.

"Lucky you. At least there wouldn't be any pictures of you."

"Pictures?"

I told him about the photos I'd found of my ass getting plowed by Lucas. "I'm online," Mike said. "I'll have to check it out."

"It's nothing you haven't seen," I said, but I heard his fingers clicking furiously in the background.

"Where is it? One of the photo sets?"

"You have a premium membership?"

"Come on, fess up. Like you said, it's nothing I haven't seen."

"Set 34," I said.

There was clicking on his end, and then a low whistle. "Man, that is hot," he said. "I'm jealous."

"Jealous why? Because Lucas's dick is bigger than yours?"

"I'm jealous because you have a hot ass that ought to belong to me," he said. "You know, last night, if your buddy Gunter hadn't come over, I might have . . ."

"I know. I might have too."

"Well. Where does that leave us?"

"You at your computer drooling over pictures of my ass. Me here remembering your dick."

"Are you naked?"

I wasn't. "I could be."

"So could I."

I closed my eyes and remembered Mike's body. His chest was hairy, his stomach flat. A trail of black hair led from the cleft of his chest down to his crotch. I'd already pulled off my shirt when I got home; as I was thinking of Mike I shucked my shorts and boxers.

"I'm naked now," I said, my voice catching a little. "I'm thinking about your body. You are so fucking hot."

"So are you. I'm stroking my nipple, and it's getting hard."

We went on, each of us spurring the other on to orgasm. Mike groaned and caught his breath, and I knew he'd come. That was enough to put me over the edge.

"Man," he said, when he'd gotten his breath back. "Are we ever going to do this in person again?"

"We might. In the meantime, I'll call my friend in the ER. I haven't seen him in a while. He's pretty hot."

"You bastard. Can't you just check the department computer and see if there's a report of his assault?"

"Yeah, but I like the idea of you being jealous."

Chapter 33

THE FEDERAL CASE

AFTER I HUNG up with Mike, I found an assault record for Fouad Khan. Then I went to sleep, thinking of Mike and how it would be to have sex with him again—this time with actual physical contact.

Frank O'Connor called the next morning. He asked me to set up a meeting with my source as soon as possible. When I spoke to Haoa, he was eager to get things moving. "How soon can we do this?"

I went back and forth between him and Frank, and we ended up with a ten o'clock meeting at Frank's office. Haoa said he would bring Sergei, even if he had to tie him up and throw him in the back of the truck. "Do we need an attorney?"

I asked Frank. "I want to get a line on who's bringing these people in," he said. "I'm not interested in putting your brother behind bars. Or his brother-in-law, as long as he's willing to cooperate."

Ray and I googled the rest of the guys on Lenny's list. We ended up with a nice selection of who's who in Hawai'i. The UH dean, a couple of corporate executives, a few politicians, a professional athlete, and a competitive surfer. All of them had something to protect.

"The next step is to see if any of these guys have been blackmailed," Ray said, when we were finished. "And if any of them are willing to swear out a complaint. What's your gut feeling on that?"

I shrugged. "If I were on the list, I'd be reluctant to air my dirty laundry. I might just sit back and hope somebody else brings the blackmailer down."

Ray looked at his watch. "Time to get moving," he said. "You OK doing this with your brother? Because I'll handle it if you want."

"No, I promised Haoa I'd look out for him. I've got to go."

A group of Hawai'ian nationalists were picketing outside the Prince Kuhio Kalaniana'ole Federal Building. Young Hawai'ian men in red T-shirts carried the Hawai'ian flag on poles, the British Union Jack in the upper left corner, surrounded by red, white, and blue stripes. Women in muumuus carried signs that read KU I KA PONO: JUSTICE FOR HAWAI'IANS. Men from *luas,* or schools of Hawai'ian martial arts, wore traditional *kihei*—tapa cloth cloaks tied in a knot—and carried staffs and other weapons. Kids carried portraits of King Kamehameha and Queen Lili'uokalani.

The demonstration was peaceful, but it took us extra time to get through the crowd and security. By the time we arrived at Frank O'Connor's office, Haoa, Tatiana, and Sergei were sitting in plush seats in the reception area. From their body language, I could tell that Haoa and Tatiana were angry, and Sergei scared. "I'm not going back to jail, am I, Kimo?" he asked me as I sat down across from him.

"This is not my operation," I said. "I'm looking out for Haoa and Tatiana."

"But Kimo, we . . . you know."

"Yes, Sergei. We had sex. It's not a secret. That doesn't mean I'm on your side in this." I knew we had to have his cooperation, so though I was angry with him for putting my brother and sister-in-law in jeopardy, I had to soften my approach. "But if you cooperate, you can walk out of this."

As Frank led us into a conference room with an oblong wooden table and comfy chairs all around it, I made the introductions. "Why don't we start with you, Mr. Baranov," Frank said. "What's been happening at Kanapa'aka Landscaping?"

"I landed here in Hawai'i about two months ago," he said. "I was kind of a fuckup in Alaska and I was trying to do a good job for Haoa. But it was next to impossible to find guys to work for him. I was bitching about it to this trick one night, and he said he could help me out."

I saw Haoa and Tatiana look at each other, and once again I remembered that magnetism that drew them together. Did Mike and I have that, too?

"Trick?" Frank asked.

"A guy I met online," Sergei said. "Stan. He puts security guys in all these big high-rises, so he said he knew what I was going through."

I looked at Ray, and both our eyebrows raised. "You know Stan's last name?"

Sergei shook his head. "Something Italian, I think. We didn't trade business cards, you know?"

"We've been following someone in a different case," I said to Frank. "Stan LoCicero. He owns a company called Mahalo Manpower."

"Yeah, that's it," Sergei said.

"We'll talk about your case later," Frank said. "So this guy, Stan. How'd you move forward with him?"

"He said he'd send a couple of guys over, but I shouldn't look too closely at their papers." He looked at Haoa. "It was just when you were getting the contract for that industrial park by the airport, and you were pressuring me to find you guys."

Haoa didn't say anything, just stared at Sergei.

Sergei looked back at Frank. "So these three Chinese guys show up the next morning. They hardly speak English, but they look like they can work. I filled out some papers for them and sent them off to Naleo, one of Haoa's superintendents."

He shifted uncomfortably in his seat. "Later that morning, Stan called. I thanked him for the guys, and he told me how it was going to work."

Frank said, "And how was that?"

"I was supposed to short each guy's pay, and give the difference to Stan. Oh, and he said I could keep a little piece for myself, too. For my trouble."

Haoa's rage was simmering, but Tatiana kept her hand on his.

"You have anything in writing from Stan?" Frank asked.

Sergei shook his head. "I wrote a check to Mahalo Manpower every week, for consulting services."

"You never questioned these checks?" Frank asked Haoa.

My brother shook his head. "We have an electric check writer and a stamp with my signature. Tatiana always handled the checks, so I got out of the habit of paying attention to it."

"Mr. Baranov, I'm going to need something I can take to a judge," Frank said. "We'll wire you up. You've got to get something incriminating on tape if you want to walk away from this."

"I can't," Sergei said. "I'm scared."

"I'll go with you," Haoa said. That probably scared Sergei even more.

"How about this," Ray said. "Stan knows Kimo, but he doesn't know me. Suppose we say I'm your new boss, Sergei. And I've figured out what you're up to, and I want a cut. I go with you to meet with Stan."

"What do you think, Mr. Baranov? You're not going to get a better offer."

Sergei nodded. "Haoa and Tatiana didn't know anything about what I was doing." He turned to them. "I'm so, so sorry," he said. "You guys gave me a chance, and I fucked it up. That's all I ever do, isn't it? I just screw up, every time."

Tatiana said, "This could be what turns things around for you, Sergei. You'll put this jerk Stan behind bars; you'll help all these people who are being victimized."

It was touching to see Tatiana still believed in her brother. I wished I did, too.

While we sat there, Sergei pulled out his cell phone and called Stan, and did a pretty convincing job of explaining that his new boss wanted a cut. "Give it to him out of yours," we heard Stan say.

"He wants more than I get," Sergei whined. "He's gonna call the cops."

They arranged to meet at the Rod and Reel Club that evening at six. Ray and I made a plan to meet Sergei at five to get him wired up and rehearse their story. "You'll keep tabs on your brother, Mrs. Kanapa'aka?" Frank asked.

"I'm not letting him out of my sight," Tatiana said.

Frank turned his attention to Haoa. "You have a list of the guys you think don't have proper working papers?" he asked.

Haoa nodded. "Six of them. All Chinese."

"I want you to talk to each one of them, Kimo," Frank said. "See if you can get anything out of them."

"You're going to need an interpreter," Sergei said. "Most of these guys don't speak more English than good morning, yes sir, and paycheck."

"I'll try, but it takes a couple of days to line up an interpreter," I said.

"We don't have a couple of days," Frank said. "As soon as these guys get the idea that something's up, they'll be in the wind."

"Aunt Mei-Mei speaks Cantonese," Haoa said. "You could ask her."

"And Harry speaks pretty decent Mandarin," I said. "You round up the guys and bring them to the station. I'll get Harry and Aunt Mei-Mei."

Haoa, Tatiana, and Sergei left, and Frank said, "Before I let you out of here, I want to hear about your case."

"It's complicated," I said.

"I may be a federal agent but I can do complicated," Frank said.

I started with the arson and the prostitution, and finished up with the blackmail attempt on Brian Izumigawa. "It looks like this guy Stan may be involved somehow," I said. "We're not sure yet."

"Federal trumps local, you know," Frank said. "I don't want you to do anything on your case that might mess up mine."

I wasn't going to get into a pissing contest with the guy, because I knew I'd lose. "You've got it, boss," I said.

Chapter 34

INTERVIEWING THE ILLEGALS

THE DEMONSTRATION WAS still going on, and I recognized a guy I'd gone to Punahou with, as well as a couple of *mokes,* or local criminals, that I'd arrested a time or two. I nodded and smiled at everybody. Including my mother.

She was wearing a formal muumuu in a Hawai'ian quilt pattern and carrying a sign that read PROTECT MY ISLANDS FOR MY GRAND-CHILDREN. It wasn't a surprise to see her there; both she and my father are half-Hawai'ian, and they'd brought us up to value that part of our heritage. I knew she'd been volunteering with one of the sovereignty groups; she said she wanted to make sure that native culture and traditions were maintained.

I stopped to kiss her hello. Ray hung back until I motioned him over and introduced him. "We just met your other son upstairs," he said, not realizing until I glared at him that it wasn't the right thing to say.

"Which son? Lui?"

"Haoa," I said. "Oh, look, there he is." I waved over Haoa, Tatiana, and Sergei. "Gotta go, Mom. Try to stay out of trouble."

"Your mom some kind of civic activist?" Ray asked, as we hurried away.

"Long story," I said. "Goes back to 1892 and the U.S. taking down the Kingdom of Hawai'i."

"Sounds like it'll have to wait. I think when we get back to the station, you ought to match up the pictures on the site to the list of names," Ray said. "I'm gay friendly and all, but . . ."

"No problem. I'll do that. Why don't you check in with Treasure?"

The time ticked by. It was a lot less fun than you'd think, looking over all the picture sets and trying to figure out who was the target and who else was involved. Lucas figured in many of the shots, but there were also a lot of unnamed guys. Some looked Chinese, some Filipino, a couple Indonesian. Whether they were hookers or escorts or illegal immigrants was impossible to tell.

The only common denominator was that they were all male. Some displayed fetishes—diapers, urine, and kinky toys. Others were just vanilla sex. My shots, from the rear, were among the most ordinary.

Treasure admitted knowing Stan LoCicero, and told Ray she found Stan creepy. Unfortunately, creepy was not against the law in Hawai'i.

I called Mike and brought him up to speed. "Stan sounds like a good candidate for the arsons," he said. "We can get a warrant for his house if you get something useful on that tape."

After scouring the Internet and police records, I found decent head shots of Richard Hu and Stan LoCicero, and put together a pair of photo arrays of guys who looked similar to them.

At three o'clock, Haoa and his superintendent, Naleo, showed up with a half-dozen Chinese men. Naleo was a Hawai'ian bodybuilder, mid to late twenties, with some kind of inscription tattooed on his neck. He wore the Kanapa'aka Landscaping polo shirt, which clung to him in places that made me miss Mike Riccardi. He didn't look happy to be in a police station, but maybe he was just nervous he'd get implicated in something.

Harry brought Aunt Mei-Mei, who had dressed up for the occasion in a bright blue pants suit with a blue-and-white striped blouse. She looked like she was going out for a ladies' lunch with my mother. Maybe they'd meet up after my mother was done protesting outside the federal building.

Naleo brought the men into our conference room one by one.

The first guy, Long, was tall and good-looking, with a shaved head and a big chest. I was pretty sure I recognized him from a couple of the pictures. He spoke a dialect that only Aunt Mei-Mei could comprehend. "Too bad Norma not here," she said to me. "She speak like him."

Long didn't want to cooperate. He knew he was going back to China, and he wasn't happy. There wasn't much I could offer him without Frank O'Connor's approval, so I brought my laptop in and logged onto the MenSayHi Web site.

It took me a few minutes to find the right pictures. Long, naked, stood over a nude *haole* man in a bathtub, a stream of urine flowing out of his fat dick, which was certainly long. The picture had been taken from the side, showing Long in profile, the *haole* full face. I'd identified him as an attorney with a prominent law firm that handled corporate litigation.

"Is this you?" I asked, showing Long the image on the laptop.

His face gave him away, though he didn't say anything.

"Too bad," I said. "If this was you, we might be able to help you."

Aunt Mei-Mei didn't see the picture, but I knew she had an idea what was going on. She translated, and Long looked interested.

"See, we want to get the guy who hired the men in these pictures," I said. "If you help us arrest him we can't send you back to China, at least not until after the trial is over. And after that, who knows?"

I could see the emotions warring in Long's face. He didn't want to admit that it was him in the photo. Maybe he was ashamed, or maybe he knew what he'd done was illegal. But he was smart enough to realize that this might be his ticket to stay in the U.S.

He said something in his guttural dialect, which Aunt Mei-Mei translated. "He says yes, this is him."

In bits and pieces, we learned his story. He had been recruited in Gansu. He did not like having sex with men, but he needed money for his wife and family back in China. He had worked at the massage parlor in Waikele for about six months, and then at a series of manual jobs.

I showed him the array of photos that included Stan LoCicero. He didn't recognize anyone. Then I showed him the array with Richard Hu, and Long said Mr. Hu had picked him up at the airport—he was the man who had brought him to the massage parlor. Long was very excited, chattering on so fast that Aunt Mei-Mei had to stop him several times so she could catch up.

It was good news for Frank O'Connor, but not for us, because Long couldn't implicate Stan LoCicero in anything. I stopped the tape, thanked Long, and then turned him over to a federal marshal, who would see that he didn't disappear until his role in Mr. Hu's case was over and his immigration status resolved.

Harry translated for two of the remaining three, Aunt Mei-Mei the last. They all told variations of the same story and could only implicate Mr. Hu, not Stan. After the marshals had taken away all six, Harry said, "I have some stuff for you on Stan LoCicero. You got a computer I can hook up to?"

He plugged a little USB drive into my computer and started printing, while Aunt Mei-Mei sat at the big table, her hands resting on the wood in front of her, like a little blue bird.

"Arrest records from New Jersey, Illinois, and Nevada," Harry said, as the aged printer started spitting out paper. "A couple for arson, a couple for petty theft, one for indecent exposure."

"Stan's been a busy guy," I said, pulling the first pages off. Ray and I started reading. I didn't ask how Harry got hold of some of this stuff, but after all, he was a police consultant, which legitimized his access.

Back in Jersey, Stan had been a breeder of Siberian Huskies. He had worked in maintenance, security, and as a motorcycle mechanic. Harry had found the incorporation papers for Mahalo Manpower, which indicated that Stan owned a 25 percent share in the business; the rest was owned by Wah Shing.

Unfortunately, there was nothing in Stan's record that we could take to a judge. Yes, there was a connection between him and the management of the acupuncture clinic, and yes, he had a record for arson. But a judge would see that as purely circumstantial. We still needed Sergei to get Stan on tape.

Chapter 35

INCIDENT AT THE ROD AND REEL

I SPOKE TO Mike during the afternoon, telling him our plans. "You need anything from me?" he asked.

"Nope. I'll let you know how it goes."

Walking back into the federal building, Ray and I saw the debris from the demonstration everywhere—crumpled flyers, crushed leis, and a lot of empty plastic water bottles. The wind had picked up, stirring the trash along the street and adding to my nerves. I was worried about the evening; Sergei was a certified fuckup, and I didn't trust Stan LoCicero.

I was relieved to see that Sergei was there and ready to go. He'd had a serious conversation with his sister, and he recognized that he didn't have any other options beyond cooperation. He was also pretty familiar with the process of getting wired up. I guess he'd been in trouble enough in Alaska to know the drill.

He and Ray went over their story a few times, getting the details straight. "Remember, we need something on the wire that shows that LoCicero knows these guys are illegal," Frank said. "You've got to pin him down."

"Leave that to me," Ray said.

Sergei rode with Ray in the Yaris, and I drove the Wrangler home then joined Frank in a surveillance van outside the club. Darkness was falling, but Kuhio Avenue hummed with traffic, and a young guy in a straw hat strummed a ukulele for the tourists, who dropped tips in a cup. A group of Japanese sightseers, led by a middle-aged woman waving a small rising sun flag, passed us, eagerly pointing and snapping pictures of an old Hawai'ian woman in a yellow muumuu.

A few minutes before six, Ray and Sergei came into sight, walking down Kuhio Avenue toward the Rod and Reel Club. Frank had just made a note in his record when I heard the rumble of a motorcycle in the background.

"That's gotta be Stan," I said.

The motorcycle came out of the alley alongside the club and turned onto Kuhio Avenue. The driver was a husky guy in full leather and a black helmet, but I couldn't see anything beyond that in the dark. I couldn't tell if he was black, white, or some shade in between. If I hadn't been watching closely, I might not have seen the flare from the gun the motorcyclist pointed at Sergei and Ray. The Harley was loud, but I thought I heard at least three shots.

Sergei fell to the ground, and tourists scattered. A woman screamed and a Toyota SUV blasted its horn as the biker pulled in front of him on Kuhio. Ray pulled his gun but didn't fire. I jumped out of the van. As I slammed the door behind me, I said, "Go after him!"

Frank's driver pulled out onto Kuhio, nearly sideswiping a tourist couple in a Toyota convertible, and took off after the biker.

I dialed 911 on my cell phone and gave our information to the dispatcher as I ran to Sergei, who was lying on the sidewalk clutching his side. Ray was already leaning over him. "Too many tourists and cars to get a clean shot," he said to me.

"Where were you shot?" I asked Sergei, leaning down next to Ray.

"My side," Sergei said. "It hurts."

"I called an ambulance, brah," I said. "You'll be OK."

"You said you'd look out for me, Kimo," Sergei said.

I grabbed his hand and squeezed. "I will." I stood up and stepped away, dialing Haoa's house, and when my niece Ashley answered I said, "I need to talk to your mom. Right away."

"I'm on a call, Uncle Kimo."

"Get off it, then. This is an emergency, and I need your mom."

My ear reverberated as she slammed the phone down onto some hard surface, and then I heard her call for Tatiana. "What is it?" Tatiana said, when she answered. "Is everything OK?"

Ray pulled off his shirt and tore it into strips, trying to staunch the bleeding from Sergei's stomach.

"Sergei's been shot." I handed him the phone.

"I'm sorry, sis," he panted. "I screwed up."

Squatting there on the sidewalk next to Sergei, I could hear Tatiana through the phone. "Don't you dare die on me, Sergei. Don't you dare."

People clustered around us, and I motioned to them to back away. "Police. Everything's under control."

The ambulance siren grew. Ray was sweating as he leaned over Sergei, shirtless, applying pressure to the gunshot wound. "Don't hate me, sis," Sergei rasped. "I didn't meant to hurt you or Howie."

Tatiana was crying when I took the phone from Sergei. The ambulance pulled up and a couple of EMTs jumped out. A patrol car arrived, sirens blasting, and a uniform from the Waikīkī station started cordoning off the area.

"The ambulance is here, Tatiana," I said. "I'll go with Sergei to Queen's."

"I'll be there as soon as I can," she said.

The EMTs leaned down to where Sergei lay. One took his vital signs while the other took over from Ray, who leaned back, breathing heavily. Within a couple of minutes, the EMTs had Sergei bandaged up and loaded into the ambulance. "I'll go with him," I said to Ray. "You all right?"

"Yeah. Just shook up."

"Go home and let Julie pamper you. I'll call you from the hospital." The ambulance ride was bumpy, and the driver had to swerve a couple of times to get around clueless drivers who didn't get out of the way.

"It hurts, Kimo," Sergei said.

I looked at the female EMT. "Can't give him anything for the pain till we get him into a bed and stabilized."

"Hold on, Sergei." I squeezed his hand. "It's gonna get better. I promise."

When the ambulance pulled in at Queen's, the crew loaded Sergei onto a gurney and wheeled him away. I went into the waiting room.

Only a few minutes later, Mike burst in. "I was monitoring the police band. I heard somebody got shot and I was worried it was you."

"I'm OK." We hugged in the waiting room and I explained about Sergei. A little later, Haoa and Tatiana arrived.

"I shouldn't have pressured him to go to that meeting," Tatiana said. "He said he was scared."

"He's a tough guy," I said, wrapping my arm around her. "I'm sure he's going to pull through."

They took Sergei up to the operating room and we all moved to the waiting room there. Eventually the doctor came out and told us that though Sergei had lost a lot of blood, they were able to stabilize him then remove the bullet and close up the entry wound.

"I want to wait here for him," Tatiana said. "I can't believe it. I was supposed to look after him."

"He's a grown man, Tatiana," I said. "You can't look after him forever."

"Of course I can. He's my brother."

I knew how she felt. My brothers had looked after me plenty.

Mike drove me over to the Rod and Reel Club, parking his truck in the alley behind the club. The first guy we talked to was Larry Solas, the crime scene tech, who had recovered the three bullets that the motorcyclist had fired. "I'm on duty till midnight," he said. "I'll see if I can get you anything on ballistics."

"Thanks, brah." I left Mike talking to him about caliber as my cell rang and I learned that Frank O'Connor's driver had lost the motorcyclist in the crowded streets, unable to get a license plate number. Though I thought the assailant was Stan LoCicero, we couldn't be certain of anything. It could have been either a man or a woman under all that leather, and the bike could have been anything from a Kawasaki to a Triumph.

"Had to be LoCicero, though," Frank said. "He's the only one who knew about the meeting."

"Unless he told somebody else, or hired somebody," I said.

We promised to compare notes in the morning. When Larry finished and packed up his big arc lights, the uniform on duty pulled up the plastic cones and let the traffic flow on Kuhio again.

I walked over to where Ray was standing under a streetlight with Julie, wearing a shirt she had brought for him, talking to Lieutenant Sampson. Tourists moved past us, and I could hear the back beat coming from the club. Life went on in Waikīkī. It was hot and humid, and a mosquito kept buzzing around my head.

"Let's meet tomorrow morning," Sampson said. "I want to re-cap. Let's get the ADA involved, too. We'll see if we've got enough evidence to get a search warrant for the gun. If we can get a ballistics match we'll have something to hold this guy on."

"Don't worry," I said. "I'm going to make it my personal mission to arrest Stan LoCicero and make sure he goes to jail for a long, long time."

Sampson looked at his watch. "I've got to roll. Call me if you need anything." He strode away down the street, and I turned to Ray and Julie. He was still shaken up, and I offered to take him out for a drink. "Julie and I are going to have dinner," he said, holding her around the waist. "I'll be OK."

"Any chance that could have been Treasure Chen on the bike?" I asked.

Ray shook his head. "I was talking to Treasure last night at dinner. She told me she had a boyfriend who rode a bike when she was in high school and she hated it. Always afraid she was going to fall off. Could it have been Richard Hu?"

I shrugged. "I don't know. I suppose."

As Ray and Julie left, Mike came over. "You want some dinner?" I asked.

"Sure. But what do you say we pick up a pizza and take it to my place?"

A dozen things flew through my head at once. Mike liked his pizza with ham and pineapple. He had a down comforter on his bed that was like resting on clouds. My Wrangler was safe in its parking space at my apartment, but if I stayed the night with Mike he'd have to drop me at home on his way to work. I didn't have any condoms on me, but I hoped Mike had some.

Had it been Stan LoCicero on the bike? Richard Hu? We didn't have anything on Stan. There was no way a judge was going to give us a warrant on so little evidence.

More than anything else, I wanted to lie in Mike's arms.

"Tomorrow's going to be a hell of a day," I said, linking my arm in his. "Let's head for your truck, Romeo."

Chapter 36

WHERE THERE'S SMOKE

AS I'D EXPECTED, Mike wanted a large pizza with ham and pineapple. "It was the first meal we ate after we moved here," he said, while we were waiting at a little pizza place just down the hill from his house in Aiea. "My parents had been talking up Hawai'i to me for a long time, and when we saw there was a Hawai'ian pizza on the menu we had to order it."

I lounged against the counter, under a faded poster of Mt. Vesuvius. Dean Martin was singing "That's Amore," and I was starting to relax. "You liked it?"

He nodded. "I'd been worried that Hawai'i would be totally different from New York. I knew we were moving here so my mom would feel more comfortable, and I was worried that everybody would look like her, that they'd all speak Korean or something. And I wouldn't fit in."

The counter clerk called our number, and Mike paid for the pie and a six-pack of garlic rolls. "So we went out for pizza after we unpacked our boxes," he said, while he waited for his change. "And I liked the mix of ham and pineapple, of sweet and savory. The next day, I met this girl next door, and her mom was Japanese and her dad was white. She even kind of looked like me."

"I always felt like I fit in," I said, as we walked back to his truck. "And then I went to college in California, and there I was exotic and different. It was weird. I'd look around, and everybody was white, or black, or Japanese, or Chinese. There were no in-betweens, like me. I'd use a Hawai'ian word, or talk about eating Spam *musubi* or something, and people would look at me like I was from another planet."

"I felt the same way," he said. "I used to go back to Long Island for summers and holidays, to stay with my dad's parents, and when it was time for college I figured I'd go there. But it didn't feel like home anymore. I'd go into this Korean neighborhood in Queens sometimes, just to hear people talking, but they'd look at me like they couldn't quite figure out what I was."

It was like old times, hanging out with Mike, talking, eating pizza, and drinking this gourmet root beer he'd found somewhere, a local Hawai'ian brand with a hula dancer on the bottle. We sat at his kitchen table eating slices and licking our fingers, and I thought of all the time we'd missed, days and months we could have spent in each other's company.

He still liked to rip all the soft dough out of the crust, then scoop bits of ham and pineapple into the hollows. And as I remembered, he'd get bits of pizza in his mustache and then snake his tongue out to grab them. It was gross, but endearing.

While we were cleaning up, he bumped into me, and when I turned toward him he wrapped his arms around me. We started to kiss and rub our bodies against each other, and within a short time we were in his bedroom. The comforter on his bed felt just as good as I'd remembered, and so did his body against mine, his tongue in my mouth, and before long, his dick in my ass.

We were slumped next to each other in the afterglow of the kind of sex that makes your eyes roll back in your head when Mike started sniffing. "You smell that?" he asked.

"What? I showered this morning, but it was a long time ago."

"Not you. Smells like gasoline."

He jumped off the bed, pulled on a pair of shorts, and ran from the room. I followed, and as I went toward the living room I smelled what he had—gasoline, and above it, smoke.

He grabbed a fire extinguisher from the kitchen and pushed

through the screen door to the yard. Over his shoulder, I could see flames licking at the back wall of the garage. "Call 911," he yelled.

I did, for the second time that night. I gave the dispatcher the address and said it was the residence of a firefighter, then I went outside to help.

If you're going to have a fire at your house, it's best to have a trained fireman there with you. Mike knew just what to do, spraying the fire with the extinguisher, and directing me to get the hose and wet down the yard.

There was little in the back that was flammable; all the landscaping was away from the house and there wasn't any of the usual junk lying around, as you'd find in my parents' yard. No broken-down furniture, wooden trellis, or anything else that might catch fire.

"Get my parents out," Mike yelled, as he sprayed the extinguisher.

The flames were moving along the back wall in the direction of his parents' half, so I ran around to the front, barefoot, wearing only my shorts, and banged on their door. It was just after midnight, and from the lack of light I was sure his parents were asleep. How long would it take me to rouse them? I looked around for a window I could break, and finding none, pounded on the door again.

His father answered, wearing a nightshirt imprinted with Japanese characters, and I had a feeling the look of distaste on his face had to do with both my presence, and my attire. "Get out," I said. "Mike's side of the house is on fire."

He turned into the house and began yelling for his wife, disappearing inside. I wasn't sure if I should wait to see if they needed help evacuating, or return to Mike. The arrival of the first fire engine told me I didn't have to do either, and I stepped back to let the professionals do their job.

Clouds covered the moon, but the truck's headlights and the flames lit up the area like daytime. The firemen hustled Mike out of the way and I met up with him alongside the house, where we had a view of the back but were out of the way.

"What the fuck?" Mike said. "Somebody tried to burn my house down."

He was agitated, yelling and jumping up and down. I tried to grab his arm, but he shook me off. We were both drenched in sweat, but the adrenaline was running down, and I just gave up and leaned back against a tree.

"Had to be Stan LoCicero," I said, when he'd calmed down. "Unless you've got some other case going?"

"Not one where they'd try to burn me out," Mike said. "Damn, we've got to catch this bastard."

I wondered if Stan was still around, if he'd found some vantage point to watch the fire and make sure he'd been successful. "He must have come back to the Rod and Reel Club after the shooting and heard me and Lieutenant Sampson talk about nailing him. I bet he thought he could get me out of the picture."

Mike's parents came around the corner then. His father had pulled on a long raincoat, and his bare calves made him look like a flasher. I couldn't laugh, though. He wore plastic rubber slippers, and his gray-and-black hair was tousled.

His wife, whom I'd only seen previously in her nurse's uniform, was wrapped in an elaborate embroidered dressing gown. She wore fuzzy pink slippers and her short dark hair hung sleekly around her face.

"It's OK," Mike said, going over to hug them. "We caught the fire before it got to your side." By then, the firefighters had extinguished the flames, but were hosing everything down just to be sure.

"What happened, Michael?" his father asked.

With an utterly straight face, Mike said, "I'll have to investigate the source and conditions of the fire before I can make any conclusions."

His father looked from him to me. I walked over to them. "I'm afraid this might be my fault," I said.

"Kimo," Mike said.

"I'm not surprised," Dr. Riccardi said. "Since you came into my son's life, detective, we've seen nothing but trouble. You break his heart, turn him into an alcoholic, now you burn down our house?"

"Dominic," Mike's mother said. She put her hand on his arm.

"No, Soon-O, these things need to be said. I'm tired of watching Michael throw his life away."

The wind picked up and I felt a sudden chill, the sweat on my arms and chest giving me chicken skin. I rubbed my hands over my upper arms and said, "You have every right to be upset. I guarantee you, if I'd known what was going to happen tonight I never would have come over here. Mike and I have been investigating a case together. The suspect we've been looking at for a couple of arsons shot at a police officer this evening in Waikīkī. I think this guy followed Mike and me up here and started the fire to keep us away."

"He obviously doesn't know my son," Dr. Riccardi said. "When he sets his mind to something, he doesn't let anything get in his way."

"I inherited that from you," Mike said. "Grandpa told me he and Grandma weren't happy when you brought Mom home, but you didn't let that stop you."

"What happened between your mother and me is a totally different story."

"Oh, let's see," Mike said. "Forbidden love. Unnatural love—isn't that what Aunt Teresa called it? White wasn't meant to mix with Asian."

"Michael," his mother said.

"No, Mom. It's time we talked about this, about all the things Grandma and Grandpa used to tell me. How you wouldn't marry Dad at first, and when he came home from the service he wouldn't talk to anybody except to argue, and he used to get drunk and get into fights."

He turned to his father. "You broke your cousin Eddie's jaw, didn't you, Dad? And you had the nerve to criticize me when I was drinking. Sanctimonious prick."

"Don't you talk to me that way, Michael."

Mrs. Riccardi reached over to take her husband's hand. "I didn't want to marry Dominic at first," she said. "I didn't want to leave my family and my country. But Dom's father sent me a plane ticket, to come to the U.S. and visit."

In the background, I could see the firemen rolling up the hoses. A crowd of birds had returned to the tree behind us, chattering noisily. "My father sent you the ticket?" Dr. Riccardi turned to his wife. "How come you never told me that?"

"He was worried about you." She smiled. "Just like you were worried about Michael. The difference is that your father overcame his prejudices because he saw that I made you happy."

The doctor looked at his wife, and a kind of unspoken communication passed between them. When I found myself hoping that Mike and I would be able to do that someday, I realized I'd crossed a line, and not just because Mike and I had ended up in bed that night. I was falling in love with him all over again.

Mrs. Riccardi let go of her husband's hand and hugged me. "We're glad you're both all right," she said. "That's all that matters."

Mike's dad hugged him, and then we switched—though his father simply extended his hand to me to shake.

I didn't take it, though. I hugged him just as I'd hugged his wife. "I love your son," I said into his ear. "I'm never going to hurt him again."

Chapter 37

A WHITE SILK THONG

ONCE THE FIREFIGHTERS had gone, Mike's parents went inside and he got a couple of high-powered flashlights so we could evaluate the damage to the duplex. Fortunately, the flames hadn't reached Mike's parents' half, and the damage to Mike's side wasn't as bad as it might have been. His back porch had been destroyed, and the rear wall of his garage had almost burned through. The yard was muddy and a hibiscus hedge had been trampled. "It's not terrible, but it'll all look worse in the morning," Mike said.

When his parents came back outside they were fully dressed. His father announced that they were going to stay with a colleague. "In case your arsonist decides to come back and finish the job."

"We're not staying here either," Mike said. Since we didn't know if Stan LoCicero was still out there watching us, we thought it would be safest to go to a hotel. As his parents drove away, Mike said, "I know a guy I can call." He stepped away from me, dialing a number on his cell, and from the way he shielded his voice I could tell he didn't want me to hear what he was saying.

"I got us a room," he said, when he hung up. "At the Halekulani. I hope that's OK. It's on the house."

The Halekulani is one of Honolulu's most expensive hotels, on Waikīkī Beach. "How did you do that?"

He shrugged. "I know a guy."

"In the Biblical sense?"

"Hey, you're not the only one who fooled around while we were separated."

"Works for me," I said. "You sleep with any gourmet chefs while you were at it? I wouldn't mind getting comped a nice meal now and then."

"Get dressed," he said. "They're not letting you into the Haleku-lani looking like that."

We had to shower before we left, to get the smell of smoke out of our skin and our hair, and we did it together, to save time and wa-ter. But the idea that Stan LoCicero might be skulking around out-side put the damper on romance, and we finished quickly and got out. The watch commander for District 3, which included Aiea, said he'd get a car to pass by Mike's house every half hour for the rest of the night, just in case.

We left Mike's truck with the valet at the Halekulani, and I walked through the lobby to the ocean while he negotiated with his former flame. The huge pool was lit up, highlighting the orchid painted on the bottom. The lounge chairs had been folded up and the umbrel-las closed. I wondered if Stan had followed us. I doubted he'd be able to cause any trouble at the Halekulani, though.

A few minutes later, Mike joined me out by the pool. "We're all set," he said.

The clouds had cleared, revealing a full moon and an array of stars splayed across the sky. The waves made a gentle rushing sound meeting the beach, and in the distance we could hear the faintest echo of dance music. Mike took my hand. "Been a busy day, huh? When I woke up this morning I couldn't have imagined what happened."

"I knew we'd end up like this, though. I guess I've known since I saw you at the shopping center fire."

"Me, too." He turned his head toward me, and we kissed. The breeze picked up and wafted the smell of salt water and plumeria blossoms around us.

The room Mike had arranged for us was the most luxurious I'd ever stayed in. It was on the twelfth floor, overlooking the ocean and Diamond Head, with a lanai, a king-sized bed, and a Roman tub in the bathroom. "This room is too nice to sleep in," I said, when we walked in. I went straight across to the lanai and opened the sliding glass door, stepping outside.

There was a glittering necklace of lights at the foot of Diamond Head, clouds massing over it, illuminated by the moonlight. "Who says we're going to sleep?" Mike asked, coming up behind me. He wrapped his arms around me and we kissed. I savored every place where our bodies touched, chest to chest, hip to hip, hands on shoulders.

Since we'd worked out the urgency of our lust earlier in the evening, we took our time. We stripped down out there on the lanai, kissing and running our hands over each other, naked against the ocean breeze. He leaned forward against the railing and I stood behind him, arching my back so my dick pressed up against his ass. I reached around and cupped his nipples in my hands, kissing the back of his neck as he breathed deeply.

We moved back inside, rolling around for a while on the lush, carpeted floor, wrestling for dominance. Then we climbed on the bed in a sixty-nine position, me on top, as if I was doing push-ups over him, and we sucked each other to climax. From there, we stumbled into the Roman tub and cuddled in the hot, soapy water. It was after four by the time we'd worn each other out and drifted to sleep.

I woke at first light, despite how late we'd gone to bed, and rolled over to kiss the top of Mike's head. He yawned. "What time is it?"

"A little before six. I think we got about two hours of sleep."

He stroked the edge of my hairline. "I wish we could stay here in bed all day."

"Me, too. But it's what, Thursday? We'll have the weekend." I stood up and stretched. His ex had arranged for us to stay at least two nights, if we needed to, and as I pulled my clothes back on I told Mike I'd call him during the day.

I would have liked the luxury of surfing for a while in the

morning, to clear my head, but I had to get downtown. I settled for a walk through Waikīkī as the city was waking up—food trucks making deliveries, maids on their way to work, street cleaners hosing down Kalākaua.

Ray was still shaken by the events of the night before, but Julie had sat up with him for a while and then dosed him with a couple of sleeping pills, and he was ready to get Stan LoCicero behind bars. I told him about the fire at Mike's, and he whistled. "The guy's a piece of work," he said. Then he looked at me. "You went back to the fireman's house."

"We may be getting back together."

"May be? Or already did?"

"Already did." I couldn't help grinning. "A couple of times, actually."

"High five," Ray said, holding up his palm. I slapped it just as Lieutenant Sampson came out of his office and beckoned us.

"I hope these high spirits mean you're making progress on this case," he said. "I don't like anybody taking potshots at my detectives. I want to catch this guy, and I want to catch him fast. What have you got?"

We ran it down for him, from the planned meeting at the Rod and Reel Club, through Sergei getting shot, to the fire at Mike's house. I admit, I made it sound to Sampson like Mike and I had just gone back there to talk through the case. I don't know if he believed me, but he didn't lecture me, and that was a good thing.

"We can't say for sure that was Stan on the motorcycle, or that he was the one who set the fire at Mike Riccardi's house," I said. "But he's our prime suspect at this point."

"Why weren't you following him?" Sampson asked. "I thought I authorized you to do that yesterday."

I looked at Ray and we both shrugged. "We knew where he was going to be," I said. "We were chasing down other leads."

"If one of you'd been following him, we'd have a case," Sampson said. "But that's water under the bridge. The question is how do we nail him?"

"We don't have enough evidence for a search warrant?" Ray asked. "Not even with everything we've got?"

"And what do you have?" Sampson asked. "You have Sergei Baranov, a felon from Alaska who says this fine, upstanding citizen supplied him with illegal immigrants. But he has nothing in writing, and the only evidence he can give you is a couple of cancelled checks to this man's business. How about the illegal workers at your brother's landscaping company—did you get anything from them?"

I shook my head. "Nothing on Stan. A couple of them implicated Richard Hu in the immigrant smuggling, and Frank O'Connor's moving forward on that."

"You have any other leads?" Sampson asked. "Any at all?"

I remembered the way that Stan had threatened Gunter. "I've got a friend who works for Stan." I explained Stan's attempt to get Gunter into his blackmail ring. "I've been trying to keep him out of this, but I don't see that we have any choice. With Sergei out of the picture, the only chance we have of nailing Stan is to use Gunter."

"Talk to him," Sampson said. I knew Gunter was tough and could take care of himself, but after seeing Sergei get shot, I was worried.

At ten, I drove over to Gunter's, leaving Ray at the station going over a couple of witness statements that the uniformed officers had collected the night before. The clouds of the night before were back, puffy cumulus piles that dotted the sky. It was garbage day in Gunter's neighborhood, and I had to nose the Wrangler between a couple of cans, careful not to bang up my new car.

Gunter answered his door in a white silk thong, and nothing else. "Why'd you bother to put that on?" I asked. "It's not like it covers anything up."

"You never know who's at the door," Gunter said, stepping back as I walked in. "Sometimes it's somebody you want to see."

He closed the door and stalked across the living room to the kitchen, and I followed. He may have been a tall, skinny guy with an average dick, but you could bounce a quarter off that ass and get change back.

"To what do I owe the pleasure of this visit?" he asked, sticking an oversized mug of water into the microwave.

"Can't I just drop in to see my good friend?" I asked, as he spooned some loose tea into a cheesecloth bag.

"Not at this hour. You want something, don't you?" He looked at me. "You want to pimp me out to Stan LoCicero. Christ."

"I wouldn't call it that."

The microwave beeped and Gunter pulled the hot water out. He poured it into a clear glass teapot, dipped the tea bag in, and put the top on.

"What would you call it?" Gunter asked, turning to face me. I was glad to avoid the distraction of that perfect ass, but it wasn't as though his dick was hidden by the pouch of white silk. "Helping the police with their inquiries?"

"Putting an asshole behind bars," I said.

We watched the water in the glass teapot grow darker. Gunter opened the cabinet for two cups and a plastic honey dispenser in the shape of a bear.

I debated whether I should tell Gunter about Sergei's aborted meeting with Stan. I knew it would make him more nervous, but he was my friend, and I owed him the truth. "We need your help." I sketched out the details of Sergei's involvement with Stan as Gunter poured the tea into the cups, squeezing honey into his and passing the bear to me.

"He shot the dude?" Gunter squeaked. "And you want me to meet with him?"

I drizzled some honey into my cup. "Yeah, but Stan had reason to be suspicious of Sergei. Sergei wanted something from him that Stan didn't want to give up. But with you, it's different."

"Different gun? Or different bullets?"

"Different because Stan wants something from you. You call him up and say you've been thinking about his offer, and you could use some extra cash. It's the holidays coming up, after all. Maybe you've been thinking about going back to Jersey for a white Christmas."

"Like that's going to happen," Gunter said. We both sipped our tea. "Where will you be?"

"Wherever you need me."

"I could tell him to come by the Kuhio Regent," Gunter said, considering. "There's a balcony overlooking the lobby. You could be up there."

"We'd have you wired up."

"Let me do this before I realize what a stupid idea it is." Gunter picked up his cell phone and dialed. "Mr. LoCicero? It's Gunter Franz," he said. "I've been thinking about your proposition."

Gunter laughed. "Well, one of your propositions," he said. "I've got my eye on a Bulgari watch, and I'm not going to be able to buy it on a security guard's paycheck. You think I could earn enough money working for you to put that little bauble on my wrist?"

He listened for a minute, then laughed again. "It's big, but not that big," he said. "Though I do have a selection of rings that fit it."

I could see what they were talking about was turning Gunter on, and I averted my eyes from the silk thong, focusing on my tea.

"I'll be at the Kuhio Regent from three to eleven," Gunter said. "OK, I'll see you later, then."

He hung up the phone. "There. I hope you're happy. If you break up with the fireman again, I am so collecting from you." He raised an eyebrow. "Unless the fireman is into threesomes?"

"I'll ask him," I said. "Tell me the details."

"Stan's coming by the Regent later today. He wants to set up a meet with that guy he told me about."

I drained the last of my tea. "Then I'd better get moving. Can you come by the station before your shift? Say, two o'clock? We'll get you wired up." I looked at him. The excitement of talking to

Stan had worn off, and it only looked like he had a coiled snake inside the thong instead of a toilet plunger. "But you're going to have to wear something more than that to cover up the wire."

"Don't make me regret this," Gunter said. He poured a third cup of tea and squeezed some honey into it. "Now, if you'll excuse me, I have a guest in my bedroom I have to say good-bye to."

Chapter 38

RENDEZVOUS AT THE REGENT

ON MY WAY back to the station I swung by the hospital to check on Sergei. Tatiana was at his bedside, sketching him. I kissed her first, then him. "How's the patient this morning?"

Sergei smiled weakly. "The doctors say I'll survive."

Tatiana laughed. "He's a big drama queen. He's fine. They're letting him out this afternoon."

I sat on the edge of Sergei's bed. "You catch that bastard, Stan?" he asked.

"Not yet. We don't have anything to tie him to the shooting other than circumstance."

Sergei sat up, his body language changing immediately. "Who else on this island has a Night Rod?"

"What do you mean?"

As if he was talking to a child, Sergei said, "I recognized the bike. Stan has a Harley special edition, the Night Rod. I'll bet there aren't that many in Honolulu."

I took out a pad and started making notes. "You know motorcycles?"

"I worked at a bike shop in Anchorage for a while."

"Until the boss caught him screwing one of the customers," Tatiana said. "How long did you last there? Six months?"

"This is good, Sergei. I'll get somebody to check the registrations."

"See?" he said to Tatiana. "I'm not a total screwup. Please don't make me go back to Alaska."

"I'll leave you guys to work things out." Back at the station, I called the Harley dealership and asked about the Night Rod. As Sergei had said, it was a special edition, and the guy only knew of four on the island. One of them was Stan's.

I added that to our growing list of information. By then, it was two o'clock, and Gunter showed up to be wired with a recorder and transmitter that would reach up to the balcony. Of course, Gunter flirted with the technician as he snaked the wire down my friend's shirt, and to my surprise the guy flirted back. Maybe he was yet another undercover homosexual at the Honolulu Police Department. Or maybe straight guys were just a lot more comfortable these days.

Ray and I took portable radios and drove over to the Kuhio Regent in two cars, parking on the street just around the corner. Gunter led us in through a back door and up to the balcony which overlooked the lobby. We tested the audio, then settled down with some sandwiches and bottled water, because it looked like it might be a long wait until Stan showed up.

It was interesting to watch Gunter work—for about the first hour. He checked in visitors, accepted deliveries, and flirted with every guy who passed his desk, including the elderly Chinese man who brought the dry cleaning, the FedEx guy, the letter carrier, and the hunky UPS guy, who filled out his brown shirt and shorts in a way that was almost pornographic. I'd have flirted with him, too, if I'd been single.

Stan showed up just before five. "Haven't seen your friend Kimo lately," he said to Gunter. "How about you?"

Gunter looked uncomfortable. "Not for a couple of days."

"You and he ever fool around?"

Gunter shrugged. "A few times."

"Pretty sexy guy. You should see him on tape. He's got some interesting tastes. Likes a big dick pounding up his ass." He smiled. "But then, who doesn't?"

I was imagining Lieutenant Sampson listening to the tape when the front doors slid open and Mr. Hu walked in, holding Treasure Chen close to him in a way that implied he had a gun on her.

"Just got more interesting, huh?" Ray said.

Stan looked surprised to see Mr. Hu. I couldn't hear what they said, but it looked like an argument.

"Shit," I said to Ray. "What the hell is Mr. Hu doing here? How did he get hold of Treasure?"

"I talked to Treasure yesterday," Ray said. "She was antsy, wanted to get out of Norma's apartment. I tried to reassure her, told her a bunch of stuff about what we've been working on. I'm sorry, Kimo. She must have gone to Mr. Hu."

My mind raced ahead. What if Treasure had attempted to use whatever Ray told her about our investigation to leverage her position with Mr. Hu? That would explain why Mr. Hu had come looking for Stan. Did he know that Gunter was my friend? Would he suspect that Gunter was wired up?

Gunter started to argue with Stan. "I can't leave the desk," he said. "Any of the residents find out, they'll complain to the manager. I'll get fired, even if I say I was with you."

"Getting fired is the least of your problems," Stan said.

Grabbing Gunter by the arm, Stan half-dragged him toward the front door, Mr. Hu and Treasure following. "Do we stop them?" Ray asked.

"We don't have anything yet." I was torn between my desire to protect Gunter and Treasure and the need to get something on the two guys that would stick. Ray looked to me as the front door slid open and the four of them walked out.

"We follow them," I said.

Chapter 39

THE HOUSE IN BLACK POINT

RAY AND I dashed for the staircase to the first floor. I radioed out to Steve Hart, who was in an unmarked car outside with his partner, a Chinese-Hawai'ian guy named Lee Kawika. Steve told me that Stan, Richard, Treasure, and Gunter were getting into a Mercedes in the semicircular drive in front of the Regent. "Chinese guy driving, Chinese girl in the front seat," he said. "The other two in the back seat."

"Follow them," I said. "We'll be behind you."

Ray and I both caught up to Steve a few blocks away from the Regent. We slid into a pattern, no one car tailing the subject too closely, trading off. We were out of transmitter range so I couldn't tell what was going on in the car, or if Stan or Mr. Hu had figured out Gunter was wired up and disconnected him.

The streets of Waikīkī were jammed. A teacher led a group of tiny kids, all wearing name badges and holding hands, across the street in front of the Royal Hawai'ian, and a man dressed like King Kamehameha, in a yellow headdress and an imitation *kihei* cloak, handed out coupons for Hawai'ian heritage jewelry.

Mr. Hu got stuck behind a bus, and we all had to drop back to avoid passing him. It looked like somebody had run into the bus shelter, knocking it into a coconut palm next to it. A few blocks on, the street was torn up for new crosswalks.

When Mr. Hu got onto the H1 he turned toward Diamond Head. "I know where we're going," I said into the radio. "Black Point." I gave the other two cars the address and directions to the house where I'd met with Mr. Hu. "I'm going ahead."

I moved into the passing lane, sped up, and zoomed past the Mercedes. It started to rain lightly and I turned on my wipers and my headlights, but by the time I got off the highway I'd passed through the shower.

When I reached the house, I radioed Steve and Ray. The three cars were bunched together down on Kahala Avenue, just about to enter Black Point. I parked uphill and jogged down to the mansion. The gates were locked, but I climbed a kiawe tree at one corner and jumped over the fence, landing hard on my right ankle.

I hobbled to the back of the house, where a cabana the size of a small bathroom sat just beyond the pool. It was unlocked and as empty as the rest of the yard, just a couple of broken-down old lawn chairs in one corner. It smelled like mold and chlorine. I saw light through a crack in the weathered old boards and lay down on the concrete floor, positioning myself so I could see out through the crack. I put the earpiece back in my ear, hoping that Gunter would still be transmitting.

"They're approaching the gate," Ray said on the radio. "Steve's gone ahead. I'm parked just down the hill."

I heard the gates opening, though they did not close again. Suddenly, I heard Mr. Hu's voice in my ear. "We will have a conversation," he said. "And depending on the results of that conversation, you may go free. Or not."

Good. That meant that they hadn't discovered Gunter was wired up.

"I already told you." The new voice had to be Treasure's. "I didn't tell the police anything."

Car doors opened and slammed. "They're here," I said to Ray and Steve on the radio. "Gunter's still transmitting. Sounds like they're going inside."

The front door opened into a wide foyer and the living room, with big sliding glass doors on the far side leading to the pool and lanai. Two sofas with oatmeal-colored slipcovers sat at right angles, with a black lacquer coffee table between them. High-hat lights in the ceiling lit the room, and a big-screen TV was mounted on one wall. To the right was the dining room and kitchen, and a door to the garage.

The bedrooms were to the left. There were three, though most of the action took place in the master bedroom, which had sliding doors out to the lanai. The other two bedrooms were smaller and faced the street.

"Wait here," I heard Mr. Hu say.

Two sets of footsteps faded away, Mr. Hu's dress shoes and Treasure's heels on the marble floor. Then I heard a fist hitting flesh.

"Ow!" Gunter said. "What the hell was that for?"

"You set me up, you little bastard," Stan said. "Isn't that what the girl was saying? You told your buddy Kimo about our deal. Somehow he managed to connect me to Richard's operation."

"I don't know what you're talking about," Gunter said. "I haven't talked to Kimo in a couple of days, like I told you. And I wouldn't tell him about this deal. He's a cop, remember? He'd turn me in. And I wouldn't get any money."

"We'll see if you change your tune when Richard hooks you up," Stan said.

The second bedroom was the dungeon. The walls were painted black, the curtains nailed to the wall so no light came in. I'd only been in there once, but the experience had both frightened and excited me. All the toys there were designed to enhance sexual pleasure, but I was sure that Richard Hu had no compunctions about using them to cause pain instead.

I didn't know what they had all talked about in the car, but I hadn't heard anything on tape that was incriminating enough to bring either Stan or Richard up on charges. As much as I wanted to swoop in and rescue Gunter and Treasure, I had to hold out a little longer.

"What's going on?" Ray said through the radio. "Can you hear anything?"

"Nothing yet. Mr. Hu took Treasure away somewhere."

"SWAT team should be in position within ten, fifteen minutes," Ray said.

I heard the sounds of footsteps returning—just one set, this time. "The girl's in the third bedroom," Mr. Hu said. "We can take your friend here into the playroom and see what he has to say."

"I don't appreciate being dragged around like this," Gunter protested. "I thought we were going to make a deal, Stan. What's going on?"

"You made a deal already," Stan said. "With your buddy Kimo. Now you're going to tell Richard and me exactly what that involved."

Footsteps. A door opened. There was some scuffling. "We can do this the easy way or the hard way," Stan said.

I wondered what they were going to do to Gunter to get him to talk. Would they take his clothes off and discover the wire? "Handcuffs," Gunter said. "Kinky." I heard some rustling and snapping, and then he said, "Hey, those leg restraints are too far apart. That hurts."

"Good," Stan said.

"I'll deal with this," Richard said. "You go prepare the house."

"The stuff's still in the garage?"

"I haven't touched it."

Footsteps faded away, and then a door closed. "Stan's on his way to the garage," I said into the radio. "Is somebody in position to see what he's up to?"

"I've got a visual," Steve said. "The door's opening from the inside." There was a pause, and then he said, "Jesus Christ."

"What's up?"

"The guy's got enough gasoline stocked there to burn down the Aloha Tower," he said. "He's picking up one can. From the way he's carrying it, it must be full. Walking around the back."

Through the crack in the cabana wall, I saw Stan come around the corner and lay a can of gasoline on the ground. He pulled a cigar from his front shirt pocket, put it in his mouth, and lit it. He puffed for a minute, then blew out a smoke ring. Once the cigar was burning to his satisfaction, he picked up the can and began pouring gasoline at the base of the house. "He's going to burn it," I said.

"Your friend has ruined a very lucrative business," Richard Hu said in my ear. "My cousin in Gansu recruited good-looking men and women and got them tourist visas. I put them to work and made a lot of money."

"The kind of work Stan wanted me to do?" Gunter asked.

"Catering to sexual desire is the oldest profession, you know," Richard said.

Gunter yelped. "That hurts."

"Good. We'll be walking that fine line between pleasure and pain, though I'm afraid things will lean more toward the painful."

Where was the SWAT team? Did we have enough yet to charge Richard? He'd admitted bringing in the aliens and putting them to work.

"Those guys Stan brought into the Regent, are they hustlers who didn't work out?" Gunter asked. Despite his earlier wimpiness, Gunter was showing himself as a trouper, keeping an eye on what he could get on tape.

"Some of them," Richard said. "Chinese women are much better at performing sexual services for pay than Chinese men. But there is always a demand for young-looking Chinese boys. I worked them until their asses were too sore to continue and then turned them over to Stan. He found them jobs in security, maintenance, yard work."

That was enough to get a search warrant. But we couldn't go into the house until the SWAT team arrived. Where the hell were they?

"Any word on the team?" I asked through the radio. "I can see Stan, and he's getting the house ready for a burn. I'm not sure how much longer we can wait."

"The team's stuck in traffic," Steve said. "There's a pileup on the H1, and they were right behind it."

"So we're on our own," I said.

Chapter 40

THROUGH THE FIRE

"LEE AND I can take the guy with the gas can," Steve Hart said over the radio.

"I'll go in the front," Ray said. "There's a uniform here, too, Portuondo. She and I will get Treasure."

Pushing open the cabana door, I saw Steve and Lee emerge from the bushes and tackle Stan LoCicero. I drew my gun and rushed for the sliding doors into the living room, feeling the pain in my twisted ankle. In my ear, I heard Mr. Hu say, "I think it's time to move to the next level, don't you?"

Something rustled, and Mr. Hu said, "You've been wired. You bastard."

I heard that flat sound of flesh hitting flesh again, and Gunter howled. The glass doors were locked, so I stood back and shot through one of them. I grabbed a lawn chair from the cabana and used it to knock away the broken glass.

Sirens howled in the distance. Ray and Lidia Portuondo burst through the front door as I made it into the living room, and I sent them to the third bedroom. The door to the dungeon room was locked, but it was flimsy plywood and one well-aimed kick at the knob knocked it loose enough that I could shoulder my way in.

As the door swung open, I saw that Gunter was still clothed, though his shirt was unbuttoned and the wire was hanging loose. He looked angry rather than frightened, and he was strapped to the wall in a position like Leonardo's Vitruvian man, his arms out to his sides in handcuffs, his feet spread and cuffed to the floor. Mr. Hu stood next to him, holding a gun to Gunter's head.

I had my weapon drawn, but we were in a standoff. If I shot Richard, there was a good chance he'd get a shot in at Gunter before he fell.

"I thought I'd see you here, Kimo," Mr. Hu said. "We seem to have a problem, though. How do you propose we solve it?"

"You give me the gun. I unhook Gunter, and we all go downtown."

"That doesn't work for me," Mr. Hu said. It was hot and close in the room, and beads of sweat clung to his forehead. It was the first time I saw him close to losing his cool.

"That's the way it's going to work, though."

He shook his head and smiled. "Ah, Kimo. Trying to be the top, are you? Forceful, determined? When we all know you're a bottom at heart. You just want a big, strong man to tell you what to do."

"I consider myself versatile," I said. "Sometimes the top, sometimes the bottom. Right now, I'm the top. And unless you want to find yourself on the floor licking my shoes, you'll do as I say."

Gunter laughed, which says a lot about his character, considering he was strapped to the wall with a gun pointed at his head.

My radio crackled. "That asshole tossed his cigar into the gasoline," Steve said. "You'd better get out of there fast." As he spoke, I smelled the smoke myself.

"Stan always did get ahead of himself." A bead of sweat dripped down the side of Mr. Hu's face. I felt the sweat pooling in my lower back, too. "He wasn't supposed to start the fire until he and I were ready to leave." He looked at me. "But that does lend a certain urgency to our negotiations, doesn't it?"

"He has a small dick, doesn't he, Kimo?" Gunter asked me. "Is that why he's such a jerk?"

Mr. Hu's attention was diverted, as if he was about to unzip right there and prove Gunter wrong. For just a moment, his gun hand pointed away from Gunter, toward the far wall.

I took advantage of the distraction, firing three shots in short succession. He fell to the ground, crying out in pain. We're always taught to aim for body mass—anywhere on the torso. But I hadn't been out to the range in a while and my aim was rusty. From where he was grabbing, it looked like I'd hit a little lower than I wanted, in Richard Hu's upper and lower thigh.

Ray burst in then, jumping on Richard and taking the gun from his hand. I pulled Richard's jacket off, looking for the keys to the handcuffs, and then Ray slapped a pair of cuffs on him.

The keys weren't in any of his jacket pockets, so I patted down his pants as he lay on the floor, loosing a stream of invective in Mandarin Chinese that was worse than anything I'd ever heard Uncle Chin say. He tried to kick me but I sat on his calves, ready to unzip his pants and pull them down if I had to.

My hands were slick with his blood by the time I found a pair of small keys in the back pocket of his suit pants. I wiped my hands on his white shirt so that the keys wouldn't slip away from me and used the back of my arm to move the sweat from my forehead. "My hero," Gunter said as I stood up. "I'm glad you showed up when you did. I was about to piss my pants."

I fumbled the keys once, dropping them to the floor, and as I bent down I felt a wave of dizziness. It was all the blood, I guess. I struggled to calm my stomach as I stood up again, my hands still shaking.

Mr. Hu was bleeding heavily from his leg. Ray flipped him on his back and said, "I'm not losing another shirt." He leaned down and pushed aside Mr. Hu's tie, then unbuttoned his white shirt and began ripping strips of fabric.

The smell of smoke grew stronger as I struggled to fit the key into Gunter's right cuff. "Where's Treasure?" I asked Ray.

"Lidia took her outside. I thought you might need a hand in here."

My hands were slippery with sweat and blood but I got Gunter's hands undone. He stayed back against the board, massaging his wrists, as I knelt to the floor to wrestle with the cuffs around his feet. "I love a man on his knees in front of me, but not like this," he said.

Ray struggled to get Richard to his feet, but Richard's bandaged leg kept buckling under him. It seemed like neither of us were making enough progress, and the smoke was getting thicker around us.

"Maybe I can just cut your feet off," I said to Gunter, just before I got the key into the lock on his right foot. "You don't need them anyway, do you?"

"I'd miss getting my toes sucked," he said. He began to cough as the smoke curled into the room around us. "Can't you hurry it up?"

Ray got Richard to his feet and pushed him out the door. They moved slowly, both coughing, and Richard wasn't putting weight on the leg I'd shot.

The lock on Gunter's left foot was tight and I had to leverage pressure on the key to get it turned. "Damn, what kind of crappy cuffs are these?" I asked. "All the money Mr. Hu was making, he could have invested in some good hardware."

I got the last cuff off and Gunter slid down the wall and into my arms. I was sweating like crazy and so was he, and we both couldn't stop coughing from the smoke. Because the windows of the dungeon room had been closed up, the hall was our only way out. I heard shouting somewhere and a siren getting closer as I focused on the smoke-filled hallway, gasping to find clean air somewhere. Ray was a few feet ahead of us, half-dragging Richard Hu.

Gunter's legs had cramped and he leaned on me. In the living room, the flames had burst in through the broken glass door and embers had landed on the cream-colored sofas. As we passed, one of the silk pillows caught in a quick burst.

There was a lot of noise outside as an engine pulled up and firefighters jumped out to combat the blaze. People were talking on the radio but I couldn't differentiate their voices. I followed Ray across the room toward the big wooden front door.

He manhandled Mr. Hu through it in front of him. The opening of the door caused a draft, though, and the flames shot across the room toward this fresh source of oxygen, blocking our exit.

I remembered the sliding doors in the master bedroom. "Come on," I said, turning Gunter back toward the bedrooms. "There's another way out back there."

We hurried down the hall like two guys in a sack race, me pushing ahead, trying to avoid putting weight on my bad ankle, dragging Gunter along behind. Both of us were choking and coughing, the smoke burning our mouths and throats. When we got to the door to the master bedroom, I had him stand back while I checked it for heat. I turned the knob and peeked in.

The drapes had been pulled back, and the room was light and free of fire. Like the rest of the house, it was sparsely furnished, just a big king-sized bed, a bureau, and two night tables. I left Gunter leaning against the bureau, gasping for breath, as I went to the doors.

They were hot, and through them I could see the flames coming our way, darting along the base of the house. I heard the fire, a roaring that made it hard to think. It would be a race—could we get out and past the growing line of flames before they burned us? I fiddled with the lock, my fingers scalding on the hot metal, but I got it open.

By the time I did, though, there was a line of flames in front of us. The deep end of the pool was just a few feet away, and I thought we might be able to run through the fire and then douse ourselves in the water—but I didn't like the idea of any exposed flesh getting burned.

Then I remembered the closet in the dungeon room. "Wait here," I said to Gunter. Leaving the glass doors pulled shut but unlocked, I raced out of the master bedroom, my bad ankle throbbing, and into the room where Gunter had been held. It was filled with smoke and I could barely see the board against the wall, the sling, and the other toys Richard had scattered around the room.

Coughing, accidentally kicking a big rubber dildo across the floor, I stumbled to the closet, where I found the two hooded cloaks I remembered. I grappled with the toys on the shelves, looking for anything that might prove useful.

I had a flash of inspiration when I saw a collection of cock rings in different sizes, stuffed into a zippered plastic bag. I grabbed the bag and the cloaks and limped back into the hallway.

The smoke was almost impenetrable, and it felt like my whole body was coated in sweat. I couldn't stop coughing and I felt an acrid burning in my throat. Using the wall for guidance I stumbled to the master bedroom, which had begun to fill with smoke as well. Gunter pointed out toward the lanai, where the flames had grown. "We can't get through that, Kimo."

"We can't wait here until the fire gets put out, either," I said, choking out the words. "We don't know how long that will take." I spilled the cock rings out of the plastic bag and said, "Give me your transmitter."

"Cock rings?" Laughter alternated with his choking.

"Gunter. Focus. Take off the transmitter so I can put it in this bag."

He pulled off the transmitter and wrapped the wires around it. I zipped it into the bag. "We'll see if these really are watertight. Now put the cloak on."

"Are you losing your mind?"

"Just put it on." I slipped the cloak on over my clothes. The effect was claustrophobic, pressing my sweaty shirt against my body, especially as I was already having trouble breathing. The hood and the long sleeves covered almost all of my skin except for my face. I grabbed a couple of pillows from the bed and dumped them out of their cases.

In the mirror over the bed, I saw our reflection. Gunter and I looked like a pair of Sith lords from *Star Wars*. "Put the pillowcase over as much of your face as you can," I said. "Then we run through the fire and jump in the pool."

"You're crazy," Gunter said. But he wrapped the cloth over his mouth.

I slid open the glass door, and there was a momentary influx of fresh air. I took a deep breath, grabbed Gunter's hand, looked him in the eye, and nodded.

Then we ran.

It felt like a hundred-yard dash through hell. There were flames all around us, and I thought my chest was going to burst. It took us a half dozen big strides to push through the flames. We opened our mouths, took deep breaths, then jumped feet first into the deep end of the pool.

My body couldn't keep up with the disorienting changes—from heat and fire to cold and wet and chlorine. I thrashed around underwater for a minute, losing the pillowcase over my mouth and shedding the cloak. The pool water doused the smoldering fabric and I didn't feel the pain of chlorinated water meeting open wounds, so that meant I hadn't been burned.

I surfaced first, choking water out of my mouth. The house was engulfed in flames, and I saw water from the fire hoses spitting over the roof. At the far end of the house, a couple of firefighters in yellow suits dragged a hose around the corner.

Below me, Gunter was having trouble, flailing around under the surface of the water, the heavy cloak dragging him below. I dove down and grabbed him, but he was frightened and tried to shake me off.

One thing about being a surfer, you get a lot of experience dragging people out of the water. I knew not to fight with him. Instead, I focused on getting the cloak off him, letting him battle on his own, and once the heavy thing was off his shoulders, he rose up to gasp for air. We were in the deep end of the pool, eight feet by the marking on the side wall. I turned on my side to swim up to the shallow end, dragging Gunter along behind me. We both collapsed on the steps, which had been inlaid with a tile pattern of hibiscus blossoms.

"You OK?" I asked, panting heavily.

He coughed, spitting out water, but managed to say, "Never a dull moment with you, Kimo."

"You burned at all?"

He shook his head. "Me neither." One of the cloaks drifted toward us, and I saw a big hole burned through the back. The other cloak spread out at the deep end like a dead man floating. As we leaned back against the tile of the pool and caught our breath, the firemen aimed their hose at the back wall of the house.

More firefighters came around the side of the house to fight the fire at the back, and one of them helped us up out of the pool. He radioed that he had two guys soaking wet, needing blankets.

I'd lost my deck shoes in the pool, but I wasn't going back for them. Gunter and I hobbled together across the lawn, as the fireman who'd helped us went back to fighting the flames. As we turned the corner, Mike came loping up the lawn, carrying blankets and throwing himself in my arms. "Don't you know I'm the one who's supposed to fight fires?" he asked, then he kissed me.

Chapter 41

GO BIG OR GO HOME

MIKE WRAPPED GUNTER and me in the blankets. I slung one arm around Mike, the other around Gunter, and we walked down the lawn together. There was a fresh breeze sweeping in from the ocean, and the air was clear down there. Despite all the chaos behind us, I felt safe and secure.

We'd almost made it to the street when the garage exploded, all that stockpiled gasoline going up in one big blast that shook the ground and sent waves of heat and fire toward us. The noise was so loud that it knocked my hearing out for a minute. I smelled singed flesh and burning grass as the three of us fell to the ground in a heap.

Waves of flame swept down from the garage. I closed my eyes and faced down in the grass. Mike rolled on top of us, splaying his arms out to keep us flat to the ground. The flames were quickly doused by the hoses, and a couple of EMTs rushed over to help us all up.

There was dirt all over Gunter's face, and he'd gotten a bunch of scrapes on his chest. He couldn't stop coughing, so they hooked him up with an oxygen mask. I saw him try to flirt with the EMT, but even Gunter is defeated sometimes.

I thought I might have a cracked rib or two, and there was a bruise on my forehead that hurt like a bastard. Mike had been wearing his yellow fire jacket, so the worst that had happened to him was that some of the black hair on the back of his head had gotten singed off.

The three of us sat down at the curb by the EMT wagon, watching the firefighters douse the rest of the blaze. Because of the spacious yard around the house, they'd been able to keep it from reaching the neighbors, though the street was crowded with onlookers and I saw a truck from Lui's station, KVOL. I ducked my head down so that Ralph Kim wouldn't see me and try to get me on camera.

The EMT insisted that we all go to The Queen's Medical Center for evaluation. None of us had the energy to complain.

Dr. Phil was on duty, and as I stepped down from the van, holding Mike's hand for support, he hurried forward in his hospital scrubs, a stethoscope around his neck. "You're turning into a frequent flyer here, Kimo," he said. "If you ever want to see me, though, you can just call. Don't feel you have to have a professional reason."

"I'll keep that in mind," I said. He took my vitals, directed the EMT to take me to a curtain, and then turned to Mike and Gunter.

A few minutes later a nurse came in to hook me up to oxygen, and I asked him for a pad and a pen. After he helped me peel off my wet, smoky clothes and put me into a backless hospital gown, he scrounged through a cabinet and found a pad from one of the drug companies, and a pen advertising a medication I'd never heard of and hoped I never had to use.

I started scrawling notes as the curtain next to me was pulled open. Mike was sitting back down on the bed next to mine. "Not what I was thinking of when I dreamed of sharing a room with you," he said.

The curtain on the other side of his bed swung open, and Gunter said, "Hey, we could always make it a threesome." Then he started to cough again, returning to his own bed, and the nurse hurried over to make sure he kept the oxygen mask over his face.

After a long while, Dr. Phil came by and said that all three of us were good to go, provided we took it easy and avoided running through any more fires for a few days. I used Mike's phone to call my parents and let them know I was OK. I called Lidia, too, and she said she would swing over to the hospital and take Gunter home. Dr. Phil lent Mike and me each a set of scrubs. We were barefoot, and the scrubs were tight and only came down to the tops of our ankles, but they were better than nothing.

Gunter said he preferred to remain in the hospital gown. "You never know when one of these will come in handy," he said. It was just six o'clock, and on our way out of the hospital we stopped in the lounge to watch the KVOL broadcast.

They had some spectacular footage of the fire, including a shot of me and Gunter hobbling around the side of the house, soaking wet. Ralph Kim's voice-over promised a full report at eleven o'clock. I knew my brother Lui would get hold of me before then, that he'd complain that I hadn't given him a heads-up on the fire. I'd make it up to him by giving Ralph Kim an interview.

Lidia arrived as the fire segment was ending. We made a quick stop at a Long's, where she went inside and bought three sets of rubber slippers, all in bright pink. Mike protested, but laughed and slid them on his feet.

A few minutes later, Lidia dropped Mike and me off at the station, then headed to Waikīkī with Gunter, who was already envisioning playing some doctor/patient games in the future. The man has a one-track mind.

Mike and I looked pretty funny, hobbling into the station, wearing the skimpy scrubs and the pink slippers. Ray was at his desk when we walked in. "Jesus, shouldn't you guys still be in the ER?" he asked.

"Can't leave you with all the paperwork," I said. "Stan in the system?"

"He's downstairs in a holding cell until they can get him in front of a judge."

The three of us began to reconstruct everything we had done, in mind-numbing detail. Ray had the transmitter, which had been protected by the zippered bag, and he played it for Mike and me. It had recorded everything Richard and Stan had said to incriminate themselves. With testimony from Gunter, Treasure, and Long and the other immigrants, we had enough to put them both away for a long time.

Around eight, Dr. Phil called. "Thought you'd want an update on Richard Hu. He lost a lot of blood, but we removed the bullet and he's in recovery."

I thanked him.

"You might be interested to know that when we emptied his pockets, he had four different driver's licenses, each one with a different name and a different address. Hospital billing is going to love tracking him down."

"We'll see if we can help," I said, and passed the news to Mike and Ray.

"I hope he has a painful recovery," Ray said.

A little later, Steve Hart and Lee Kawika showed up. They had gotten a search warrant for Stan's house in Hawai'i Kai, where they found enough incendiary materials to burn all the way down to the Pacific.

"I've never seen so much stuff," Steve said. "It's a wonder the whole place didn't just spontaneously combust."

"What about the dog?" Ray asked.

"Had to call the Hawai'ian Humane Society," Lee said. "Beautiful dog, that Husky. They'll take care of him until the bastard makes arrangements for him."

"You know we have a mountain of paperwork ahead of us," Ray said. "Tracking down everything about Richard and Stan, about their businesses, and then finding all those illegal immigrants."

"Frank O'Connor can handle the Mahalo Manpower stuff," I said. By ten o'clock, we were all ready to call it quits. Steve and Lee were finished with their inventory of Stan's house, and Ray wanted to head home to Julie. There was still a lot more paperwork to do, but that would take time. I called Brian Izumigawa and let him know he was off the hook, and suggested he find himself another closeted guy, maybe another banker, rather than meeting strangers online. I'm not sure he appreciated the thought.

I e-mailed Fouad Khan and let him know that Stan wouldn't be contacting him anymore. After the cool response I got from Brian, I didn't make any suggestions to Fouad. Though I did think for a minute or two about hooking the two of them up.

Mike and I agreed to stop at Raimundo's for dinner. We were surprised as we walked in to see Doc Takayama and Lidia Portuondo, sharing an intimate table.

"So, you guys have discovered our little romantic hideaway," I said.

Lidia blushed. She had her hair down around her shoulders, instead of up in her regular French braid, and she looked pretty in the candlelight.

"Officer Portuondo and I were just discussing a case," Doc said.

Mike and I both laughed. "Come on, Doc, you're busted," I said. "Though I can't say I see what a lovely young woman like Lidia sees in a ghoul like you."

"Paul is not a ghoul," Lidia said. She reached over and took Doc's hand, and I realized I'd never known the medical examiner's first name until then.

"Enjoy your dinner," I said, smiling, and Mike and I sat down at our own table, still wearing our scrubs and pink slippers.

We didn't talk much; the day had taken a lot out of both of us, and we'd already talked through everything about the case at the station. Instead, we just sat back and enjoyed the antipasto salad and the restorative powers of pasta, chicken, and tomato sauce in various combinations.

When we got back to the Halekulani, we pulled a couple of Big Wave Pale Ales out of the minibar and sat out on the lanai together, drinking and staring at the view of Diamond Head. I felt ready to tackle the unspoken issues between us.

"That was a pretty ballsy thing you did today," I said, sipping my beer.

"Which thing was that?"

"Running up to me, hugging and kissing me. All those firemen watching you. Pretty dramatic way to out yourself."

"It was going to happen sooner or later," he said. "You know what they say, go big or go home."

"So we're going to give this a try again?"

"That is my intention."

He looked at me and took my hand. "I went out to Tripler at lunch, and my dad and I had a talk," he said. "I think it was the first time in a long time that we actually communicated, you know? Not him lecturing and me arguing. We talked. I was pretty surprised to hear that stuff my mom said last night."

He looked out toward Diamond Head. "He said that I was a lot more like him than either of us wanted to admit. He did go a little nuts when he thought my mom wouldn't marry him. And he recognized I was doing the same thing, and he just wanted to make things easier for me."

"He cares about you."

"I know. Like your folks care about you." He smiled. "I was jealous, you know? Seeing you with your parents. How much they love you and accept you. I didn't think I had that." He squeezed my hand. "But now I know that I do. And knowing that, I can get on with things. I'm sure I'm still going to have some issues. But you can help me out."

"It is handy having somebody around who's been through it before."

"So we're back on? Together?"

"Just try and get rid of me." We leaned across and kissed, and then I yawned.

He said, "Am I boring you?" But then he yawned himself.

I stood up. "What do you say we go to bed?" I asked.

"Those are words I hope I never get tired of hearing," he said, standing up beside me.

We stood together for a moment, staring out at Diamond Head.

In the distance we could hear car horns, late-night revelers on Kalākaua, a far-off siren. I was in the city I called home, within sight and sound of the ocean. My family and friends were safe out there in the darkness, and the man I loved was beside me.

It didn't get better than that.